For April, who helps me despite myself. Thank you for your honesty and know that I strive to make you want to read my stories.

In Memory of David Farland.
Irreplaceable mentor of so many. You are loved and missed.

DEMON'S LAIR

BOOK FOUR OF THE ANGELSONG SERIES

KEVIN A DAVIS

Inkd
Publishing

Cover Design by Warren Designs

Created with Vellum

DEMON'S LAIR

CONTENTS

INTRODUCTION

This is *Demon's Lair,* Book Four of the AngelSong series.

When Thomas disappears on a solo mission against the leader of the Unceasing, Haddie has to evade the police and coerced FBI to bring together a team to save her dad.

After the sacrifices she's already made, she doesn't want to lose anyone else.

PART 1

I often doubt that I am the best for this task, given my particular skills.

CHAPTER 1

HADDIE ROLLED over in the sheets to blink at the ceiling. The smell of cooking pancakes roused her. *This is what I want to wake up to every day.* The air conditioner vents in David's apartment hissed out cool air, forcing her to throw on a T-shirt.

"I'm hungry," she called out, yawning. He would have hot tea ready, as he refused to serve cold tea for breakfast. Smoothing her hair and rolling it into a bun against her neck, she smiled and walked into the next room.

"Almost ready." David was wearing a pair of blue boxers and sported a lean, muscular body as he worked a skillet at the stove.

His apartment had been neat when they'd arrived last night. Now, her jacket and helmet were piled in a beige easy chair, her pants lay on the floor beside the couch, her shirt and sports bra tossed on the top. One sock peeked from under the coffee table. *It must drive him crazy.* David lived an orderly, chaos-free life, except for her. He said he liked it, but she had to wonder.

The teapot waited on a decorated tile, and he had a

padded cozy to keep it warm. Cups and saucers had been arranged with a sugar bowl near his. *At least he hadn't placed the silverware.* "You're spoiling me," she said. She added a spoonful to his cup, then poured tea for both of them.

David turned with a plate of pancakes. "Just trying to tame you." He leaned over for a kiss before putting her food down. As he retrieved butter and syrup, he said, "Just work today? Nothing crazy?"

"I promise." She sat down and sipped a robust tea, possibly his Assam black. They'd had a wonderful holiday weekend, and she'd gotten to ride her bike a little, though the midday heat in September still made for a warm ride. She had an appointment with Liz this morning before heading to work. "What's the weather today?"

David finished stirring his tea with a light tinkle of the spoon before he spoke. "Sunny and hot. No rain 'til Thursday." He took a sip, then smiled. "Nelson's tonight?"

"Sure. I guess you're in town, then?"

"Yep."

It bothered her when he ended up out of town overnight on a job, but she never said anything. *Who am I to speak?* San Francisco and her skirmish with Lady Erica had been a nightmare, and it had taken her a week to fully recover. She still couldn't be sure the police wouldn't question her about the lost burner phone with her fingerprints all over it. At least Terry hadn't been harassed by the FBI since before then, and Josh appeared to be settling down to a survivable, though certainly un-Josh-like, lifestyle.

Her life had almost reached normal the past week. Liz, as expected, had been ecstatic about Haddie's time traveling. *She must have taken a quart of blood by now.* Thinking about Aaron still left a pit in her stomach, and she kept promising herself to go visit his grave soon. *I need to call Kiana, check on her leg.*

"Where'd you go?" David asked.

Haddie shrugged. "Just thinking about everything. Mainly Taco Tuesday."

"I could have made tacos for breakfast."

"Dinner's fine. I may call in that offer another day, though." Haddie stuffed in another mouthful of sweet pancakes. She had to get to Liz's apartment in time that neither of them would be late for work. David would hit the gym. She'd gone with him a few times as his guest, but preferred her own stretching and walking Rock.

The sun colored the few thin clouds pink as she strapped on her helmet and strode to her Fat Boy. The jacket felt warm, but the cool air brushed against her neck and cheeks. She fired up the Harley and connected her phone to dial Kiana. They tended to get going early on Dad's farm.

"Hey, Haddie." Kiana's voice sounded as though she'd been laughing. "Riding your bike?"

"Yeah." Haddie pulled out of David's parking lot and turned toward Liz's house in east Eugene. "How's your leg doing?"

"Itchy. I've got a couple weeks left in the cast. I seem to have bad luck with my left leg, eh?" There were voices in the background, perhaps Sam or Meg. "Are you headed back to work today? Have fun with David?"

"We hiked yesterday morning. I imagine the doggy day care was busy."

"Mrs. Mitchell, from the farm across from the kennel, helped out. Crow came by Sunday night, and we played poker with Sam and Meg."

Haddie's lips pursed, imagining Crow, oversized and

tattooed, playing cards with little Meg. They lived like a real family, something she hadn't had when she'd lived with Dad. *I can't be jealous.* She'd made her choice. If the police came after her, she'd likely end up with poker nights on the farm as well.

"Sam drove into Bent last Saturday, alone."

"Wow. She's driving?" Haddie had offered to teach her when they'd first met. *Sam's growing up because of Dad.*

"She has been. Still gets nervous on the faster roads, but does okay. I think she got motivated when Thomas gave her a forged driver's license. This was the first time she drove alone."

When she finally hung up, Haddie's stomach burned, not from the breakfast, but from Sam, Kiana, and Meg getting all the best time with Dad. He'd had to leave with a warrant from Boise hanging over his head. *Do I really want him to be lonely?* She didn't, but the call left her feeling empty.

Preoccupied, she pulled into Liz's driveway in front of the odd-shaped house with a single peak high to the front. No one had built anything else on the side street, which dead-ended at the woods. Liz opened the downstairs door as Haddie walked up. The bike had likely announced her arrival.

"How was the hike?" Liz asked, motioning Haddie inside.

"Fun, but it got hot near the end. Happy to cool off at David's pool. One benefit to a condo association, I guess."

Liz led them toward the large room that served as both a living room and dining room. The black and white picture of Sid Vicious hung over Liz's red couch. Smaller photos covered the wall above her glass dining table. Needles and vials waited on the tabletop.

"Any symptoms?"

"Aching knees and hips," Haddie answered.

"The usual." Liz gestured toward one of the black padded chairs at the table. "I really hoped to have found some abnormalities in your blood from being pushed through time."

"Sorry to disappoint." *I'm not.* Haddie surely didn't want anything unusual happening to her. *I'd like to be more normal than I am.*

Liz tied Haddie's arm and prepped a syringe. "How's Josh? I forgot to ask Saturday." She still pined to get some of his blood and an MRI of his brain.

"Same. He acts too normal. He's a better worker, but there's nothing there."

"Sounds like my coworkers."

"I am able to get him talking about whatever he's reading, though. The others assume it's depression after his mom's death."

Liz waited as a vial filled. "I've looked through some of the medical news, waiting to see if cases such as his pop up, but there haven't been any conclusive situations. I wonder if that was part of the selection process — people not too connected to family or friends, like Josh. It doesn't sound like this Lady Erica made that decision. Maybe. I think there's someone more logistically minded in charge. Military maybe. Those types run every scenario."

Haddie couldn't bring Dad's letter into the conversation; they still kept that to themselves. Whoever wrote the letter had obviously penned the Unceasing manifesto. When Liz or Terry discussed the Unceasing, it always came to her mind, but if they learned that the Unceasing were trying to recruit Dad, it might make Terry and Liz uneasy.

"You're thinking about Aaron," Liz guessed.

Haddie lied with a nod and began rolling her hair in a knot. "He came to Eugene to check out the Unceasing because of me. He should have left that day."

Liz moved to the second vial. "That was the attack by the bus station. The time-pushed gunshot."

It had confused Haddie when she'd heard the roaring and thought it unnatural, but didn't realize until afterward that she'd pushed the explosion back in time. When she'd described it to Dad, he'd had a similar experience in one of the wars, of course. *Hell, Liz is going to ask again.*

"I really want to do that experiment. It doesn't have to be an explosion — a ringing bell would work great."

"No."

Liz pouted.

"Can you see my skin?" Haddie asked.

Liz leaned in. "It looks fine."

"I'd like to keep it that way. I'm not using my powers." The visions and the accompanying nightmares were worse than the purpura. After the abuse she'd put her body through in San Francisco, Haddie had no intention of using her powers anytime soon.

Liz dragged a random hair from her face and shrugged. "Can't blame a girl for trying."

Haddie frowned. "Yes, I can."

Liz laughed and bandaged Haddie's arm. "Is our Thursday game night back on? I haven't seen Livia in a bit. Terry either, but we've been texting."

"I'm looking forward to it. Friday night beers?" Haddie asked.

"Of course, we need to get back into the swing of it. Classes start soon." Liz looked at the vials in her hands. "Matt's not coming back. He got out of rehab and took a teaching job in a middle school. Somewhere in Alaska."

"Sorry to hear." *Not surprising*. Matt had been exposed to Sameedha and the raves, along with demons. *I'd move to Alaska*. Haddie couldn't leave. She'd brought the FBI down on Terry. Dad and Kiana were wanted criminals. Aaron had died. All to fight something they didn't understand. Perhaps they fought what the Unceasing wanted, the downfall of society. It seemed to be why they were trying to recruit Dad. She couldn't just go hide.

I need to get refocused on school and my job. "I'm going to be early for work, second time in a week. Maybe Andrea won't fire me after all." Haddie gave Liz a hug.

CHAPTER 2

DETECTIVE DALE COOPER sat inside the department's Ford Interceptor parked under the branches of an old oak. The chatter on the Eugene police band focused on the shift changes. The sun had risen to shine on the four-story building he watched, so there would be little chance to see if anyone entered the third-floor office. They wouldn't need to turn on the lights.

The aroma of pastries wafted from the nearby bakery. He could leave the back windows of the SUV down for a while and continue to enjoy the cool night air. It wouldn't get too hot until later in the day.

His display rang with an alert.

Allison, the desk sergeant coming on shift, sent Dale a message. "FBI inquiry on someone in your case files. You asked to be notified."

He frowned and shook his head as he typed. "Who?" Probably the same jerks as before, looking for ex-agent Wilkins.

"Terrence Lipton."

He glanced at the building and fastened his seatbelt before responding. "When?"

"Last night, previous shift."

Damn it. He'd specifically marked the people the FBI were interested in. What was the night shift doing? *Deal with that later.* The FBI had been clear that they'd dropped their interest in Terrence Lipton.

Whatever Thomas Dawson was up to, the FBI had been relentless. Dale couldn't get anything out of them or his chief. There had been something strange going on ever since the Colman murders and Mel Schaeffer. The chief had shown his hand then, pressuring to close the Colman case quickly, until Harold Holmes had gone missing. Then the FBI had come in, and the bodies at Harold Holmes's estate had cleared Mel Schaeffer, since she was in custody. What did Thomas Dawson have to do with all that? He'd enlisted his daughter and her friends, though Dale hadn't realized it at the time.

Despite the FBI's warning, he'd tracked the group as best he could, especially after Thomas Dawson picked up a warrant for charges in Boise. That was when the FBI had questioned Terrence Lipton. The FBI wanted Dale to be their hound, but kept him in the dark. *Doesn't work for me.* He'd picked up on the connection between Dawson's daughter and Lipton, but hadn't mentioned it to the FBI. They were the ones who said the investigation on the student was closed. Now, they were back.

This specific group of FBI were a little zealous.

If his chief and the FBI were both being pushed, who were the real players? Someone higher up in the government? What could Thomas Dawson be doing that attracted so much attention? *I hate being out of the loop.* Mark

Colman's death had come three days after Dale's divorce. Since then, the job had become frustrating. Harold Holmes had gone missing with the FBI hot on his trail, and no one would give Dale any information. He had the highest conviction rate in homicide until that case. If he weren't being stonewalled, he might have made some headway. He blamed the chief and the FBI more than Dawson or his daughter.

Dale drove toward Lipton's apartment as the morning traffic started to grow heavy. *Damn it.* Eugene would be the size of Buffalo soon, and working homicide made for a grim outlook anyway. He'd already considered a move. Someplace on the coast perhaps, where the town's biggest trouble consisted of illiterate drunks. His résumé had the right stats, and he was pushing fifty.

Terrence Lipton's car wasn't in the apartment parking lot. Still, Dale got out and rapped on the door. Other than a baby crying in the apartment next door, there were no sounds from inside. He sighed. He hated putting out an APB on the car without a good reason. *I'd like to stay off the FBI's radar.* They'd been clear about keeping out of their business. Trying to find out what the FBI were up to in his town wouldn't go over well if the chief got wind of it.

He'd have to head over to the girlfriend's place. He did have the kid's phone number and could call. Climbing back in his SUV, he started it up. He'd get some sleep once he found out what the FBI were up to.

CHAPTER 3

THOMAS WALKED to the back pens of the kennel where Meg and Louis were causing a stir among the three boarded dogs. The wolfhound was the most vocal. Meg, dressed in blue overalls and a yellow T-shirt, stopped at each of the cages with treats. Beyond the scent of the dogs, he could smell the marigolds and geraniums they had planted outside the fence. The wind blew cool from the west. *Might get rain this afternoon.* The farm and the kennel were exactly what he'd needed after living on the edge of Eugene for over two decades. So much had changed in the last couple of months.

I miss Haddie. He might have been able to ignore everything else that the Unceasing were up to if she were here. *Almost.* Whoever was in charge of this movement, their recruitment letter led Thomas to believe they wouldn't go away.

Sam opened the back gate and leaned into the leash as the German Shephard lunged in, excited after its walk. "Pepper. Stop."

Fearless, Louis scampered over and danced at the dog's feet.

"How'd she do?" Thomas asked.

"She's good. I let her off for a quick run; she comes when called." Sam opened Pepper's pen and coaxed her inside.

Thomas grabbed Louis before he ran in. "Good. We'll try her with the Collie later."

"Derringer," Sam corrected. She locked the pen and stood with the leash trailing behind her. Like Meg, she wore overalls at the kennel, and her pink and blue T-shirt was adorned with multiple pins, including her trans pride favorite. She'd easily adjusted to a rural life and appeared more at ease outside the city. She could do with more confidence, but she'd been growing since she began dealing with the dog owners regularly. Her only resistance to their new life and identities had been a fictitious first name, but she insisted on keeping Sam as her middle. He understood the reluctance.

Meg ran over. "Yennifer next?" She pointed to the Wolfhound.

Thomas nodded. "Put Louis on a leash until we see how they do."

Meg pouted, then smiled and ran for the back door of the office.

He smiled at Sam. It looked like a good day, even if they did get some rain later. His phone vibrated in his pocket. One of his contacts had commented in a game app. One of the people from Eugene. His eyebrows drew together, and his muscles tightened. "Be careful with the Wolfhound – Yennifer." He opened the app as Meg bounded from the house with Louis scampering on his leash.

The message was short: "There's a cat watching the jaybird's nest."

Thomas sighed. Someone had gone back to staking out Haddie's apartment. "Siamese?" he typed.

"Negative."

So, not the FBI. They'd been on her for ten days after his warrant had come out. Who then? "Did the bird fly this morning?"

"Nest has been empty all night."

Haddie had likely been at her boyfriend's for the holiday weekend. She'd checked in with Kiana this morning.

The FBI had been nosing around for Thomas. Had someone picked up prints from San Francisco? That would be worse. *I need to get Crow up to Eugene.* Together, they could draw out whoever was watching and maybe even learn a little bit in the process. Crow could be fairly intimidating, and Thomas had lost all measure of patience in this. These could be people connected to whomever wrote the letter. It would be far more dangerous to Haddie if they tried to use her for leverage.

He turned to Sam, who had just opened the gate for the Wolfhound. "I'm going for a ride. You good today?" They were down to just the four, and the Shepherd would be picked up by noon.

She shrugged. Her hair had gotten a little long, and she'd started wearing it in a ponytail. It swung behind her. "Guess so. Kiana's staying here?"

Thomas nodded and headed inside.

Kiana sat at the desk; she'd started handling some of the bookkeeping. With a smile, she looked up when Thomas entered, then frowned. "What's wrong?"

"Someone's watching Haddie's apartment." He started to dial Haddie.

"You think it's him? What are you going to do?"

"I think Crow and I should ask them some questions. Maybe bug the car and see who they call afterward."

Kiana leaned down and scratched at her leg under the desk. "He seems pretty good about keeping insulated, but what choice do you have?"

Exactly. Haddie might have to let go of her life in Eugene. *She won't.* He inhaled into a tight chest. No matter how close they'd come, she resisted the idea of losing her life. He understood that, but she'd have to learn someday when people started to notice she wasn't growing older. Right now, she might be in danger though, and it might not wait until she was ready. If she rejected the idea, he could lose her. Kiana was right. If they rousted these people watching Haddie's apartment, it might only lead them one rung up the chain of command. They'd send others after Haddie. *What choice do I have?*

Kiana studied him.

"I'm going to Eugene." He started dialing Haddie.

CHAPTER 4

Haddie rode down Franklin past the university and ignored Dad's second call to her burner phone.

Terry had been near panic when he called. The FBI had picked him up driving home the night before. "I wish you'd been there with your super vision. They are spooky. Coerced I'd bet. They want to know where Aaron is and his connection to my searches on Lady Erica. I said he might be in some of our groups, because they'd know that already. I'm still shaking."

If they were coerced, how were they functioning any better than Josh? Andrea must be livid. "What did Andrea say?" She took a deep breath of air still cool from the night, but heavy with exhaust from the traffic.

"She's actually pretty cool. She said something about them needing medical treatment after she chewed their asses off. She is the best. Thanks for getting her on my side."

Andrea would be on a rampage. She'd likely be at the firm already. *So much for being early.* Haddie swallowed and her pulse quickened. "I meant, what did she tell you to do?"

"She suggested finding a quiet place at the university to relax and only answer her calls. Later, she wants to meet and get a detailed report. Maybe at the office? Guess I'll see you then."

Probably. Dad called again. "I'm sorry. Dad's just called for the third time in the past minute. Can you call me back when you get somewhere?" She was almost to work anyway, and Andrea would need all her attention.

"You got it, Buckaroo." Terry hung up.

She couldn't help feeling guilty that Terry's situation originated with their friendship. The FBI had started focusing on him after Terry had researched Lady Erica for her. He'd always been there, ready to help. Haddie wouldn't have been able to save Liz without him.

She neared her turn off Franklin and answered Dad's call. "What's up, Dad?"

"Where are you?" His tone sounded sharp.

She frowned. "Almost to work."

"You're on the bike. Turn around, wherever you are. Take side streets to Colburg and head over the bridge to Alton Baker Park. I'll stay on the line."

"Dad?" She slowed, then passed her turn.

"Do it, Haddie. You're being watched, your apartment at least. I need to see if they're following you."

A cold chill raced across her neck and she slowed, picking a right onto Hilyard Street. One car, a blue Camry, followed behind, and Haddie put her blinker on for a left turn onto East 8th Avenue. The sedan continued as she turned, and she took a breath. Ever since San Francisco, she'd been waiting for the hammer to fall. *Well, it has*.

"I think I'm clear. I'm getting onto Colburg now."

"I've got someone at the park. She'll make sure you don't have anyone following."

"Is it the FBI at my apartment?"

"We don't think so. They appear to have given up on you leading them to me."

"Because, last night the FBI picked up Terry, looking for Aaron."

"Hell. He okay?"

"Yeah, Andrea's going to go after them."

Haddie started north, taking deep breaths to calm her nerves. Who was watching her apartment? Would Dad say, if he knew? She'd grown almost relaxed after a harrowing first week back from California. Dad had wanted her to go on a vacation — disappear — until they knew for sure if they'd left any prints connecting themselves to Lady Erica. Liz had kept an eye out for them using the crime lab computers. Nothing had happened, Haddie had gone back to work, and she'd been having a wonderful time rekindling her relationship with David. *Now this.*

Alton Baker Park was huge. "Where in the park?" She rode the bridge over the curving Willamette River where the park stretched along the northeast shore.

"Pull into the first parking lot, walk quickly to the west end, and then head north. I'll be on the phone. If needed, I'll have you cross under the bridge. I haven't gotten much past that." He sounded angry. "Hell Haddie, if you'd just moved on."

Her jaw tightened. Unless he could prove these people were from the Unceasing, or a warrant came out from the FBI, she wasn't going to give up everything. School barely mattered anymore. Her childhood dream of becoming a lawyer hardly seemed important. She wouldn't give up on David, though. *Or Liz and Terry.* She didn't respond to Dad. That could wait. She'd continue with school and her job. *I'd make a lousy lawyer.*

"Haddie?" Dad's voice almost sounded pleading.

"Almost there." The bridge had massive green girders and red rails. It had always looked old. Dad had probably seen it when it was new. She'd come to the park to walk Rock when he was a puppy. It had been a few years, but she knew the large circle that led to the entrance. *No one is following.* A work truck continued straight when she entered. "I don't think anyone's following."

"Good."

She picked a parking spot on the west side, disconnected the Bluetooth speakers, and locked her helmet in the saddlebag. Haddie raised the phone to her ear as she crossed the lawn, ignoring the paths. "You still there?"

"Yes." A faded horn sounded in his background.

"You're driving?" she asked. She rolled her eyes. "You're coming here, of course."

"I am. This is serious. You know what we're up against."

I do. If this turned out to be Lady Erica's boss, Haddie wouldn't have a lot of choices. She'd already risked Terry and Liz. *Rock.* "We need to get Rock and Jisoo out of the apartment."

"We will. They won't bother with them. They're after you." His phone dinged in the background.

Haddie sagged as she reached the walk along the river. *This might be it.* She might have to leave Eugene and her life. "I'm at the path along the river."

"Walk north, past the walkway that leads over the river. She's got eyes on you."

Haddie glanced around, phone to her ear. There were some older couples walking. Two men rode bicycles. There were too many people to watch. Her regular cell buzzed with an unknown number from Portland again; that was two this morning, and they'd left a message. It would have to wait. The little pond in the middle of the park had walkways around it and bridges. More people than she would have imagined seemed to be out early. The weather still held, despite the sun. Fresh grass and water scented the air.

To her left, the Willamette snaked past, and the sound of traffic rushed through the trees. A footbridge suspended from the walk in front of her to the opposite side of the river where the park continued and the bike trail through Campbell Park started. *Where I was attacked by Harold Holmes's men*. That had been a nasty cut, and she'd learned about her powers soon afterward. She shivered at the memories. Cal Young, where the Colmans' house had burned down, lay to the north. The echoes of Eugene had become a lot darker over the past year.

She strode past a small set of falls splashing into the Willamette River. The two men on bicycles rode ahead of her, where the trees of the park thickened and the path wound down toward the traffic on Colburg. How far did he intend her to go? "I'm past the footbridge, heading along the path toward the road. I've never gone this way."

"There's an intersection coming up with some green directional signs. You can sit there on the curb. I need to do something. Haddie, you may have to leave anyway." His voice had that grave tone that she'd begun to notice during their more trying times. "I'll be on mute."

He's really worried. What did he plan on doing? She found where another path joined hers and two rust red lampposts sprouted along a six-inch curb. She sat awkwardly with the burner phone to her ear.

Andrea would wonder if Haddie didn't show up. *I can call her on my regular phone*. She had a while before she'd have to make that decision. The day had started out so well with David; now her life seemed on the brink of falling apart.

I'm not going to leave. She flushed at the thought. It sounded childish. She couldn't put Rock, Jisoo, and her friends in that kind of risk. *I won't leave on a whim.* Dad would have to prove to her that this was a real danger. What was he doing, anyway? *Something that he needed to do.* It sounded ominous.

CHAPTER 5

THOMAS DROVE along the mountain highway in his newly purchased green and white '72 Ford van. It had a wooden bumper bolted to the front, rattled like it might lose a floorboard, and had Grateful Dead stickers on the side window. Despite the repairs and cleaning, it still smelled like weed. He'd left the newer van for Sam.

He watched the pines trail by as he made his decision. It wasn't easy, but they were closing in on Haddie, and he couldn't let that happen. She'd resist letting go of her life. One little mistake or a threat to one of her friends, and she'd be back in Eugene. *This is the only way.* He let another mile of the green forest settle his nerves before he slowed and pulled off the road.

The grassy shoulder slanted upward, and the old van leaned top heavy toward traffic. Coming to a stop, he could hear the sounds of the park around Haddie. She would be livid if she knew what he intended to do. Hopefully, she'd never find out.

He opened an email account, typed in the address he'd

memorized, and composed the message. "Let's talk. I'll be in Eugene in an hour and a half. Tempest."

He didn't wait after hitting send. Returning to the call, he unmuted himself. With his jaw tight, he shifted the van into drive and checked his mirror. The sun bathed the road in blinding light.

Waiting for a semi to pass, he checked his operative's last message. Haddie wasn't being followed. He needed to get her out of Eugene, even if just for a day or two. "Haddie?" he asked.

"Still here Dad. Not very comfortable, and it's going to get hot soon."

He sent a message to Crow; hopefully the man hadn't been drinking last night, or he wouldn't be up for hours. The semi rattled the van as it passed. "I'm trying to arrange someone to get you and your pets out of Eugene until I can clear this up. For now, stay in the park. Head south along the trail, and you'll come to the covered pavilions. There's water and bathrooms." Thomas pulled onto the highway. "Take the battery out of your regular cell if you haven't already. I'm working on fixing this."

Before he'd come to America, early in the nineteenth century, he'd dueled a man in Newcastle. A minor English lord had taken fault with a business venture Thomas had started while masquerading as a Dutch merchant. He'd tried to avoid the man, but the lord had made things uncomfortable for a kindly father-in-law. When the entire family had been on the verge of poverty, Thomas had faced their antagonist knowing that he risked both their lives. Pistols were hardly very accurate at the time and took forever to load. Both of them had gotten off a shot without hitting each other. The lord had managed a second shot that caught Thomas in the ribs. Thomas had killed the lord with a bullet to the neck with his second shot. Thomas had healed, but the family never had. His sacrifice hadn't fixed things. It might not this time either, but he had to try.

"How can we fix this, Dad?"

He sighed. "Best way I know how." *Headfirst into the belly of the beast.*

PART 2

Let us work together so that we can offer mankind a way out of their self-destruction and the endless torture of their siblings.

CHAPTER 6

BRUCE LEANED back in his seat, watching the dark water of the Gulf pass under them. The thudding whir of the Sikorsky helicopter killed any other sounds, but it created an excellent time to think. The back smelled of metal with an occasional whiff of the oil fumes. Stanton, dressed in his navy Brooks Brothers suit, reviewed reports and messages on his tablet. *The FBI still hasn't checked in.*

Inside the hour, they would land just outside New Orleans to meet with the CDC officials under Bruce's control. Everything had to be ready before New York happened. China was ready to proceed. Tempest's daughter had been an opportune find. She'd been the pink-haired woman he'd been looking for since Sameedha had disappeared, and she'd slipped right under Bruce's nose. He'd actually coordinated a lunch with Hadhira, hoping that she might know the whereabouts of Harold Holmes. He'd been on track looking for her, and assumed it was Tempest after Barbara and Araki disappeared. It would make sense that Tempest would have a daughter of that age. Were they working together? Maybe as far back as Harold Holmes, she'd been employed at the agency involved in the whole mess. He had never realized how close he'd been when he'd met Hadhira Dawson at the law firm. At the time, he'd been focused on tracking down Harold Holmes and believed that the agency was hiding something. *A shame.* If he'd known, it might have changed everything.

Stanton faced the screen toward Bruce so he could see the email he'd received from Tempest. *Finally.* A simple email and to the point. "Let's talk. I'll be in Eugene in an hour and a half. Tempest."

Bruce looked at the time and switched his com to the pilots. "Turn around. Head due west. Coordinates to follow." He leaned into the seat as the helicopter turned sharply and the sun shone through his window.

What was Tempest planning? *Tempest knows I've got his daughter marked.* Tempest had devastated much of Bruce's network, but late in the game. If Tempest had taken out Erica early on, things would be very different. Why reach out now? Just to save a daughter? *Perhaps.* This could be a mad dash at Bruce. *I can stop that, easily enough.* Maybe the daughter could be a hostage to gain Tempest's compliance. *I need a strong base for that plan. And the daughter.*

If he hadn't had Erica cede control of so many of her people to him, they'd be in a worse situation. At this point in his plans, Tempest would be a worthy trade for her abilities. Her skill had been remarkable, though her drive and performance lacked for the most part. He'd come close to losing her to suicide multiple times. *Eventually I would have lost her.* Most of her people were tightly under his management, where they belonged.

I need a strong position to negotiate with Tempest. The man would make his move, no doubt. The best place to settle their differences was deep in home territory with a visible force. Tempest had never met one of the perfected mutations. The scraps had gone to the others. Dylan had the real army hidden in the caverns.

He switched to the pilots again. "Albuquerque, New Mexico." Dylan's ranch would impress a military man.

Tempest's overture only made sense in light of his daughter. Bruce switched his com to Stanton. "Check on the FBI; I want this woman immediately." His own mercenaries had likely blown the stakeout, but it had stirred up Tempest. "Tell Dylan that we might be having company. I'll keep him updated on an ETA."

The opportunity to bring Tempest in would mean more now than at any other time. Sameedha and Erica had been instrumental in preparing the groundwork. Once New York triggered the Chinese, military might would matter most. *It's more than just his powers.* How long had he'd been alive, shifting identities? That took some intelligence; Tempest had altered his driver's license just enough to avoid a digital comparison. Even in Bruce's visions, Tempest's ancestor had been a brilliant ally, and then a troublesome enemy. *Time to reverse that mistake.*

He nodded toward the tablet and reached out for it. A timely and appropriate response would be expected.

CHAPTER 7

HADDIE SAT at the picnic bench, trying to ignore the older man who'd been reading at one of the tables when she arrived. He appeared nice enough and hadn't bothered her when she'd sat down, but he did glance over occasionally. Under the pavilion it was still cool, but she wanted to take off her jacket. The air had begun to smell warm, like grass heating up in the sun. Something had died in the bushes somewhere and had the dull scent of decay. She twisted her hair into a knot and checked the time. *I need to get word to Andrea.*

Pursing her lips, she texted Liz.

"Sorry to ask, but could you call the firm and tell them I'm dealing with the rash and won't be in today?" *Maybe never.*

"What's wrong?" Liz would already be at work.

"Dad found out some people are watching my place.

He's all nervous and wants me to stay out of sight for a while."

"Wow! Who's watching? The Unceasing?"

"Don't know. Dad doesn't want me to be at work, and he's got me turning off my cell. I don't want to use a burner."

"I'll call."

Haddie stared at the screen, unsure whether they were done or Liz would be calling. Another text from Liz came through.

"I don't want to lose you."

Haddie's throat swelled. All the frustration of the past hour and a half rose up inside her. "You won't."

Haddie choked down a sob, then noticed the man put down his book. She sucked in a breath and stood. *This has gone too far.* Leaving everything and everybody wasn't an option. Neither was putting Rock, Jisoo, and her friends at risk. *I need a third option.* Her muscles tensed as she paced. She wanted to go back to her apartment and search every car until she found whoever Dad was worried about.

Her phone dinged as Liz sent another text. "I don't think Andrea was happy."

Haddie deflated. "Did you speak with her?"

"No. But I could hear her yelling that you better not be calling out."

Haddie almost turned to her bike. She could see the parking lot from where she sat, and Dad's spy could probably see her as well. That wasn't what stopped her. Dad was right. They needed more information. Maybe Crow could beat the truth out of them.

Liz texted, "You okay?"

"I don't like this. What can I do though?"

"Nothing stupid."

Haddie laughed. Liz knew her well enough to guess what was going on in her head.

"I'll wait for Dad. He's on his way. Thank you."

"I'll call at lunch."

"Okay."

Andrea would be angry, partly because the FBI took Terry for questioning without his attorney. She did everything she could to avoid that scenario. Terry made it sound like the FBI had abducted him. If they were coerced, why hadn't they turned like Josh? Maybe they just worked on their last instructions. What were their directions? What had they hoped to get from Terry? *Aaron. Accomplices. Me.* If Haddie disappeared, would they give up?

Haddie dialed Terry.

He answered quickly. "Hey. Sorry for not getting back to you. Everything okay with your Dad?"

"His people figured out that I'm being watched, so I'm hiding out, and his people are keeping an eye on me."

"No way. Is it the FBI?"

"Dad didn't think so."

"The Unceasing then. Do you think it's because of the phone you left in San Francisco?" Terry asked.

Haddie stiffened, pausing a step in her pacing. "I didn't leave it, they took it. But, yeah, maybe." She looked back at the pavilion where the man read his book. "Where are you?"

"School. Worked on the San Francisco lady's tablet some more. Running a program on the data, actually. The apps have their own security, military grade, but I've been cross referencing the network activity with external data. I think I've matched up a few packets. I've been looking for a trend there and they have a couple servers in the south. One that does a lot of traffic in the southwest, primarily New Mexico, and another for Texas. Today I'm focusing on the New Mexico server. In case you want to do a road trip."

Haddie smiled weakly to herself. *I don't want a road trip. I want Rock and everyone safe.* "That's cool."

"It is. I've got a guy pulling tower data from the carriers. He does a lot of work for the airlines down in that area."

She didn't ask what planes had to do with cell towers. Terry's answers just got weirder when she tried to understand what he was talking about. "Did you tell Livia about the FBI?" What did she think about all this? *David expects to have dinner tonight.*

"Of course. Except — not about nearly pissing myself when they took my phone and stuck me in the back of the car."

Haddie's eyes opened wide. "They got your burner?"

"Nah. Tucked that in some fast-food container while they headed to my car. Kept the regular cell on me so they wouldn't dig too deep."

A police car cruised through the parking lots. It was a regular sight in the parks, but still she swiveled on her toes and headed away from the road. She twisted her hair, conscious of how white it was.

"So," Terry said slowly, "I might know where they were communicating in New Mexico."

Haddie stopped. "How? Where?"

"I've been rebuilding my data from the Coos Bay pictures Kiana got, cross-referencing the different companies under the one corporation in India, and finding all the properties they own. One is in New Mexico, in Albuquerque. The Unceasing have a hidden training site for the apocalypse. Supposedly, you go down there and learn military survival techniques. I'm on their mailing list."

Of course he was. "Where in Albuquerque?"

"Some ranch in the hills. Coyote Canyon? If they have roadrunners there, then I'm all in for a week of survival training."

"I should let Dad know. Can you text me the address?

I'll forward it to him." Actually, she wanted to call him. Sitting here with an old man reading a book would not last long. She'd burned up some time and it had started to get warm in the jacket. The sun had risen high enough that she had to get close to the pavilion to get any shade.

"I could be wrong, you know." Terry sounded smug.

"Not likely, Maestro of the Web."

"Emperor of the Digital World."

"Nerd."

The police car continued its tour, heading east toward the dog park. She couldn't leave Rock and Jisoo alone in the apartment. If someone tried to break inside, Rock might get shot again. Her muscles tensed. *I can't just sit here.* Still, she walked toward the pavilion.

"I'm going to call Dad. Let him know about the New Mexico place."

"Tell our fearless leader that I'm ready to join the Unceasing at their base, infiltrate and all that."

She knew Dad's response would be a clear no. "I'll mention it."

"See yah later, Buckaroo."

Haddie wanted to sit. Her joints ached; they always did lately. The smell of baking grass made her thirsty. She'd walk over to the restrooms.

Dad answered after a minute. "Everything okay?"

"Yes." He knew that though. His lady would have told him if Haddie had left or there were trouble. "I just talked with Terry. He's got an address for us. It might be where the Unceasing are doing survival training."

"Hmm. Okay. Send it to me." He sounded distracted.

"You still driving here?"

"Yes. Crow might have to pick you up, though. I want to see these people watching your apartment."

"Are you going to hurt them?" She didn't cringe at the idea as she might have before.

"No, no." The sounds of city traffic told her that he was close.

"How long are you going to be?" she asked.

"A bit. Crow will be there soon."

What is he doing? She'd done what he asked and kept out of sight, leaving Rock and Jisoo at the apartment, and he wasn't telling her something. Crow would stick her in some motel and nothing much would change. They just expected her to sit there and be safe. "You'll make sure Rock and Jisoo have someplace to go?"

"Yep."

Haddie glared at the phone. All this trouble and now he kept her out of his plans. She stormed past the old man and headed toward the bathroom.

"Are you going to tell me what's going on?"

"Not yet." Dad cleared his throat. "Just stay put for a while. See if I can clear this up. Let me go. Traffic is its usual mess."

Haddie clenched her teeth, her eyes flitting at the people in the park. "You'll call?"

"Yes. I love you."

The tense energy she'd been holding dissipated with her words. "I love you too, Dad." She needed to calm down until they had more information. Without much purpose, she reached the bathrooms and drank some water. Somewhere around her, Dad's people watched her.

CHAPTER 8

DALE COOPER DROVE the Interceptor through the parking lot of the university where a few cars clustered close to the buildings. The police band centered on two accidents and a burglary at a warehouse in western Eugene. The air had warmed with the rising sun heating the asphalt. He'd rolled up the windows and the car took on the scents of empty coffee cups and stale sandwich wrappers from the night before.

He didn't see Terrence Lipton's car, but the school spread through the city; students could leave their car on a street and walk to the buildings. *I'm not about to put out an APB.*

His phone rang with a call from the Portland office of the FBI showing on the display.

He answered, "Detective Cooper, Homicide."

"This is Special Agent Jeffrey Lawrence. We're looking for Hadhira Dawson for questioning. Your desk sergeant suggested that we call you. Are there any known associates or locations that aren't in the file?" His voice had a slight nasal quality.

"Let me think on that. What are you looking at her for?" Dale asked. He'd been the most frequent liaison.

"Can you think of anyone or anyplace we haven't looked at? Something outside of the file?" The FBI agent's tone tightened.

"I'll look at the notes. Is this in connection with her father, Thomas Dawson, or Terrence Lipton?"

"She's not at her work, Detective Cooper. Where would she be?"

"This time of day? She should be there. I'll got though my notes. Is this a new matter, or just a follow up?"

"Let us know if you come up with something." The call disconnected.

Dale rang the desk sergeant as he sped for the parking lot exit. *The FBI aren't letting me in on their investigation.* He was back in traffic before Allison picked up.

Dale interrupted as she answered. "Is there an APB on Hadhira Dawson yet?"

"Just got the call from the FBI to put one out."

"Put one out from me. No contact. Just have them let me know immediately if they find her vehicles or spot her."

"So – block the FBI's?"

"Effectively, yes. Any problem?"

"Not at all, Detective. I'll queue their request behind yours, in case the chief asks."

"Thanks, Allison."

Dale made a loop past the boyfriend's apartment. The FBI would have already looked at her work and home, but neither her or the boyfriend's car or her bike was in the parking lot. If the FBI were looking for her, then something had changed. He might get a hint from Hadhira, though he doubted it. She lied badly, but diligently. He'd never been able to pin her down on one, but likely Thomas Dawson took care of that. The man had connections with nearly every biker group on the west coast.

The traffic on Colburg was thicker this morning, but he got to the bridge and kept right, intending to take the quicker loop past the park to get to the police station. He raced down the back scenic path, watching the bicyclists carefully; they had the tendency to jump out without a look. Civilians weren't the brightest.

It's the FBI who have the information I want. Dale had never been able to put together the larger picture. The FBI worked on a case, and if something was going on in Eugene, he didn't want to find out from the media or his chief. Those four burning deaths surrounding the Harold Holmes disappearance still hung against his record. Clearing those, either before or with the FBI, would be the best outcome.

He pulled up to the station, noting the chief's car and hoping he could get into evidence without too much notice. *He'll string me up if he gets wind of this.* The FBI weren't going to let Dale into their information willingly, so he'd have to get creative.

Luckily, Gibson worked the cage and let him in without a question. "Nelson case. Domestic dispute. Ton of crap in the box. You want a table?" A small table, big enough for three boxes, sat inside the fenced-in room.

Dale nodded. "You get off for the summer with the kids at all?"

Gibson dropped the box on the table and climbed back in his chair. "Hell, yeah. Anaheim. You have no idea how damned expensive. Could have gone to Hawaii and back with the wife."

One of the bugs and receiver had been paired off in a Ziploc left at the top; a quality job from one of the local spy shops. Ms. Nelson could have stuck to divorce instead of trying to cut off Mr. Nelson's goods, but then, her electronics wouldn't be in evidence. Dale kept Gibson chattering about the price of theme park burgers and city restaurants while he palmed the bag in his left hand and leaned in to block the security camera. It focused on the pass-through in front of the desk and caught the table from behind. Tucking the equipment behind his belt buckle, he dug to the bottom and frowned, flipped the lid, and read the list.

"They've got it wrong. I've got the wrong box. I'll be back, Gibson. Let me sort this out." Dale shrugged and headed out into the hall.

He pulled out his cell and paused by the door to call Agent Lawrence. It took a moment for the man to pick up. "This is Detective Cooper. I've got some printouts of my notes that might help. Where can we meet?"

Lawrence muffled the phone, but there were voices in the background. "Scan it and send it to my email."

"Damn. I should have thought of that, but I'm driving now. Where are you? I'll drop it off."

The agent snorted into the phone. "We'll call you when we're done here."

"Gotcha. Let me know." Dale frowned as he pocketed his phone. Who were they questioning now? The boyfriend? Maybe the crime lab tech, Elizabeth Backhus. *That would be convenient*. He headed for the stairs.

His phone buzzed as Allison called, and he almost lost the call in the stairwell. "The FBI put out a warrant for your APB suspect. You want me to keep your status?"

Damn. "Yes." He doubled his pace.

CHAPTER 9

One block from Haddie's apartment, Thomas pulled into a parking spot under a drooping maple tree. He marked each car parked along the street. He didn't expect anyone this far away, but that was no reason to be reckless. His knife and ID he stowed under the passenger seat. Texting a picture of the license plate to Biff, he sent the address and "5pm." The van would be gone tonight, before it became an issue for the local police. Biff would know where the spare key was.

Sam had lived in the apartments across the alley from Haddie's. Thomas walked to the front of the building. A sidewalk cut from the streetside of the building back down to the alley where Haddie parked. No one paid any attention to Thomas as he headed down the concrete path between the apartments and the neighboring wooden fence. The air had started to warm, despite the shade, and the spicy scents of the plants mixed with the pungent city.

He slowed as he came near the end of the walk and inventoried each car as it came into sight. In some of the parking spots, cars were stacked two deep. A gray Chevy

Suburban was parked nose to the alley in a slot with no other cars. Tinted windows hid all but the slightest movement inside. *Not FBI*. They used sedans for surveillance.

Thomas backed two steps and checked his email. He had a response to his overture. "I'm happy to hear from you, Tempest. I'm assuming we can suspend hostilities and discuss our positions amicably. I can make arrangements to have you brought to my location at your convenience." *No signature.* The timestamp was over an hour ago, shortly after Thomas had sent his email.

He sighed and glanced at the window of the apartment in front of him. *Sam's old place.* The curtains were thick and hadn't moved. Stairs led up to the door two paces away. The foundation was concrete masonry with a pattern of blocks in the middle row turned sideways for ventilation. Hopefully his loitering wasn't alarming anyone.

He wiped his hair back, sent a few last messages, then texted Haddie. "Stay put. Go with Crow when he gets there. Two hours." He couldn't be sure she'd hold put. *I have to try*.

Quickly he returned to the email and typed a reply, "Assuming the boys in the gray Suburban outside Haddie's place are yours?" He sent the email and waited, glancing at the apartment window and down the walkway. A bit too open for this.

The response came immediately. "Yes. I'll have them escort you to a helicopter I have waiting. All operations cease immediately."

Thomas frowned. Not likely that he could trust them. "Tell them to expect me." Without waiting for an answer, he disconnected the battery, walked to the apartment, kicked in the screen of a ventilation block, and slipped his phone under the building.

Two men had just opened their doors to the SUV when Thomas turned the corner. *Easy now.* Even with their orders, the driver's hands paused, ready to reach for weapons. Mercenaries? Most were good at taking orders, unless it meant losing their lives. Everything about the letter's author stunk of military. He would pick a secure location to meet with Thomas, well defended with the hopes of impressing and dissuading any assassination attempts. Helicopter? Perhaps Terry's theory on New Mexico would bear out.

None of them spoke as the driver opened the door, then patted his back and sides as he moved to climb in. These people were hardly any concern. Once in the air, any attempt to neutralize him would have to be dealt with carefully. A missing pilot wouldn't do him much good. It was more likely that the author of the letter wanted to convince him than kill him. *Belly of the beast.*

CHAPTER 10

Haddie threw her hand in the air as she read Dad's text. *Two hours?*

She glared at the old man as she peeled off her jacket. The air had warmed, and the park visitors had thinned out. Bicyclists and dog walkers didn't appear to mind the heat. She texted back, "What am I supposed to do? I'm more obvious sitting in a park doing nothing. I'd rather be sitting in a coffee shop."

Air conditioned preferably. She expected a quick response, even an argument, but he didn't reply. Driving still? Shouldn't he be here by now? If he'd left when he first contacted her, which he likely did, then where was he? Her skin around her neck prickled. What is he up to?

Haddie dialed him. If he was driving, he'd answer. It went directly to an out of service area message. She stared at the phone. *I can't sit here all day.* Who was getting Rock and Jisoo? She twisted her hair and glanced back toward the bathrooms. *I'm not pacing in the sun.*

Her phone vibrated and she jumped.

Terry texted, "Need to call David. He's upset. Says your phone goes directly to voicemail. It does."

"What's wrong?"

"Didn't say. Didn't ask. Your boyfriend. I've got enough going on with Livia. She thinks I'm an international hacker. Which is kind of cool."

"Thanks."

Haddie fumbled out her regular cell and put in the battery. What would possibly get David upset? She hadn't even told him about missing dinner. *Maybe this will blow over and I won't have to.* She bounced her knee as she waited.

She had four messages: three from the Portland number and one from David. Ignoring them all, she dialed David.

His voice was strained. "Did you know the FBI have a warrant out for you?"

Haddie chilled. "No."

"They pulled me over and questioned me in some van. What's going on? I know I said I wouldn't ask, wouldn't get involved, but — what's going on?"

She slumped. So, it *had* been the FBI watching her place. Dad was wrong. What if they got a hold of him? Is that why he's not answering? "I'm sorry. I never meant for you to get caught up in any of this. I shouldn't be calling you. If they track this call, tell them you tried to talk me into coming in. You probably should call them and tell them I called. Just say that I promised to turn myself in, okay?" He didn't respond. "David."

"Okay, so I guess — no tacos tonight."

Haddie's chest tightened. *He sounds hopeless.* "I'll work this out, okay?" And if she couldn't? "I love you."

"I love you too, Haddie."

She couldn't stand hearing him sound so empty. "I've got to go."

"Okay."

She hung up, fighting tears, and resisted throwing the phone. Instead, she listened to his message and the near hysteria in his voice. The only part she really heard was when he said, "I don't want to lose you." Maybe she should just face up to the FBI and let them interrogate her. What did they have on her but maybe a burner with her fingerprints on it? Maybe Dad's?

She listened to the other messages from the Portland number. "Ms. Dawson, this is Special Agent Jeffrey Lawrence. Please call me back." The other messages progressed in tone to "you need to call us back." Was it as simple as a question about her and Dad's burners? Taking a deep breath, she called Dad again. It gave the same recording of an out of service error. *What are you up to?*

Haddie removed the battery again from her regular cell, though she had no idea why. Terry, Kiana, and Dad had all mentioned it. *I'm just winging it.* Flailing around in a world outside her comprehension. FBI and operatives. Hiding. Getting a burner phone. Secret codes. She wanted to slam her cell down and stomp on it.

Calm down. Did the FBI have Dad? No. He sounded like he planned on doing something. *And he doesn't want me involved.* She could call the FBI and give them an interview over the phone. What would be her story? Haddie paced away from the pavilion. The man reading his book had become annoying just because he'd stayed so long. He could probably say the same about her.

She opened her burner and called Kiana. "Do you know where Dad went?"

Kiana took a moment to answer, and a dog barked in the background. "He should be with you."

"Yeah, that's what I thought. I think he's doing something else — I mean, he's not here, so he has to be. He made some vague comments about taking care of this. I'm supposed to wait for Crow."

"What did he say exactly?"

"He wanted to see the people watching my apartment at first. Then he started saying that he was 'taking care of it,' no, 'clearing it up.' Then just, 'stay put.' His phone is off. I've tried twice. Maybe they surprised him. Kidnapped or shot him. I'm getting worried." Haddie's concern grew worse as she spoke it out loud. She knew he wasn't as invulnerable as he thought. He could be hurt. "I can't just sit here. The FBI are looking for me."

"What?" Kiana's response came through startling and loud.

"Yeah, they've been calling and even questioned David. They grabbed Terry last night, but that was about Aaron and Lady Erica. Terry's hiding out." Haddie spun in the grass, moving back toward the shade of the pavilion. "So, Rock and Jisoo are sitting at the apartment, and I can't get them. My dogwalker was scheduled to take care of them this morning and today, but what if someone goes into my apartment and ends up shooting Rock — again? I can't just sit here. I'm at least going to go home and get them out. I'm not waiting for Crow."

"Haddie." Kiana spoke calmly but firmly. "Wait. We'll come up there and help out. Sam can coordinate with your dogwalker to get them out of the apartment and pick them up. I'll get with Crow, and we can get you someplace safe until we find out what Thomas is doing."

Haddie stood still and took a breath. *Think for a minute.*

"Okay." That still meant sitting in the park for two more hours. Somehow, it seemed more bearable knowing that Kiana would be coming. "Thank you. Can you drive? I imagine it's not easy with a cast."

"A stick shift would be difficult, but an automatic is easy enough. Besides, Sam can give me a break here or there. She needs highway time."

Hurry. "Okay. Call me when you're on the road so I can know how long. Do you have Crow's number?"

"I'll coordinate with him. One of us will be there soon. Just after 10 a.m. now, sit tight."

"Wait. What are you driving?"

"The Transit. Thomas bought a beat-up green van."

Another van. Haddie tucked her phone away listened to the water of the Willamette River. *What are you up to, Dad?*

CHAPTER 11

THOMAS STEPPED out of the Suburban and tolerated a more thorough search by his escorts while standing on the tarmac of the Eugene airport. A Sikorsky helicopter idled with a slow thumping rhythm on the field. He didn't recognize the model; the equipment had come a long way since his Vietnam years. There were two men in the cockpit wearing gray flight suits. His escorts had stopped beside a private jet office, and he'd been urged to use the facilities, which he had. No telling how long the flight would be. After a thorough search, the mercenaries found nothing.

He hadn't tried to chat them up. These, and even the pilots, might not even know who they worked for. Either way, he wouldn't get any decent intel. If he gauged his correspondent well enough, he'd get plenty of information soon. *Or I'll be dead.*

They pointed him to the open door of the waiting Sikorsky, and Thomas trudged across the tarmac. The blades blew the hot scent of the engine and oil against him. The sun had warmed the airfield. He'd dressed lightly for the van. The helicopter looked more military than commercial, but it had no armaments. Inside, two rows of three seats waited in the back. Pure transport for troops. Thomas climbed inside. *Belly of the beast*. His escorts closed the door behind him.

He put on the headset after he strapped in, not expecting any more conversation than with the mercenaries. Surprisingly, one of the pilots checked on him. "All set back there?"

"Clear." Thomas shrugged. "So, where we headed?"

The pilot laughed. "Wherever we're told. Going to have a couple refuels, but there's water in the locker along with piddle packs. We've got a path of clear weather planned. Easy ride."

"Thanks." He'd picked the middle chair facing forward so he could keep an eye out both windows. The pilots were trained enough not to engage him on any details.

He'd spent a couple years of his life accustomed to helicopters. Sometimes he'd been with a full team heading into the jungles of Vietnam, and in a couple instances, wounded on a stretcher on the floor. The trips out were always filled with bravado and boisterous chatter to quell the nerves. The other trips proved deadened with regrets and the thudding blades above. The war had been futile and wasted so many good lives. In other wars he'd believed he protected someone, even if not his own family. The times were few and far between when killing other soldiers had meant any semblance of safety for those he loved, but he had tried anyway, as he would now. *I have a choice*. He always did. This choice might end up with him dead and Haddie no more secure than when he left. *Or, I'll end this*.

They took off in a southerly direction over Eugene, then set a direct path to the southeast once they reached the edge of the city. A couple of refuels they'd said, but how far would this helicopter go on a tank? They could be heading for Nevada, Texas, or any one of four or five states.

I still don't have a solid plan. He could negotiate for Haddie's safety, or try an all-out attack. A lot depended on the environment, and the author of the letter would likely pick a setting that forced negotiation. *It's time to face this head on and put a face to the enemy.* He'd tried to get a handle on the organization, but he and Haddie had inadvertently dismantled parts in the attempt. Thomas looked out the windows and tracked the mountains and sun as the helicopter leveled and locked on course.

CHAPTER 12

Dale strolled through the squad room to avoid the hall that would take him near the chief on his way out. A phone rang among the desks, but the morning patrols had emptied most of the room, leaving the ringing phone and the scent of coffee strong in the air. The pair of officers who did notice him nodded and quickly busied themselves at their monitors. His reputation as a lone wolf in the division had long ago spread beyond Homicide and extended into the entire force.

The chief had made the situation worse during the Colman case. *I didn't help.* They'd fought openly over closing the case with Mel Schaeffer's arrest. It hadn't appeared that the chief cared who was to blame in the high-profile case, just that it was closed. Dale had initially chalked up the rush on getting out of the media spotlight. Burnt corpses couldn't help but draw out every news outlet. However, there'd been more to it — an urgency without all the usual political positioning that came with morbid cases. One solid alibi and the case would have crumbled, leaving Dale appearing incompetent. His own ego and fear of failure had put him and the chief toe-to-toe over the situation. The chief had won out, and Dale had been tasked to making sure the arrest stuck, despite Andrea Simmons and her intern, Hadhira. Someone had been pressuring the chief. When the second set of corpses were found on the estate of Harold Holmes, the whole matter was dropped, and the FBI began their games. Dale had been thrown to them as fodder, and the chief retreated from any concerns about the Colmans — without demoting Dale as promised. The chief's accusations that Dale wasn't a team player weren't unfounded, but the allegations reverberated inside the police department.

His Interceptor had warmed considerably since early morning, and he'd emptied his thermos. He could have grabbed coffee at the station but wasn't about to head back inside. The FBI were on the move, and he wanted to be mobile if the APB called in. Besides, hanging around the station had never been his MO. He tossed the manila envelope of randomly printed notes and the plastic bag containing the listening device on the passenger seat.

The police scanner woke with his engine, and Dale headed out of the parking lot before the FBI decided to visit and find him at the station. The city had come fully awake, and civilians busied themselves scrambling down sidewalks or clogging up the streets on their errands. Most clung to their phones, desperate for their dopamine fixes from social media. The population of Eugene acted like a herd sometimes, more so than before. *I'm just jaded.* The city had begun to represent loss to him, and its inhabitants acted like shallow drones.

There were some, such as Hadhira and Thomas Dawson, who broke that mold. They might even exhibit some intelligence. Hadhira's interference during the

Colman case had been both refreshing and frustrating. She had no idea how close she came to voicing his own concerns, but he could never let her see that. Besides, a civilian investigating a police matter was every detective's nightmare. He'd wanted to lock her up at least twice during the investigation, though her activity had brought its own repercussions. How much had Thomas Dawson been behind that incident? *I still don't see the correlation.* That was the worst part — not knowing. It kept him up at night.

Allison messaged him on the tablet. "APB alert. Suspect's motorcycle identified. West parking lot of Alton Baker Park. Apprehend or monitor?"

Damn. He hit the lights and pulled around in the two-lane road. He'd been heading southwest. He called her. "Who picked it up?"

"Two six three. Taylor and Jax. What do you want them to do?"

"Get them out of there. I'm on my way. Three minutes out," he lied. Taylor and Jax would let everyone know. If the FBI were monitoring, he had a chance they'd meet him there.

The last thing he needed was to arrive after the FBI. If they came in slightly behind, he could plant his bug on them and see what information he could get. They were done burying their investigation. He'd find out what game they were playing, and maybe, for whom. If he came out of the park with Haddie, he had even better leverage, though he doubted they would budge too far. Best to pull them out to the site and plant the device in their car while they took her in. It might work out best that way; they'd think Hadhira or Thomas Dawson was behind it. His lip curled at the edge of his mouth. *This might just work out.*

CHAPTER 13

HADDIE LEANED against a post of the pavilion, farthest from her companion. It appeared that the old man intended to finish the novel where he sat. The weather would become more stifling before Crow or Kiana showed up, and already she found herself thirsty and ready to head back to the bathroom. Whatever had died in the bushes had begun to reek.

Terry talked on her burner, threatening to finish off her battery. "I've got a program running, but it looks as though they've been getting a ton of messages out of the southwest and New York; both have known Unceasing installations. It'll take a few hours to get details, and I'm pretty bored and hungry at this point. Andrea says it won't be until late this afternoon before she's ready to get a statement out of me."

Lunch actually sounded good. "I'm in the same boat, but I should wait for Crow or Kiana."

Her phone vibrated and a message from Liz popped up. "FBI just left crime lab looking for you. A warrant."

"Hell," Haddie said.

"What?"

"Liz said the FBI was just by looking for me. They've got a warrant."

"I feel slighted, the most they had for me was bad breath. How'd you rank?"

"San Fran? Maybe?"

"Guess you're stuck hiding out, but that might free me up. I've got a great idea."

Haddie raised her eyebrows. "Should I be concerned?"

"I'm thinking sushi. I can grab some right over by the bike trail, leave my car there, and walk over the footbridge to your park. We can do lunch."

Haddie leaned her head back against the pole. It would kill some time. *I am hungry*. "Okay. You know the kind of stuff I like. Thank you, Terry. This will help."

"What are friends for, Buckaroo, if not sushi delivery to your secret hideout?"

Haddie checked her phone's power. *Sixty percent*. She had a charger and plug in one of the saddlebags, and there was an outlet under the eave of the pavilion that she could reach.

Would Dad send Biff for her bike? She sent him another text. "What are you up to?" He hadn't answered the other four. *He's not been arrested*. She closed her eyes, hoping the thought was true. He'd made it clear he planned on doing something, but what? Beating up and interrogating the people who watched her place? She wanted to believe he wouldn't do that, but he might look at it as protecting her. Who was watching her anyway? He'd said it wasn't the FBI. Maybe he believed they were the Unceasing or whoever wrote that letter to him? Deciding to charge her phone before it got too low, she threw her jacket over her shoulder and headed into the sun.

Sameedha and Barbara Stevens had made it sound like

someone was in control. It had to be the person who tried to recruit Dad. So, the people who watched her apartment were likely hired by that person. Maybe Dad would find out who that was. But for over an hour? She didn't like that the FBI just happened to be looking for her at the same time. Then again, Kiana and the others believed the FBI might be working for this person. *Maybe they did find my fingerprints.*

Haddie rummaged through her saddlebag and came out with a plug and cord for her charger. The sun had become brutal and would leave her sweating on the return trip. With less than an hour until noon, both Kiana and Crow were an hour away. Terry would help her kill some time, and then her sentence at the park would be over.

She stood on her toes and just reached the outlet. Propping the charging phone on a ledge, she turned at the sound of a scuffed footstep. Her heart froze in her chest.

Detective Cooper wore his black shirt, silver badge, and a scowl. A black Ford Interceptor had been parked on the edge of the grass. His thin mustache drew forward as he spoke. "Hadhira Dawson, you're wanted for questioning by the FBI. You'll need to come with me." He jerked his head at her companion in the pavilion with a dismissive motion. "Leave."

The older man looked from her to the Detective, and slowly closed his book. For a desperate moment, Haddie imagined the man's presence might help. Her eyes flickered to the few other people still at the park in the heat. Dad's spy would be here, watching. No one could help her. Her shoulders sagged. The reader stood and backed out of the pavilion, staring at both her and the detective. He slipped at the edge of the concrete, regained his balance, and stumbled across the grass, glancing back every other step.

"Turn around," Detective Cooper said.

Haddie raised her hands. "Please don't let the FBI get hold of me. They're being controlled by someone else." Her throat seemed dry.

His hand paused at his waist, thumb touching his belt. His gun holstered there. "Why do you say that?"

Could she actually reason with him? For the first time since she'd known him, he seemed to waver. How much could she tell him? If he gave her to the FBI, she might not have any option but to kill them. Enough people had died. She cleared her throat. "Kiana — Special Agent Wilkins found out that a group of the FBI were acting on orders outside the FBI. It's why she left and why they are looking for her." *Not all of the truth, but close.*

"Who is controlling them?" He tilted his head toward her, leaning in, as if unsurprised but almost hungry for the information. Did he suspect?

"The Unceasing, we believe. A group that is planning for an Armageddon-like event." Her pulse pounded in her ears.

The answer appeared to annoy him. He reached back and produced a pair of cuffs. "Turn around. Hands behind your back."

What should I do? She couldn't kill Detective Cooper. If he worked for the Unceasing, he wouldn't be disappointed or annoyed at the mention of them. *He was played as much as me over the Colmans.* How, she couldn't be sure. The FBI were her enemy, at least this group of them. Sighing, she turned around and offered her wrists. She could make the cuffs disappear later.

She swallowed a lump in her throat as he clasped a cuff around one wrist. A simple spin and she could take him down, but then what? She stared at the trees lining the path by the river as he locked the second cuff. "Are you going to give me to them?" she asked.

"Are you going to tell me why the FBI wants you?"

She could. He wouldn't believe it. Haddie turned and watched him over her shoulder. "I know too much. I know that they work for the Unceasing. I know that Sameedha collected money for the organization through the raves. I know that Lady Erica recruited people for their cause. I know that they plan on doing much worse, very soon."

"And your father?"

"The same, he knows too much. And Kiana, Special Agent Wilkins."

Detective Cooper studied her, rubbing a thumb across his mustache. "Do you have any proof?"

What would he consider proof? The connections Terry had drawn between the financial organizations and the properties they owned? Probably illegally obtained information. "Some, yes."

He was going to rub off his mustache. His scowl changed; evidently, he had different versions of her claims. "Sit."

Haddie fit her hands under the top of the picnic table and sat down, elbows against the edge. She faced out of the pavilion in that position. Terry stood, in the path by the river, with two bags dangling from his hands. *Lunch.*

Detective Cooper followed her gaze. "There's room for two in the back," he said with a low growl to his tone. "No. That makes sense. Terrence Lipton is the one who digs up a lot of this information for you. Which is why the FBI have been questioning him." He turned and waved Terry forward.

Terry lifted a bag and freed a finger to point to his chest.

"Yes, you," Detective Cooper called out. With a slight snarl, he said, "He's not an idiot."

Maybe; Terry *had* just stood there watching when he should have dropped their food and run. Finally, Terry walked across the grass toward them.

"He knows everything?" Detective Cooper asked Haddie with a sidelong glance.

She nodded. How much should they tell Detective Cooper? *Maybe just enough to get free?* Careful not to let him see, she scanned the parking lot. When would Crow or Kiana arrive? Surely they'd be more careful. Well, Kiana would be. What if Dad showed up?

Terry wore a sheepish smile; his hair looked tousled and hung down across his eyes. "Hey — Agent — Detective Smith. I didn't really buy enough for everyone, but I guess we can share."

"Detective Cooper. Put the bags down and sit."

The plastic bags clinked on the picnic table, and Haddie found herself thirsty. What could they tell Detective Cooper that wasn't too much but would convince him not to turn her over to the FBI? He obviously wanted information.

"Why are the FBI questioning you?" Detective Cooper asked Terry.

"Well, they're looking for Dr. Aaron Knox. He's somewhat famous on the forums — for hunting demons."

Detective Cooper's lips tightened. "Demons?"

"Yeah. They look like humans, until their skin falls off, then they're just flesh underneath with fangs and teeth — usually. They're all different, from what I've seen. The government disappears the pictures as soon as they show up on the web, but we've got most of them." Terry had gotten animated, gesturing with his fingers, and then sat subdued.

"There's room for both of you in the back of the car. Maybe the FBI would like a second run at you, considering that you were bringing their fugitive food." Detective Cooper spoke with a sharp tone. "Are you going to tell me the truth?"

Terry looked up with the sheepish grin. "I know it sounds crazy, but we've got pictures. And I've seen them. They attacked Aaron — Dr. Knox at the bus station last month. And —" He stopped and grinned sharper as Detective Cooper cocked his head. "You heard about it."

Detective Cooper's thumb returned to his mustache. "I dismissed those statements as they came up in the original reports from the responding officers, and the witnesses recanted. It made no sense."

"Yeah, they've managed to intimidate people into believing that they'd be considered insane. Which happened; some reporters have been pretty brutal. Anyway, Aaron thought they might be some government experiment trying to create a super soldier. Then, the FBI started harassing me and him over the research we did."

"Where is Dr. Knox now?"

Terry motioned. "Somewhere east of here."

Haddie felt her chest hollow. She hated using Aaron, but Terry built a compelling story of the truth that might persuade Detective Cooper that the FBI were not to be trusted. Would it work?

Detective Cooper shook his head lightly. "You can show me your evidence? Can we get hold of Dr. Knox?"

"I've rebuilt most of it, since the FBI burned me. I've got people on the forum that can dig out the older stuff. As far as Dr. Aaron, you'll need a psychic. He's under deep cover."

Haddie closed her eyes. Terry might have gotten her a small break, but his humor stung. "Can we show you?"

she asked. "Then you decide if you want to trust the FBI?"

Detective Cooper shifted scowls, then nodded and walked over to her phone. "I'll keep this. You stay cuffed. We'll all take a ride and Terry will get me some evidence." He stood on his toes to yank her burner down. "Then we'll see."

He jerked around as a car door shut.

A silver Pontiac G6 had pulled onto the grass behind Detective Cooper's Interceptor. Two men, both in black suits, were walking toward the pavilion. *FBI*. Her heart raced, and Haddie slumped. They'd been so close. How had they found her? She couldn't go with them.

Detective Cooper strode toward them. "They're in my custody. You can get them when I'm done, Special Agent Richardson." He spoke in a balance tone of authority and geniality.

Both men stopped. Their eyes were dark rimmed, as if they hadn't been sleeping much. The closer agent stood on the edge of the pavilion. "She's coming with us," he said. His eyes locked on hers, not with fear, but apprehension. Did he know what she could do?

"They are staying with me. Discuss it with the chief," Detective Cooper said. His voice carried a grisly determination that drew the eyes of the closer agent. Detective Cooper blocked the path down the pavilion to the picnic bench.

The agent didn't blink. "No time." He reached back and drew his gun, his partner following his lead. In a two-handed grip, he pointed the muzzle at Detective Cooper's chest.

"Stand down, Richardson," Detective Cooper barked. His right hand shifted, but he didn't reach for his gun.

The closer agent gave the slightest shrug and his supporting hand tightened. Muscles on his finger tensed and the pad of his finger spread as he put slow pressure on the trigger. They were going to fire. Haddie's heart jumped.

"Stop," she yelled, and her tone rang inside the pavilion.

CHAPTER 14

DALE FLINCHED from Hadhira Dawson's shout, expecting the shot from Richardson's gun. Special Agents May and Richardson faded away in the space of a heartbeat. Dale's pulse began to race. Where Richardson had stood, an ugly slick of dark red stained the concrete. What had happened to them?

They were gone, leaving their car still idling on the grass. *What just happened?* They had been about to kill him, just to get to the suspect. On its own merit, that appeared impossible. "Where?" he asked out loud.

People don't disappear. The FBI does not shoot local law enforcement. His eyes dilated and the grass appeared to brighten around him and he searched the cool dark of the pavilion, as if he'd missed something and the two agents were hiding.

In shock, he turned around to confirm. "They're gone," he said to Terrence and Hadhira.

Terrence nodded, a bit stiffly. Hadhira sagged forward, her arms still cuffed behind her back and her white hair trailing down her pants.

The moment repeated in his mind. People didn't just vanish. Dale glanced down at his chest, as if he might have missed being shot and he were dying — hallucinating. "They're gone. You saw that?" He asked both of them, but only Terrence reacted with another nod. Hadhira acted sick. She leaned down, chest to her knees, groaning lightly. Her friend moved slowly, pointing to her as he slid down to the seat beside her. His eyes watched Dale's hands. Then he rested his fingers gingerly on Hadhira's back and pulled hair out of her face.

Dale looked down at the cell phone in one hand and his drawn gun in the other. He barely remembered pulling it as the men disappeared. *Richardson would have shot me.* He raced through the past few moments of his memory. *This isn't happening.* Glancing around the park, he slid his gun back into his holster and dropped the cell phone into his shirt pocket. *I need to call this in.* What would he say? *The FBI tried to shoot me, but they disappeared into thin air.* Anything he composed sounded absurd.

Terrence had Hadhira's hair back off her face. "Are you okay?" he asked her quietly.

She nodded. "I had to." Her voice wavered as if crying or in pain. "They were going to kill him, possibly you afterward."

"I know."

She acted as if she'd done something — more than just yelling at the men. "Is she okay?" Dale asked. His body pulsed with each heartbeat.

Terrence nodded. "Could we maybe lose the handcuffs, at least for a few minutes?" He glanced at Dale, then at the cars. "Also, we might want to get out of here."

In this heat, the park looked empty. "Not until I understand what just happened."

She turned up to him, and he saw that her face had purple red splotches on skin that had been smooth a minute prior. She acted as though it were painful for her to speak. "You wouldn't understand, wouldn't believe."

Ears pounding with his heartbeat, his face tightened. "I'm not in the mood for theatrics or mysteries. Are you saying that you understand what just happened?" Part of him pleaded for her to have an answer, but nothing could make any sense. She'd been right. Anything she said he would likely not understand, or not believe. *Still.*

She leaned back, a sad expression tugging at the ends of her lips. The mottling dotted across her cheek and down her neck. "I did that. I made them disappear. It's an ability that I have. I did it to save you — us. I would have likely had to do it anyway, if they worked for who I believe they report to."

She seemed serious.

How? He didn't ask.

Her being able to do what she said made no more sense than the two missing FBI agents. How did he explain the marks on her face? They weren't there earlier, and they didn't seem to be growing or spreading like some sudden rash. A trick? To do so, she would have planned on this happening. Anger flushed up his cheeks. She offered an answer that he couldn't accept.

Terrence nodded. "Believe it. Crazy, huh."

Dale staggered back. His heart pounded in his chest. *I'm almost fifty*. He could be having a heart attack. Would that cause delusions? *This isn't real*. He felt the heat under his shirt and the sweat. The air smelled rank with decay. *This is real. Impossible*. He stared past them into the green beyond the sidewalk. Trees and brush rustled in a thin wall at the edge of the grass. Through the branches, the dark blue of the river splashed white in one spot. *I'm losing it.* The brightness that had come earlier faded, and the leaves turned dark. He took a deep breath, trying to slow his pulse.

"How?" he asked without taking his eyes off the leaves. There was an emptiness to his voice, as if someone else spoke.

She sighed. "I don't know exactly. I make a sound and have intent." Her head shook, white hair rolling. "It hurts afterward, and I get purpura."

"Purpura?"

"The markings on my face and hands."

He stopped himself from looking at her hands. What was he going to do? If he believed her, she'd murdered two FBI agents who were going to kill him to get to her. A self-defense case wouldn't make it past a sanitarium. If he didn't believe her, then two agents had disappeared before they could shoot him. *I can't go to the chief with this.* Dale would be out of a job either way. Since the divorce, the only thing he had was the police force. His head hurt; his pulse throbbed.

When his father had been shot on patrol in Buffalo, Dale had been thirteen visiting his grandmother for four days in the summer. She'd lived on a farm in a green place they called Sand Hill. *Not a town. Just a church, fields, and houses.* He'd been throwing seed in the dirt for the chickens when she came out teary-eyed to tell him. The chickens had already been fed; he just liked watching them chase the pieces.

He hadn't believed her. *Impossible.* He'd just kept feeding the chickens. He could see his father in his mind. Tall and thick with a smile that barely curled the edges of his lips, but he knew the rare times it showed. He spoke firm but caring words — never harsh or angry, just firm, like stone.

An Aunt Bela had come out to Sand Hill. Even with his father's body motionless in the polished box, Dale hadn't cried.

The impossible simply had become possible. He was moved to the place called Sand Hill and had lived there until he talked his grandmother into letting him go off to prep school.

His neck felt stiff as he turned down to study her. *The impossible simply became possible.* Terrence sat awkwardly beside her. "You believe this?" he asked her friend.

Terrence shrugged. "Ever find the demon or the coerced who chased Aaron at the bus station?"

Coerced? Dale blinked. "No." Those ridiculous reports. "You?" he asked Hadhira.

She nodded. Sweat trickled down the side of her face and she looked like she was still in pain. "Not much choice."

How many people had she killed? A headache grew at his temples where his pulse pounded. His neck hurt. "What are coerced?"

She glanced at Terry and he blushed. "There was someone who could make people obey her. We call her victims coerced. We think that happened to the rogue FBI."

The agents had seemed fanatic and acted outside what he expected from them. "She *was*? What happened to her?" Dale shook his head. *I'm acting as if I believe her. Do I?* He never could help himself wanting to drill down to the truth. It was an aspect that both aided his career and worked against it. What career? *I'm done*.

A woman spoke from behind and he jumped.

"I need you to move very slowly, Detective Cooper."

The tone had a marshal authority to it, one that threatened death if he didn't comply.

He put his hands out to his sides and turned slowly.

Leaning against the side of his Interceptor, holding a Sig Sauer P320 at her waist and aiming it at his torso, was ex-FBI Special Agent Kiana Wilkins. She had a cast down her left leg covered in colorful art, and a crutch leaned against his car.

CHAPTER 15

HADDIE TURNED with a wince at Kiana's voice. Detective Cooper stood a pace away from Haddie's knee, his hands splayed at his sides. Kiana wore a dark green shirt, a colorful cast, and shorts; her braided beads dangled over her left eye, and she positioned herself as though relaxed, but she was a good shot. Dad had commented on Kiana's skill a number of times. Part of Haddie felt relief, but her chest tightened. *Kiana won't shoot him.* Where were Meg and Sam? There was no sign of the big Ford Transit. In this heat, there were few cars left in the parking lot at all.

She started to say something, but fell silent. Detective Cooper wouldn't try anything, but he might not react well to Haddie interfering. Kiana's arrival brought a sense of support, but Haddie imagined the detective had been close to releasing her anyway.

He tilted his head as he spoke. "What do you intend to do, Wilkins?"

Kiana smiled, leaning on his Interceptor with a crutch propped beside her. "I've got a couple suggestions that might make us all relax a little. First, take your gun out of the holster very slowly and toss the magazine in the grass, empty the chamber, then toss your backup magazine. Then we'll move on to releasing Haddie."

"Why would I release her?"

"Well, two of the agents who were looking for her are gone. I know you noticed," Kiana said.

"There's still two more." He shifted a heel. "You were here? You've seen this before?"

Kiana tilted her head and nodded. "Let's work on cooling down this situation first. Magazines?"

Haddie let out a breath, but Detective Cooper didn't move immediately. The smell of decay hung in the pavilion, and she wished for a breeze. *Something to drink.* The stress over being caught by the detective and then the FBI left her frazzled along with the fatigue of using her powers. She couldn't argue for staying in Eugene anymore. The FBI were willing to kill to get to her, and now the police would know about her.

He moved slowly, reaching with his left hand to draw out his gun. Haddie jumped when the magazine clattered against the concrete; a bullet followed, and he kicked them into the grass. He had another magazine clipped on his belt. The keys to her cuffs he pulled from his pocket and tossed to Terry. "This isn't going to turn out well," he said.

Haddie shifted to give Terry access to her hands and the cuffs.

Kiana lowered her gun, keeping it in hand, but pointed at the ground. "Agreed. But none of us have a lot of choices."

"Come to the station, and we'll hash this out." He slid his gun back into his holster.

Shaking her head, Kiana watched as Terry fumbled with Haddie's cuffs. "I tried that after Portland. Didn't work out too well for me. I think you'll find things turning pretty nasty for yourself, despite whatever happened to us."

Haddie winced as she pulled her left arm forward. They had to get Rock and Jisoo, then she had to leave Eugene, permanently. Detective Cooper had found them with the FBI right behind. Were the police watching the park now? Would Detective Cooper tell her if they were? They had to get out of the park.

Terry freed her left hand. "Can I keep the cuffs?" he asked.

"I think it best that we give them back to Detective Cooper," Kiana said. "Put your hands behind your back."

Detective Cooper raised his hands up. "I don't think we want to go there."

Haddie stood, picking up her jacket. Along with aching joints and burning skin, her arms felt numb. She walked out of the pavilion to the side, circling toward Kiana. Terry stood, lips tight, behind the detective. They didn't need Detective Cooper following, but handcuffing him seemed a bit excessive. He had been willing to stand up to the FBI over her. Had he been alone, or were there officers waiting at the entrance to the park?

Kiana studied Haddie's face. "You okay?"

Haddie shrugged. "You know."

Leaning over, Kiana spoke quietly. "I think Thomas went to meet with the guy who wrote the letter. He might think it was the best way to deal with this. I've been thinking over some of his comments to me. We need to get you out of here and figure out what to do next."

Haddie's chest tightened. If Dad and Crow planned on interrogating the people who watched her house, wouldn't she have heard from them by now? Kiana could be right. *That's suicide.* She couldn't let him do it. If he killed the leader, would the Unceasing stop? Was that his plan?

Detective Cooper studied them. "I can help." He had not put his hands behind his back, and Terry stood awkwardly with cuffs in hand. "First, I can send the station a message, you've gotten away, last seen heading over the footbridge toward the west. The other two FBI agents might be listening to the scanner. Maybe we could trap them over at Campbell Park."

"Hands behind your back," Kiana reiterated. "You're trying to delay us."

He scowled. "No. I'm not. But I need to make sense of this." Any pretense of concern for Kiana's weapon disappeared as he stepped toward Haddie. "You. Was that you with the Colmans?"

Haddie shook her head. Kiana had raised her gun slightly.

"Someone like you?" He waited, scowl growing harder. "Who?" He wiped his mustache with his thumb. "I need to know. Was it one of these demons or coerced? How?"

Kiana didn't look over, but asked, "What were you guys talking about over here?"

Haddie smoothed back her hair and twisted it into a knot. "I was trying to get out of the cuffs." Some part of her did want Detective Cooper to understand — to believe her. He'd been close to accepting, before, and he would know how to get them out of the park. Speaking louder, she looked up at him. "Harold Holmes. He could burn people, and so could his brother."

"Dmitry? Where did they go?"

Haddie grimaced and pointed toward the smudge in the grass left from the FBI agent. Detective Cooper had stepped in it.

He sidled out the dark stain and shook his head. "It does explain it. But that's impossible." The later statement came out with less conviction.

"What are we doing?" asked Kiana. "I'm not comfortable here."

What am I doing? They needed to go find Dad. Maybe he was at that New Mexico ranch. What would they do about Detective Cooper? The entire county would be looking for them if he got back to the station. If the police didn't already have them surrounded. He'd been surprised by the FBI. *I'm missing something.*

"I can help," he said. "I can't say I believe you. However, something happened that I can't explain. I don't have much of a future if I can't explain it. I only ask that you help me understand some of this. I'll help you get out of here, if you promise me that."

Haddie raised her eyebrows. *Take him with us?* "I have explained, and you don't believe me."

He stepped closer, eying Kiana as she raised the gun slightly so that it aimed at his feet. "I'll try. Agent Wilkins is right, though. We don't have much time. Someone, police or FBI, will be here soon, and everything will get very complicated. Let me put them off track so we can leave and discuss everything." The scowl appeared to have been replaced by a pained grimace. "I need to understand this, and I'm pretty sure that won't happen in the interrogation room of the police station."

Kiana's face tightened. "We don't have time to find someplace where we can all sit around and chat."

"Why?" he asked. His tone hardened, but still there was a sense of pleading to it.

We have to leave. Rock and Jisoo needed out of the apartment. Sam and Meg were around somewhere. The quicker they wrapped everything up and left Eugene, the better. It truly seemed that Detective Cooper wanted to understand, first and foremost, but they couldn't fully trust him. Haddie stepped over to his window and looked in at the driver's seat.

She took a deep breath and put out her hand. "Give me your phone."

"What are you doing?" asked Kiana.

"Something stupid, most likely."

Detective Cooper reached into the front pocket of his slacks and produced his cell. Haddie disconnected the battery. "Get in your car. You're going to send that message, then you and I are driving to the police station where we'll drop off the SUV."

His eyes widened, surprised.

Kiana hissed. "What are you doing? What if he tries something?"

Haddie jerked her head toward the inside of the Interceptor. "There's no sludge in his front seat, so I didn't have to defend myself." She wasn't sure if that were exactly true, but it certainly caused Detective Cooper to stiffen. "We can't leave his police car here. They'd track it and find the FBI's Pontiac." She couldn't wait any longer to get started after Dad. They could always just abandon Detective Cooper far enough in the woods that it took him until nightfall to get back to a phone. "Besides, if he truly does get them off our trail, then we'll have a good start."

"I thought you didn't trust him."

"Don't. But he didn't hand me over to the FBI."

"Thomas would hate this idea."

Haddie raised her eyebrows. "And where is Dad?" She gestured to Detective Cooper. "Get in. Don't make me do something I'll regret." She brushed her face, knowing he looked at the purpura.

Kiana slipped her gun into the back of her belt and touched Haddie's arm. "This is insane, but — where do you want me?"

Until they had better control of Detective Cooper, Haddie didn't want him to know about the van or Sam and Meg. "Park in the lot east of the police department. Turn left at the entrance up there. There's an office building on the same side as the police station; you can park there. I'll walk him down the road and text you to come pick us up."

"Dumb idea, Haddie." Kiana shook her head. "Thomas is going to be pissed I agreed to go along with this."

"What choice did you have?"

"Shoot him?" Kiana hobbled with her crutch.

Bottles clinked as Terry retrieved their forgotten lunch. *I really am hungry*. She opened the passenger door to the Interceptor and slid inside before Detective Cooper. He climbed in and took a deep breath as he started the car. Picking up his radio he called in. "Suspect Hadhira Dawson spotted crossing Peter Defazio Bridge heading west toward Campbell Park. Pursuing on foot. Backup officers to Campbell Park." They listened to the response, and then he put on his seatbelt.

Kiana and Terry waited by the pavilion. Where had she parked? Kiana wore a frown and Terry looked a little paler than usual.

"Seatbelt." Detective Cooper's face had settled back into his everyday scowl.

As she pulled down the belt, Haddie's phone buzzed in his shirt pocket. "Damn." Did he forget, or plan on keeping it? "Give me that." She glared as he handed it over. Her charger hung in the pavilion. "Terry, grab my phone charger hanging at the pavilion."

Crow texted, "Found the park. Where are you?"

"I'm leaving now," she replied. "Meet us at hillside. Do you need the address?"

"Nope, but I'm supposed to take you to Creswell."

"Change in plans. Have you talked to Dad in the last couple hours?" she asked.

"Nope."

She waited but he didn't add anything. *Where the hell are you, Dad?*

Detective Cooper pulled slowly onto the road. "Was that your father?" he asked.

"Nope." *What am I doing? This is a bad idea, Haddie.* She might end up having Crow pin Detective Cooper down and using his handcuffs anyway. At least, if the FBI were listening, they were headed in the wrong direction. She didn't look over as they passed Dad's Ford Transit parked just behind the bathrooms. Cooper might still pull something once they were in the police station parking lot.

CHAPTER 16

Fifteen minutes later, Haddie strode with Detective Cooper down the sidewalk of the street just south of Cal Young where the police station was located. Fumes from passing traffic wafted around them. Sweat trickled down her sides, and she kept waiting for a police siren to whoop behind them.

Once she'd passed the buildings where Kiana had parked, she texted as they continued to walk. "On the road. I told Crow hillside."

The sun had become brutal, and the heat caused her skin to prickle with pain. The effect of using her power had subsided, but she felt like crap. She regretted her plan with each step. *I need to find Dad, not babysit Detective Cooper.* They were out of the park, at least.

"What will they do, when they don't find you at Campbell Park?" she asked.

He took a deep breath. "Radio. Then cell. Track the vehicle while patrols search the area. When they find the SUV at the station, they might assume I'm inside, but they'll continue searching until they're sure. Then an APB. I think you've got an hour before it's county wide."

Haddie doubted they'd be too far by then. She'd have to either drop him somewhere or hide him. She still couldn't be sure where they'd find Dad, but guessed they'd start in New Mexico. Hopefully, Crow might have some details that would help. Dragging Detective Cooper around became a less attractive idea the more she thought about it. He'd end up seeing Sam and Meg.

The bright white of the Ford van pulled up beside them, and Sam slid the door open. There was only a bike lane to pull into, so traffic had to pass. Kiana studied them from the driver's seat. In the front, Meg's mop of auburn hair jostled as Louis wriggled to get a view over her shoulder. Terry sat in the first row eating sushi. Haddie jumped in ahead of Detective Cooper, climbed into the second row, and left her jacket on the seat beside her.

"Hi, Aunt Haddie." Meg's voice still had a light, bright tone, but she kept her voice subdued. A red tanned nose peeked around her curly hair.

"Lose the jewelry, Detective, and lie down in the back row," Kiana said.

As he passed, Detective Cooper took the silver badge off his black shirt. "What's the plan?"

"The plan is you lie down in the back row."

He started to speak. "I –"

"Silently." Kiana's tone reminded Haddie of when her friend had been an FBI agent – and a danger.

Sam slammed the door closed and dove into the seat beside Haddie, grappling her with a hug as the van pulled forward. "I missed you. Are you okay? Your rash is back."

Haddie closed her eyes and felt her throat thicken. *I can't start crying*. She missed Sam – all of them. Now, she may be joining them as exiles from Eugene. *We need to find Dad first.* She'd have to leave Terry and Liz. *David.* Her heart dropped. Louis wiggled against her knees, and despite a horrendous morning, she felt like she was home. Sam wore overalls. When had that started?

"Why is Detective Cooper with us?" Sam asked, whispering in Haddie's ear.

Haddie pulled back and rolled her eyes. "Maybe because I'm not that bright."

Terry waved a takeout in her direction over the seat. "If you don't want this . . ."

She grabbed the food. "Thank you, Terry. I'm starving."

Sam nodded toward the back seat with a questioning look.

"Later," Haddie said. She grabbed the bottle of green tea when Terry offered it. "We need to get Rock and Jisoo."

"That's what Kiana said." Sam leaned back into the seat, hunching a little. "I finally learned to drive. She mentioned I might be driving back on my own — with Meg."

"Probably." Haddie dipped sushi into soy sauce, wishing she could mix in some wasabi, but not willing to take the time. It wouldn't take long to get to the hillside house. Crow wouldn't like seeing Detective Cooper with them. Terry seemed to think New Mexico was a hub for the Unceasing, but that didn't mean Dad was there. Toenails clattered behind her where Louis had gone to investigate Detective Cooper. She took a swig of the unsweetened green tea and sighed. Hopefully, they could figure out where Dad had gone; he had to have said something to Kiana or Crow that would give them a hint.

Terry passed back a napkin and looked over Haddie's shoulder. His eyes held a haunted and somewhat desperate look. In a whisper, he said, "Technically, we just kidnapped Detective Cooper, didn't we?"

Detective Cooper answered, his voice seeming to come from under her seat, "I'm a willing participant. I would, however, like to know what the plan is."

Haddie raised her eyebrows at Terry whose lips formed an O. "We'll let you know," she said.

"So, no plan. Is this how you end up in these messes, Ms. Dawson?"

Pretty much. Haddie dipped more sushi and didn't answer. They'd be at the hillside house and would need to keep him out of the way until they had a plan. *A willing participant? I can't trust him.* For their own good, Sam and Meg needed to be kept out of earshot as well. She'd finished her food by the time they approached the house. The last time she'd been there, Aaron had been alive.

Her chest tightened as they approached the drive. An older, gray Toyota Highlander was parked at the mailbox. It had a magnet on the side advertising "Kelly's Kleaners." The windows were tinted, and the driver flashed the lights. Crow rolled down the driver's window and smiled. He wore a black leather vest with nothing but hair and tattoos underneath it.

"Crow!" Meg shouted as they rambled up the familiar road.

The house looked quiet, like it always had. So many memories were there, but the ones that pushed to the front were of Aaron and how miserably Haddie had treated him. She took a deep breath, trying to shove those regrets down with the other emotions that bubbled inside of her. *I need to focus on Dad.*

Kiana parked the van and released her seatbelt. "What do we do with him now, Haddie?"

Detective Cooper shuffled behind Haddie with a grunt.

We need to talk without him listening.

Sam stood up, looking behind, and then opened the van door to let Louis out. "C'mon Meg, let's walk Louis." She gave Haddie a quick glance and jumped out.

Terry followed with a bag of trash, and Meg peered over her seat before jumping out.

Picking up her jacket, Detective Cooper sat down beside Haddie. "You've got to take some time and discuss your options. I understand I represent a problem. The FBI and even my own chief have been giving me the runaround on this. What happened at the park likely ended my career. I won't be able to explain my way around it. So, the only thing I have left is finding out what's going on. Why are the FBI after you and your friends? Who's behind all this? That's what I'm looking for." He paused, pursing his lips through a scowl. "You need to decide how far you're willing to go, to let me get those answers. Talk it through, I'll sit outside until you come to a decision." Handing her the jacket, he stood and stepped out the door.

Kiana, struggling against her cast, twisted to look at Haddie. "I'll turn the air conditioner on inside, you explain this to Crow." She opened her door and maneuvered out.

Haddie drew in a deep breath and gathered her trash. *What now, Haddie?* Crow wouldn't like Detective Cooper there, and neither would Dad if he were there, but they'd gotten out of the park with his help. At least, he'd helped keep everyone's attention elsewhere. Whether the police had been watching the park entrance, she would never know. Terry followed Kiana as she hobbled into the house.

Detective Cooper had wandered over to the shade of a short oak and sat awkwardly on the ground there. Crow stood in his open door of the Toyota, thick arms resting on the door and roof, and watched the man. He turned as Haddie jumped out and gestured for her to come over.

Tilting his head, he spoke in a low tone. "That's Detective Dale Cooper, y'know."

"Yeah, I didn't imagine you'd like that. How do you know him?"

Crow snorted. "I know everybody that's a problem. And he's a problem. This your idea? It ain't Kiana's." He tugged at his beard with tattooed fingers. "What're you going to do with him?"

"We need to talk about that. He got the FBI and police off our trail." She had to be careful what she said. Crow didn't know directly about their power, and didn't ask.

He stared at her a moment and then glanced back at the detective. "I might guess what your dad would do." He pulled a revolver from between the seats and stuffed it behind his back.

She started for the stairs and heard Crow huff before closing his car door. She'd worry about Detective Cooper after they decided what to do about Dad. The house had a musty smell and the heat stopped her at the door. Terry lingered in the kitchen, across the counter from where Aaron used to sit. Kiana rested on the couch, her crutch propped against the cushions and her cast elevated on the coffee table, and she was trying to scratch under its top edge. Haddie moved toward the garbage under the sink, then stopped and placed hers with Terry's on the counter along with her jacket. Sweat resumed trickling down her sides after the reprieve of the cool ride in the van.

"What's he doing here?" Crow's tone rumbled and carried into the room behind her. The door closed with a thud.

"Haddie felt he'd get us a head start," Kiana answered.

"Ain't that gonna bring them down on us?" Crow strode into the living room and picked an easy chair.

"I think we've got a bit of time."

"You let him keep his gun?" Crow pulled at his beard and stared up at the ceiling.

"Tossed his magazines and cleared his chamber."

"Still."

"Law enforcement can get weird when you want their weapons."

"You'd know." Crow's smile spread out his beard.

"I would."

Haddie sat at the counter, waiting for them to stop. "Crow, do you know where Dad is?"

"Nope. Said he had to take care of something, and to pick you up quiet-like." He pointed toward the kitchen and the door. "Nothing about the LEO outside and the nerd in the kitchen. You didn't mention them either."

"Hey there, Bigfoot, I didn't expect to be part of this either." Terry pushed hair off his eyebrows. "I'm not sure if I just made the most wanted list or not."

Haddie didn't have time to waste. Dad was missing. The police and the FBI would be looking for them quickly. They needed to make some decisions and get out of Eugene. "Kiana," Haddie interrupted. "Where do you think he's gone?"

Kiana tugged on her earlobe. "I'm guessing he found a way to go directly to the top. I'm afraid he'll try something rash." She held Haddie's eye. "To the author of all this."

I agree. That made the most sense. He might have gone for the men outside her apartment, but that wouldn't have done much to stop anything. Dad only needed to respond to the letter. "Where do you suppose that is? New Mexico?"

"That could be Texas or New Mexico, if I read the flow

of the encrypted messages correctly." Terry moved over to stand beside Haddie.

"New York?" Kiana asked.

"Not since San Francisco." Terry shrugged. "Not one." He pulled out his phone. "I've got some data being analyzed over the past week, but I could just have my friend flag these packets over the past two or three hours. Maybe pinpoint present activity. If it's all in one location, then we've got a starting point."

"How long?" Kiana leaned forward. She acted calm and in control, but there were tight lines around the edges of her mouth.

"Hour or so? Can't hurry mad skills." He started typing. "Besides, he's got a job."

"Would a few thousand put a rush job on it?"

Terry looked up. "For me or him?" He cracked a smile. "There is a video card he's pining for. Bit pricey."

"Done."

"I'm guessing the FBI found your burners." He still typed, but Haddie sensed he talked to her. "If so, they could be tracking everywhere they were used."

"They were new phones," she said. "Remember we had to change phones before we left?"

"Also, they'll get numbers for everyone you called. And then their locations." He turned off his screen and held up his phone with a somber frown. "Meaning, everyone needs to power down and start fresh. Might be too late. And, I've got important information coming, so we'll need to keep mine on until then." His mouth curled up at the side in a smirk. "That means you too, Sasquatch."

Crow grumbled in a low laugh. "Gotcha, Dweeb."

The door opened and Meg stood silhouetted in the sunlight. "Aunt Haddie? Can you come out?"

Haddie's pulse had started to race. They would know Liz's location if they dug as far as Terry suggested. And Dad's new farm. She glanced over at Kiana who had her phone out and was removing the battery. Dad couldn't contact them. The wide-eyed expression on Kiana's face suggested that she too, had begun to wonder about their new home.

"You just realized this? That the lost burners could be used to pinpoint our locations?" Haddie asked Terry. A flush of anger raised up across her cheeks.

"Sorry, Buckaroo. I've been wracking my brain trying to figure out how the FBI decided to focus on you. The burner came to mind, and I started thinking. A bit late, I know." He tilted his head, as if he were going to say more, but just stared down at the floor. *Livia. David.* They were all at risk.

"Aunt Haddie?" Meg repeated.

Crow had his phone out as well. "If we get a lead, me and Kiana will get down to New Mexico or Texas. I'll call in some people. We'll drop you and Poindexter off somewhere safe. Meg and Sam can pick up the animals, and I'll find a place for them to drive to. I still don't know what you plan to do with your detective."

"Aunt Haddie?"

Haddie stood up from her chair. "I'm not getting dumped off somewhere. I'll be going with you. I can spot things you can't." She couldn't say more. "Coming, Meg."

"We'll see." Crow dropped his burner in his lap.

Terry and Crow wouldn't know why Dad would be in New Mexico or Texas; they didn't know about the letter. She wasn't about to get left behind. Dad could be in a bad position. Why had he done this? Just for her? Or was it for all of them? "I'm going, with or without you. You'd be safer with me."

"Until your dad found out, that's who I'm really afraid of." He had a smile, but there was a tone to his voice. *How much did Crow know about Dad?*

"Let me see what they want." Haddie approached the door as Meg skittered off ahead.

Haddie blinked against the sunlight so that she fumbled to close the door behind her. Heat prickled her skin and brought back the memories of pain that had begun to subside. Detective Cooper sat under the tree with his elbow propped against his knee and his head tilted into his palm – he didn't look up. Meg's auburn mop bounced ahead as she ran toward the field in the back of the house. Sam waited there, and Louis dove through the grass like a dolphin. Where was Meg going? The woods around were quiet. In this heat, perhaps everything had settled in until it cooled off.

She started to say something as she passed Detective Cooper, but he'd just ask about their plan. It sounded like they were in for a long drive, and he wouldn't be invited.

His eyes flicked toward her, but he didn't move. It didn't seem like him to be quiet. *I don't have time for games.*

Meg had stopped in the field beside Sam; Louis danced around them both.

As Haddie approached, Sam stood tucked her hands behind her back with a sheepish expression on her face. "She's seeing Angels."

CHAPTER 17

THE AIR SMELLED OF PEPPER, spice, and sweet grass. Yellow and white flowers dotted the deep, tawny tones of the field, and the tops of the pine trees sprayed out in a thousand shades of green. Each needle appeared to reflect the sunlight differently, shifting with breeze. Meg pointed to the two angels lingering at the edge of the woods. Sam couldn't see them, but Aunt Haddie sometimes did.

Ribbons of white light rippled up and down into the tunnels behind the two angels. The number of stripes changed when she tried to focus on them. Each band had markings that rolled past the side facing Meg so that her eyes darted from one to the next, trying but never able to fully capture the designs. Music wavered as quickly in her mind. *So beautiful.* Light poured from the ribbons and flowed out past the edges of their tunnels. The trees behind didn't suffer from the brightness; if anything, their colors grew richer and more vibrant. Brown trunks turned opulent, as lavish as any flower petal.

"Do you see them?" Meg pointed for Aunt Haddie.

Her aunt searched across the field, then stopped, staring in the right direction. *Good, she sees them.*

The angels knew that Aunt Haddie saw them as well. It pleased them. They cared so much for her. *All of us.* Something had happened — or would happen — to Thomas. He'd gone far away; Kiana had said so too. Meg didn't like the feeling. Everything had become okay, finally. The bad things shouldn't happen again. *Ever again.* Meg smiled. *Sam and Louis are here.* Thomas, the angels, and Aunt Haddie would keep the angry people away.

Aunt Haddie had to save Thomas from the Angry Man. Meg didn't want Haddie to risk it, be in danger herself. But it would be. The Sad Man had to go with her.

Meg turned and looked back at the house. The police officer, they had called him detective, sat under a wilted oak. He looked wilted too. The colors had faded, and the tree, all the trees, needed rain. It would rain soon. The angels knew it would. Aunt Haddie had to leave — soon.

CHAPTER 18

As HADDIE STARED at the rolling lights, wisps of white feathered away from them. She'd never seen them this clearly before. Despite her surprise, the world felt right and calm for the moment. It shouldn't, considering all that pressed in on her. Is this what Meg feels? Each time she tried to focus, her eyes drifted off the feathery plumes, found the forest, and shifted back again. Is this what Meg sees? They appeared to be dwindling. Why had they come?

"Are they saying something?" she asked Meg.

The lights were almost gone, not moving away, just smaller and less intense.

"They know that you have to go to Thomas with the Sad Man."

Haddie didn't want to take her eyes off the lights; they were almost gone. Which sad man? No one seemed particularly happy at the moment, at least inside the house. "Who's sad?"

"The police officer." Meg shifted and gestured.

Haddie looked to where Meg pointed toward Detective

Cooper. His back was to them, resting against the tree. She couldn't convince herself that it was wrong. How could it not be a bad idea to kidnap a detective and drag him across state lines? *A willing participant.* He could always change that statement later. They'd effectively disarmed him and threatened him with handcuffs and death.

Haddie snapped her head back, but the lights were gone. "They're gone."

"Just can't see them," Meg replied. "If you listen though, you can hear the music and feel them."

Music? "What does their music sound like?"

"Waves and wind, maybe." Meg shrugged and jumped after Louis.

Haddie stared after her. *Thirteen.* Meg didn't stand very tall, and her actions spoke of someone younger than a teen. The thought of these lights, angels, didn't disturb Meg. Should they? Should I be alarmed seeing them? She glanced over at Sam, studying her with a somber expression, hands behind her back.

Sam offered a lopsided grin. "You okay?"

Haddie nodded. "You don't see anything? Lights?"

"No. Must be a family thing."

"Has Dad?" What else might Meg have inherited?

"He's not around when Meg sees them."

What if Meg did have the power? Haddie shivered. She wouldn't wish it on anyone. Her dreams combined the nightmare visions, her day-to-day life, and the horrors of her own actions. Rock had gotten used to her waking in the middle of the night when she mixed everything around until her friends were dying by her hand or burning in hellish buildings. *I hope Meg never has to live this way.*

Meg ran back and slammed against Sam to lean against her. "You should go. Soon," she said to Haddie.

Haddie raised her eyebrows. *I should.* Feeling an urgency, she left them in the field and strode back toward the house. Sweat trickled under her shirt, and the grass smelled hot. Still, the woods around were quiet. Detective Cooper remained in the same position and barely glanced at her as she made for the door.

Inside, the air conditioner seemed to be working against the summer heat. It wasn't much cooler, but some of the musty smell was gone.

Crow had been talking but stopped as she entered. Terry rested against the counter, typing on his phone. Kiana leaned back into the couch.

"We should go soon," Haddie said. "Cooper's coming with me."

Crow guffawed and began smoothing out his beard. "Neither of those are happening. Me and Kiana will —"

"Do whatever you see fit." Haddie interrupted. "If Dad's in New Mexico, then I'm heading there, with Cooper." The sad man? It didn't seem to fit.

"I'll tie you both up and leave you in the downstairs rooms, if I need to." Crow leaned forward and the chair creaked.

Kiana tugged at her earlobe, her lips pursed. She knew that wouldn't work with Haddie.

"Let's get it over with." Haddie said. "Either way. What's the plan with Rock and Jisoo?" She needed to let David know somehow that she would be leaving. *Maybe I should leave him out of it.* Keep the focus off him.

Kiana stood. "Sam worked it out. We just need to send them on their way. She'll meet up with the dogwalker and get them home — no — I'll give her some cash and have them stay at a hotel until we figure out how badly we've been compromised." She turned toward Crow. "We are not tying Haddie up. I'm not sure how I feel about her going along, but we'll deal with it, either in New Mexico or Texas, when we get there."

"Cooper's coming," Haddie said. Why? He didn't offer any benefit that she could see. They wouldn't trust him with bullets. *Why am I pushing for this? Angels?* They'd delayed too long already. Sam and Meg needed to be on their way. She could deal with Cooper the same way Kiana intended to deal with her, later, once they were out of Eugene.

"Looks like New Mexico is the winner," Terry said. He motioned toward his phone. "Preliminary numbers are pointing solidly at an eastern cell tower outside Albuquerque."

Haddie had expected New Mexico. *Is that where you are, Dad?* Some part of her didn't doubt it. "Let's go," she said.

Kiana gave Crow a smile. "You heard her."

Terry opened his phone and disconnected his battery. "C'mon Papa Bear. I call shotgun."

Crow's beard spread in a smile. "Your scrawny dork ass in the front with me? I might just shoot ya."

"Someone's got to keep you fed, or else you might wither away."

"Damn right." Crow clapped Terry on the shoulder. "Sounds like you got the job."

Haddie forced a smile and headed for the door. The sooner Rock and Jisoo were safely away from Eugene with Sam and Meg, the better she'd feel. *I'll feel better when I have eyes on Dad.* He shouldn't have gone without her. *He's trying to protect me.* He could have left Eugene with Haddie and determined what to do then. Terry's concern with the lost burners added a twist to the situation, but still,

Dad shouldn't have gone alone. It was unlikely that the author of the recruitment letter would have allowed escorts.

"Haddie." Kiana lingered behind, balancing on her good leg and holding her crutch.

Letting Crow and Terry leave ahead of her, Haddie walked into the living room.

"What did Meg want?" Kiana asked.

Haddie twisted her hair. "Angels. They were in the field out back."

"You really see them, like in San Francisco?" Kiana frowned lightly.

"Yeah. Better this time, actually."

"What did they want? Any messages like the harmony thing last time?"

Haddie nodded. "Not to me — I don't think. Meg said I had to go to Dad, with the Sad Man. She said she means Cooper."

"Are you sure you weren't affected by them? You seem pretty sure about bringing him." Kiana smiled. "Sad man fits if you ask me."

"I'm not so sure about Cooper. Maybe they did put something in my head." Haddie shrugged. "Why angels? Why does Meg call them that? I just see twirling lights. Why don't they help?" They were frustrating, like when Dad first talked about his powers and his age. *I didn't believe him. Maybe I don't believe in them.*

"Can Meg contact them?" Kiana asked.

"Doesn't seem like she can. I imagine we can ask, when this is all over." Haddie gestured toward the door. "I want to get out of here. I know we can't talk during the ride, with Cooper and Crow there, but we'll have to stop to pee sometime."

The men had left the door ajar; Haddie opened it,

blinking at the bright light.

PART 3

We could save this world, with your help; in fact, that is the reason we are here.

CHAPTER 19

THE MOUNTAINS to the east of Albuquerque ate the horizon, and the myriad ravines and canyons of the foothills marbled the ground. Thomas leaned to get a view as the helicopter curved downward after passing over the city. Dark trees dotted brown and gray earth. Light roads trailed through terrain like rivers.

His pulse quickened as buildings and ranches became visible. Thomas would finally meet the author of the letter. *I would love to know what he's talking about in some of his rants.* Wording in some of the lines had been specific, like the man actually understood their powers and some mysterious beginnings. What are his powers? *I'll probably not learn anything.* Thomas would bide his time, but eventually he'd have to take the head off the snake. If he could do so without dying himself, he would. *I've lived more than my share of years anyway.*

Turning south, the helicopter flew over a ridge and dropped altitude. A complex of buildings flashed along the sparse wilds, one massive barn and smaller ones surrounded by leveled ground. Ponderosa pines dominated the larger trees. The area would make a beautiful place to visit if it weren't for his present circumstances.

He had to hope that Crow had gotten Haddie safely out of the way by now. She'd be starting to get concerned at his absence, but Crow could handle her. Hopefully, his host would keep to his word and claw back his people. *Not that I trust him.* The sooner this was over, the safer she'd be. *Patience.* A quick reaction would be expected, so if Thomas let the man lull himself with inaction, then he could strike with some hope of success and possibly survival.

The pilot brought them to the compound Thomas had spotted earlier. The massive steel building stood with a peaked metal roof and wide, open hangar doors. The property had been an obvious ranch at one point. Now, it had been converted to a military training site. The government had to have noticed. Armored transports ranged outside the leveled area, and men fought hand to hand on tan dirt. Everyone carried weapons, even the combatants. Officers in dark green trained men in khakis. Paved roads bordered the complex and trailed off in multiple directions. The helicopter dropped into what had once been a paddock.

An armored vehicle waited on the paved road, its back open with the stairs down; two men stood outside it. One, over six feet tall, wore a tan, three-piece suit and a bright red tie. He was clean shaven, though the helicopter ruffled his curly black hair. *What is your power?* The dark-haired man next to him acted as an attendant, carrying the same type of tablet that they'd brought back from Lady Erica's; his eyes marked him as coerced. He wore a black suit flapping in the breeze, but his bulk and stance said military. Under his jacket, he had a holstered weapon.

The pilot's casual voice came over the com: "Final destination. Thanks." There was a tone of relief to the voice. Had they expected trouble from him?

Thomas unbuckled and opened the side door closest to his host. He stepped out, wincing against the afternoon sun. Even with the blades churning overhead and the exhaust, the air smelled of dust and spent gunpowder. Gunshots from a range inside one of the buildings echoed dully. The engines of the roving armored cars rose and fell in the hilly terrain around them. Occasionally a grunt or yell sounded from the sparring soldiers. The heat pulled at his shirt. The paddock gate swung open to a dirt path leading to where they'd parked the tan armored car. Boxy, it didn't look very different in shape from his Ford Transit, though perhaps bigger. He studied it as he walked, trying not to focus on the men.

"Tempest," the man in the tan suit said. "A pleasure to finally meet you." He extended his hand, leaving Thomas to walk the two final steps to grasp it. "Call me General."

There was a tone in the air, deep and subtle. A protection of sorts? *Likely.* "Thank you for meeting me, General." Since Thomas had received the letter, he'd memorized every leader of the Vietnam war. The man's name was Bruce. *General is fine.* They weren't going to be friends.

The general motioned toward the back of the armored car. "This risk was yours. I appreciate that you were willing to meet me."

Little choice. "And operations against Haddie?"

"All operations ceased. I've pulled back my men; there's no need for them to be out there. Not now." The general's smile was wholesome and genuine. Likely as much a politician in the war as a military man. About as trustworthy as a snake.

Thomas followed him to the back of the vehicle. He managed not to react at what he saw.

Inside the shade sat a demon, skinless and closer to the size and shape of any human than any of the creatures had ever come. Other than the naked flesh, the only indication that this creature wasn't a man came from the orange glow in its eyes, two oversized bottom canines that pushed out its upper lip, and black fingernails that came to pointed claws on its hands and feet. Muscles rippled as its head turned; it had no eyelids. "Welcome, Tempest," it said. It wore camouflage fatigues with the sleeves cut off.

General seemed pleased. "I believe you've only met our rejects. This is our final prototype. What do you think?"

Thomas unclenched his teeth and studied the creature. It tilted its head in a human-like fashion, not seeming to expect a response, but perhaps enjoying the surprise or attention. "Impressive." This was meant to intimidate, to set the stage as being weighed in his host's favor. Had the sole purpose of keeping it in the vehicle been to surprise Thomas, or were the trainees unaware?

"It pleases me that you say that. You'll likely meet the rest of the troops tomorrow."

Further intimidation. "I look forward to it, Bruce." Thomas barely hesitated to see the general's reaction before he climbed up to sit beside the demon. *I was right.* The creature had a foul odor, like a man whose bowels had been cut open.

Bruce pursed his lips in an appreciative expression and nodded slowly. "Very good. You've done your homework, Thomas." He climbed up to take the seat on the opposite side of the car.

Thomas kept his expression neutral. Bruce did not

know his present identity, or he would have used it. That boded well. "Obviously, not as well as you."

Bruce's aide pulled the stairs up behind them and took his place opposite the demon. The driver hadn't been visible from the paddock, but in the relative darkness inside, the yellow glow of coercion was clear. A wire wall separated them, and a monitor and electronic equipment sat on a stand behind the driver's seat. This was a far cry from the Hummers Thomas had ridden in before.

He waited until they jolted forward and turned north on the road. "How'd you find Haddie?"

Bruce studied him for a moment. "The bus had a camera. I had you on it, as well as a clearer image of the pink-haired girl I'd been looking for since Sameedha was killed. Facial recognition on social media did the rest. Took longer than I would have liked, but I'm missing some key people now. Experts in fields that I'd left under Erica's control."

Control can be swapped. Terry and Liz had both suggested it. Better to get off the topic than dwell on options Bruce might not have considered. Hopefully, local looters had taken the burners. "How are your plans now, after Lady Erica's disappearance?" *If Bruce intends to recruit me — this is his opening.*

"I was hoping for some preliminary conversation before we dug into details. However, I will say that despite some obstacles, we've continued with all plans and contingencies. This society, as we know it, will fall. We just need to be here to bring it back up and mold it. Your timing is opportune."

How? There was an implication to the statement. Did Bruce have something planned? Infrastructure could be far more fragile than anyone expected. People in wars learned that quickly. The ability to have coerced people in key positions gave Bruce dangerous power. Did "being here to bring it back up" offer a threat to Thomas that if he did assassinate Bruce, it would doom the world? Demons and coerced hardly seemed like the best alternative, no matter how corrupt present authorities were. Thomas shook his head, blowing out the stench of the creature sitting next to him.

"I'm glad you're mulling this over." The vehicle pulled off the paved road and jostled along a dirt trail. The hills and brush gave no sense that they were headed anywhere except into the New Mexico wilds. Bruce leaned forward and put his chin in his hand, resting an index finger on his lip. "Before we head up to the house, I need to show you something."

Thomas looked through the windshield. The dirt road circled around a dry pine, seeming to end at a dusty roundabout. "What?"

Bruce just smiled as they veered partially around the circle and stopped. The assistant shifted past to open the back.

Thomas pushed down a rising pressure in his chest. He wouldn't have been brought here for an attack. The strongest position had been at the compound with overwhelming manpower; they knew his abilities. Then, what is this? The dry air filled the back, and he quickly followed the assistant out, leaving Bruce to follow. Drawing in fresh air, he turned sideways to watch Bruce and the demon following him. The creature moved like any man, though disturbing with its muscle and tendons sliding against each other. Intelligence gleamed from its eyes along with the familiar red glow. It seemed to enjoy his discomfort.

Thomas didn't cringe when Bruce put his hand on his

back in a way that said they were familiar and cordial acquaintances. They were neither. As they moved away from the others, he began to hear a tone, a low pitch like a Tibetan bowl. He jerked away, but nothing seemed to be happening. Purpura grew along Bruce's face.

"Stop it," Thomas growled, his power nearly coming out. *He's protected against my abilities.* "What are you doing?" Haddie had tried to show him how to use protection, but it didn't work. His fingers clenched into a fist. He might be able to snap the man's neck. The man deserved it for killing Meg's family and relatives let alone every other atrocity he'd perpetrated through his people — soldiers that followed this man's orders. Pulse pounding, Thomas ground his teeth, muscles tense and ready.

Bruce smiled and the tone grew stronger.

I need to kill him. Now, before it goes any further. Bruce didn't carry a weapon, but his physique said toned military. The fight wouldn't be fair, once the demon joined in. *One move to kill him.* This is what he'd come for, though the timing wasn't right. It didn't matter. Rage made it hard to breathe.

Thomas screamed and his tone rang out and squelched against Bruce. The rebuke against his power was solid.

Bruce smirked arrogantly. "There, we've taken care of that." He tilted his head in a manner that mocked Thomas. "You can't touch me that way."

The world dimmed around them, and Thomas could see only the enemy. Body tense, he uncoiled in a raging leap, trying to get his hands around the man's throat. Bruce blocked easily, but Thomas got a grip on the man's forearm, yanking him down with him. Dust flared into the air around their scuffle.

Thomas took an elbow to the chin before he threw a leg

over Bruce's hip and tried to gain leverage over him before a moist foot slammed into the side of his face. Dirt sprayed into his eyes and mouth. The world spun as he flipped over Bruce, catching a glimpse of the red body of the demon standing above them before the sun blinded him.

CHAPTER 20

Bruce rested on his back with his eyes closed, waiting for the last vision. In his test with Tempest, he'd already had two. They lasted longer for him than for others, but they appeared throughout his tone instead of starting at its end. *I still don't understand why I'm different.* It hadn't been this way for his ancestors.

Without Bruce pushing the rage upon him, Tempest would relax immediately and begin to realize what had happened — how he'd been controlled. *He needs to know that assassination is futile.* No one, except Erica, had developed the ability to resist before they met him.

The sun glowing red against his eyelids brightened to sunshine and stone in the vision. Bruce stood in a rock-filled valley, somewhere likely in Greece. Shepherds and militia, dressed in rough wool tunics tied at the waist, lined up to face those who would attempt to depose him. The enemy troops came with a descendant from Azazel, allied with half a dozen of the other children of the Noveilm. He didn't see her, but she would be here. His own allies had been conveniently occupied in other battles. "Hold," he told his troops.

His voice carried the song, and he focused it deep in the enemy ranks. At first they stirred forward, and then as the intensity of his tone grew, they jostled and struck at each other. In moments, a battle roiled in their own ranks as Bruce whipped them into an uncontrollable blood lust. He would wait until they beat down their own before he pushed his soldiers into a more subtle frenzy and unleashed them on the remnants.

The red glow of his eyelids returned, and Bruce leaned up, dusting off his suit. The demonstration had been necessary. It cleared up the question of Tempest's deficiencies and highlighted how impotent an assassination attempt would be. There would be some residual resentment over it, but the point had been made. They could move on.

Specimen E626 stood quietly with his foot on Tempest's chest. Thomas rested his hand on his forehead, keeping his eyes shaded.

"Are we done? Have I seen what you needed me to?" asked Tempest.

Bruce's eyebrows furrowed. *He recovered quickly*. No hint of resentment in the man's voice as he lay there defeated. *Maybe I'm underestimating him.* Standing up, Bruce dusted off his hands, then jerked his head at E626 to get off. "I suppose. You understand why I did this?"

Tempest rolled up with a wince. "I guess. Hopefully we won't need to spar often?" He stood and dusted off his pants, then rubbed his hair smooth. Blood marked the side of his mouth.

"Just know that I can intensify it so that your blood pressure will soar and either render you incapable or give you a stroke." Bruce nodded. "Hungry?" he asked.

Tempest strolled behind, as if nothing had happened. "I could do with a bite."

I'm never going to be able to trust this man. Maybe the daughter would be more pliable. Or the grand daughter. Hopefully his men would be successful in rounding them up. Their last message, just before Thomas had landed, had been promising.

CHAPTER 21

Dale stood up as the oversized biker, who he assumed was nicknamed Crow, and Terrence Lipton stepped outside the house. He slipped the earbud and cord into his pocket discreetly and suffered a glare from the giant in the leather vest. *Best not to antagonize him.* The situation appeared tenuous, at best. Crow headed into the field and waved in Sam Johnson, who had disappeared at the same time as Thomas Dawson, and the child who had suddenly appeared, and quickly disappeared, with the name Meg Dawson.

Why did Hadhira suddenly push for him to accompany them? And what or who were they rescuing Thomas from in New Mexico? Their conversation had left him with more questions than answers. The part about the FBI being coerced, he could somewhat believe. *The chief too? Maybe.* It wouldn't matter much for his career. Whichever way he spun this, he'd be lucky to stay out of federal prison.

Right now, he had a chance for answers. It was all he had left. His mouth felt dry, and an empty desperation hung in his chest. In a morning, the remains of his life had been torn away by his own doing. Then, within a few short hours, he'd seen the impossible when two FBI agents vanished in front of him. Special Agent Richardson had been about to shoot him. *I can't accept that, any of it.* But, somehow, it had happened. None of it made sense. Eventually, motives and actions made sense, but not when they flew in the face of reason.

And what were they talking about with angels? Tracy had been obsessed with angels, until the end.

Two years ago, he'd been sitting in a cold hospital waiting room to see if Michael would make it through another flare up in his lungs, a complication of his cystic fibrosis. Tracy had brought an angel figurine to pray with. It was white with wings that wrapped around its ankles — small enough to fit into the palm of her hand. He thought she'd break it, she held onto it so tightly. Dale would have done anything for Michael to have made it through the night. He'd even prayed with Tracy and her angel. It hadn't worked. The emptiness growing in him now reminded him of the quiet desperation and regret he'd felt the weeks afterward. Tracy had left the family during that time, though it took longer for the divorce to come through. The only thing he had left were questions that needed to be answered. Compared to the liveliness of Hadhira and her companions, he could be dead.

He shook the morose thoughts away. The others grouped at the stairs as Haddie walked through the shadow of the house toward the door. Crow's large back blocked most of the others. He was a dangerous biker from the looks of it, but the dogwalker and the young girl acted as if they liked him — even the puppy jumped on his legs.

It didn't matter what Dale believed about the disappearing FBI agents or angels; he needed to get to the bottom of all this. The FBI had their motives and goals, as did Hadhira and Thomas Dawson, which Dale needed to understand. He'd stretched boundaries to investigate before, but today he broke right through them. Crow, it appeared, was the only obstacle at the moment.

A twig snapped in the woods behind Dale, and he turned. It wouldn't have been so noticeable if it were not for the otherwise silence of the trees in the midday heat. Not even the birds were out.

CHAPTER 22

Haddie walked toward the door, catching Crow's eyes as he stood just beyond the stairs; his face softened quickly, but he seemed angry. Detective Cooper stood in the shade, looking into the woods. Sam and Meg chased Louis at Crow's boots.

She blinked in the sunlight, and a reflection caught her eye in the field to her right, a bright flicker of white light. A red blur flitted from her left, but she already had started to turn. Something bit into her left shoulder and chipped into her bone. Instinctively, she flinched and crouched with her hands on the steps. The wood felt warm and rough against her palms. The woods were too silent.

A gunshot rang out from the trees and Crow grunted, wrenched forward. *They found us.* As a second shot rang out, he lurched to his knees and looked up at her almost apologetically. Haddie jerked toward a flash in the woods. FBI? Who was out there?

The crutch rattled down the stairs, and Kiana brushed past with her gunshots ringing in Haddie's ears. A bullet thudded into the wall of the house.

On the ground below her, Sam laid on top of Meg in front of Crow; she looked up at Haddie with wide eyes.

Cooper's gun flashed, firing into the woods as he jumped to a tree for cover. *He doesn't have bullets.* Kiana shot almost continuously in a tight rhythm that obliterated any other sounds.

Haddie tasted medicine. Turning her head, she saw a red-tailed dart stuck in her shoulder, and blinked. They were trying to drug her. "No," she yelled. Her tone rang and the dart disappeared. More than that, she'd tried to make the tranquilizer vanish and some of the taste went away, but her mind still faltered. The pain that ripped across her skin felt different than usual, distant. It still hurt. Kiana kept firing and the noise deafened Haddie to anything else. Someone shouted something, maybe Kiana. Haddie dropped to a knee and looked from Crow to Sam; they both watched her as the visions took her.

The world turned dark with night and mud, while explosions and gunshots lit the trench around her. Dad wrestled with a man wound in wire. The barbs dug into her skin as she held a foul-smelling man tight with her right arm and kept his long blade away from her throat with her left. A blast lit the sky, silhouetting another enemy jumping into the trench. The first man had cleared the way, and another had followed. Dad's growl banished them both.

The second vision could have been in the same trench, on the same night. Her ears rang with gunshots, and Dad dispatched a man who stood at the edge and fired in. Two men, momentary comrades, were dying at her feet.

Daylight, green trees, and calling birds broke into her vision of a dusty road with the smell of a fireplace and baking bread. There wasn't a house in sight, just fields and trees. Then a young teen with a gun and a dark uniform began firing from between the trunks. Dave, the last man of their unit walking beside Haddie, spun with a spatter of blood. Dad called out and the young enemy faded away. He'd been just a kid.

The hot sun of a Eugene summer beat down on Haddie as she knelt and shook off the last of the visions. Kiana's gun rang out above her, and Cooper continued to fire from his hiding place beside a too small tree trunk. Louis might have been barking, but between the tranquilizer and Kiana shooting so close, it sounded faint.

Someone had shot Crow. *I need to help.*

He still knelt in the same spot, looking up at her with big legs wobbling as he tried to rise. She imagined the expression he wore came from his loyalty to Dad. His job was to protect her. *We've got to help him.* She shifted, and spilled down the stairs, driving her face into the sand. Her muscles weren't working right. At least the pain wasn't bad.

The gunshots stopped, and Haddie tried to turn to look up at Kiana. *Is she alright?* Haddie squinted at Crow, who knelt only a few feet from Haddie's elbow. He didn't appear to be bleeding. *So many gunshots.* How long had they been firing?

Fingers came to Haddie's throat, and Kiana spoke, a faint echo beyond the roar. "Are you okay?"

Haddie drooled. "Drugg-ed." Her lips weren't working well.

Cooper was backing toward them, his focus still on the woods. Haddie's ears rang. Crow slid onto the ground and groaned.

Hands tugged at her arms, and Kiana flipped Haddie, then dragged her legs off the step. It didn't really hurt, but it jolted her knees.

Haddie's ears might have been pounding with heartbeats or the ghosts of gunshots. Her vision dulled, but she could make out Kiana and the dots of color that were her beads swaying over her eye. The sun seemed even brighter than before.

Sam crawled over and touched Haddie's shoulder. "It's gone." Her eyes were wide, and she kept swallowing. For a long moment Sam blocked the sun and seemed the only shape, then she moved to the side and Haddie blinked at the light.

Everyone seemed to be moving, and Haddie just felt slower. She wanted to get up and react to the attack, but she could feel the drug slowing her down as she drifted deeper inside.

Kiana moved over to Crow. "She'll probably be okay."

Haddie blinked, wondering if she'd sleep. She'd meant to get rid of the poison, surely that was the intent. It seemed so long ago.

Cooper's voice came from somewhere to Haddie's left. "Is he hit?"

Crow grunted. "No, but the bastards might have broke a rib or two."

"You wear a Kevlar biker's vest?" Kiana asked. Her relieved tone had a tinge of sarcasm.

"The newest fashion." Crow chuckled and groaned. "Did I really need to be shot twice?"

Terry came into view above Haddie. "Biggest target." He grabbed her hand, but she barely felt it. She could sleep, if they let her. Sam and Terry were joined by Meg, and Louis whined against her ear. They seemed to surround her, blotting some of the sun.

"Help me up," Crow coughed. "We need to get Haddie outta here."

"Are you sure you can stand?" Kiana asked.

"Ya, I've been beat up worse than this and still rode away." He grunted and shuffled his feet in the dirt.

Haddie wanted to sleep, and at least Crow hadn't been hurt too badly. Dad would be pissed if his friend had died. She wanted to say something, but her throat was too dry and her mind too dull. Everyone had turned into blurry silhouettes.

Sam spoke from one of the blurs. "Are you going to be okay?"

"Aunt Haddie needs to leave," Meg said. Small fingers brushed hair off Haddie's face and whisked sand off her cheeks.

Haddie tried to nod, not sure if her head moved or not. Where would they go? The farm wasn't safe, not if the burners had been found.

"You can walk?" Kiana asked.

She appeared to be talking to Crow, as he answered. "Ya." A zipper sounded. "You need to keep an eye out, in case there's more."

"I haven't seen any movement," said Cooper.

"Cooper, where the hell did you get bullets?" snapped Kiana. She sounded angry.

"In my car. I keep them in my side door storage." Cooper's voice had a calm indifference to it. Was he really the Sad Man?

Kiana responded with something, and Terry as well. Their voices seemed to blend together.

CHAPTER 23

As Kiana steered Crow toward the SUV, Dale veered wide of the big man. Dale's ankle still burned. *A scratch.* The bullet had gone through the cuff of his slacks and sock. Blood soaked that side of his shoe, but the bleeding had stopped. *An inch off, and I wouldn't be walking.* He'd just shot two men, and it would have been a clean shooting, if he were staying to file the paperwork. They would match his gun to the bodies if a patrol didn't respond before they left. Any chance of getting out of this mess without jail time appeared less likely by the hour.

Hadhira was still calling him Cooper, and so was Special Agent Wilkins. If he wanted to find out what they were up to and who was trying to stop them, then he'd have to adopt a more familiar stance with them. Crow would as quickly leave him here with the other bodies, though the others wouldn't agree. *And if I do answer all my questions, what then?* It didn't matter. He found it hard to be concerned. His pulse had slowed, now that the attack had ended. Still, he checked the woods for movement. There had been three, two in the woods to the south, and a third downhill to the east.

"The tranquilizer put Haddie out. We'll have to carry her. We've got to get out of here. Someone's going to call in the gunshots." Kiana tried to angle Crow over to the passenger door as she spoke, and he bullied toward the driver's door. "You're in no shape to drive."

"Bruised. I'll be fine." Crow grumbled, though he walked with a distinctly stiff gait.

Dale cleared his throat. "I can drive, if you want. Kiana." Her name sounded awkward as he said it; perhaps Wilkins would have been easier. Driving would get him a clear sense of where they were going, and more reason to join conversations.

She gave him a sharp look, beads swinging from her eyes. "No." Studying him, she shook her head. "Crow can drive. Your gun goes in storage, or you stay here."

Crow opened the driver's door. "Check him for a backup weapon while you're at it. What did they even teach you in FBI school?"

Kiana steamed and jerked her head toward Haddie sprawled in front of the house. "Help me get Haddie in the car." She hobbled with her crutch toward the cluster around Haddie, pulling out a wad of cash. "Sam, you and Meg need to get in the van. We're leaving." She reached the young woman, whispered in her ear, and handed off some of the cash.

What connection did the dogwalker have with the Dawsons? He hadn't seen anything worth consideration during the Colman case. The younger Dawson relative, Meg, had picked up the wriggling puppy and walked over to Dale. She didn't say anything, just stopped and smiled until Sam came along to whisk her away. The way she had looked at him left him awkward, like she pitied him in some way. He turned to watch them climb into the large white van. What did she know? Haddie had been called out of the house by the girl, but he'd been too busy listening in on the other three to pay attention. Tranquilizer? When had that happened?

"Cooper." Kiana motioned him to take the other side of Haddie, she braced awkwardly with one hand on the crutch, colorful cast out to the side, and a hand firm in Haddie's armpit. Terry picked up Haddie's feet.

Hadhira's — Haddie's — face was speckled with more reddish bruises. *Purpura*. She claimed it came from using some imaginary powers, but it was more likely a reaction to stress. *Richardson and May are gone*. He still could remember them slowly fading into nothingness. *That doesn't happen*. Neither did the FBI threatening to shoot at local law enforcement over jurisdictional issues. None of it made sense. Now, they'd been attacked. It wasn't an FBI operation that had tried to tranquilize her. This was some other group.

He leaned down, putting one arm under her shoulders and the other just above her hip. "Who did this?" he asked.

Kiana grunted and started them hobbling toward the car in precarious jerking steps. "Why don't you stay here and investigate?"

He could, actually. There were only a few routes to Albuquerque, but he'd find out more if he went along, so he told her the truth. "I've got nothing left here. I'd rather find out what this is all about."

CHAPTER 24

THE SANDIA MOUNTAINS were most impressive when viewed from the plains where Albuquerque sprawled. Thomas kept his focus out the windows of the armored vehicle. Here in the foothills, the peaks lost some of their impact as nearby hilltops and ridges blocked the hazy horizon. The air in the enclosed space reeked of the creature sitting beside him. Fast and strong, it had acted with precision and restraint. Perhaps Bruce had created the super soldiers that so many governments sought.

Bruce did not appear insane or delusional. He acted with forethought and experience. That was obvious from the fight. He'd planned every bit of it. *He stripped me of everything but rage.* Lady Erica's power had been different, and would have been permanent if not for Aaron. How much use were Bruce's powers? *Enough to disable me.* Thomas would have to come up with a serious plan. Bruce had the ability to send him into a blinding rage at any moment. The military man had solid training, and probably sparred regularly.

They swung in a circle around a statue within a fountain and pulled in front of a long house with a stone block façade. Large, arched openings had multiple windows to create expansive views. A recessed entrance included a sitting area. It appeared to be a rich, isolated residence. A mansion.

"Dylan should have some afternoon refreshments ready for us." Bruce waited for his attendant to slip past and open the back. "I'm a tea man, myself."

"Tea's fine." An incongruous conversation after Thomas had tried to kill the man mere minutes before. He followed Bruce out and took a deep breath of the mountain air. It likely got chilly at night, but for now, the afternoon sun left the air dry and hot. The few plants and the gurgling fountain gave off an earthy smell. To his right and behind him, a ridge climbed quickly to the southeast, while the building spread out across the north and blocked much of the horizon.

The demon followed them inside, its nails scraping on the flooring as it walked. Someone smoked cigars. The entryway rose two stories and had an elaborate chandelier over a single table and vase. The walls were a drab beige with few adornments. Lit alcoves broke the plainness, but were lacking highlighted paintings or décor in them. Whoever lived here had little use for eloquence. Hallways opened to the right and left, but Bruce's assistant led them toward the back room. It was tiled and walled to match, with large windows looking out to arid hills. A sizeable table sat to the left with six high-backed chairs. A large man lounged on one of two couches that looked too small, padded, and ornate for the room and the size of the man. An embroidered pillow had spilled to the floor where the man sat.

He rose with a reserved, almost suspicious look in his

deep-set eyes. A tall forehead gave way to reddish blond, almost orange, hair that swept back across the top and sides while curly sideburns spread down to the base of his jaws. "General." His voice sounded gravelly, like he'd been a smoker, but he looked twenty-five at most.

"Dylan. Meet Tempest." Bruce waived them toward each other while he moved to the table.

Dylan stepped forward and offered a hand. He wore pocketed khakis and a zippered jacket that could have come from a high school's football team. "Tempest."

Thomas took the hand, ignoring the excess pressure. "Dylan."

Bruce's assistant had moved off to the side, standing with the demon two paces back from the table. Tea and coffee pots rested on a platter along with cups and a pitcher of water. Dry looking cookies had been placed on separate trays. Thomas took a seat one away from Bruce, and Dylan sat similarly, creating a triangle between them.

"I think Tempest is quite impressed with your work, Dylan. E626." Bruce flipped over two cups and poured tea. He handed one to Thomas and motioned toward the sugar and cream. "I promised that we'd review the barracks and troops tomorrow."

Dylan's head didn't move, but his eyes flicked toward Bruce. "Of course." He didn't seem to relish the idea. The man had a military presence to him, but that might have come after he began working with Bruce.

There wouldn't be a lot of opportunity to dispatch Bruce with the demon guarding. Did they sleep? His best option relied on keeping his recruitment on the table. *They'll discard me once I'm not a prospect.* "How did you end up working for the General? Did you serve together?" he asked.

One of Bruce's eyebrows rose, but Dylan just frowned and glanced at his leader. "Not exactly," Bruce said. "Tell him."

Dylan scowled and tapped the lacquered wood of the table. "I was a kid. Scottish mother, Irish dad. Joined up with the IRA and ended up twisting up a Brit who tried to interrogate me." There was no accent to his words except a Texan or southern drawl.

"Twisting up?" asked Thomas.

"I didn't realize what I was doing at the time." Dylan shrugged. "Skewed the DNA in his cells. He was beating on me."

Bruce finished his tea, and poured another. "It's a messy and quick death."

Thomas took a slow sip of his tea. Without Haddie's ability to resist other powers, he'd have to be careful with Dylan as well.

"Anyway. They started looking for me and I had to go into hiding. General heard about it and found me." He took a deep breath and stretched, locking his hands behind his head. "Moved to Texas in '76." He shrugged as if to end the story.

"Tried to twist me up. You forgot that part." Bruce offered a smug look to Thomas. "Didn't work." He raised his cup as a salute. "I was looking for you by that time. I'd started to build a network of people looking for unusual deaths — or disappearances. Dylan popped right up on my radar. Thanks to you."

Thomas rubbed back his hair. "So that's how Harold Holmes came into your focus."

"Exactly." Bruce tilted his head with a question. "So, I can assume he's — not around?"

Thomas shook his head.

"Relatives?"

Keeping his expression pasted on, Thomas shook his head. A cold chill rose in his chest. Could he lead this into the conversation around Meg? There wasn't much question that Bruce organized the deaths, but why? "Not that I know of. Would you just kill them off?"

Bruce didn't flinch at the comment, but shook his head. "No. I had hoped you wouldn't hold any resentments over that. You've had plenty of family, since at least WWII."

So, either Bruce found the images before Haddie suggested he take them down, or the man Thomas had hired wasn't thorough enough. Likely the latter. He waited for Bruce to continue.

"I'm not sure how much of our history you've seen." Bruce paused to check for a reaction.

The visions? Thomas nodded without any commitment, hoping for Bruce to continue.

"But the descendants of the Noveilm have a tendency to fight among each other. Keeping a singular role tends to help avoid that. Learn from history." He blinked as if something occurred to him, and looked down in his cup. "I know I can't purge all of it, and I can't risk losing another lineage; our ancestors still mourned Makabetza. So, I've kept a small nursery established, to maintain the ancestry."

Thomas couldn't help but swallow. One, or some of his family survived, besides Meg. "How old are they?" His goals shifted slightly, perhaps Bruce planned on that.

Bruce shrugged. "Young. Obviously, I would prefer a working partner who is older and experienced. This is a crucial time. Two weeks before the first domino drops."

"What's that going to be?" Thomas felt his chest tighten. The man seemed too assured. How far along had his plan to destroy civilization come? Bruce did not seem like someone to leave much to chance.

Studying him dramatically for a moment, Bruce shook his head. "I think we'll leave that for a later conversation. I still don't believe that you are convinced." He slid his chair back and stood. "Relax before dinner. You've got a couple hours. Dylan has a room ready for you if you'd like to rest. There's a pool and plenty of clothes in your room to change into. Sit outside and enjoy the view." He jerked his finger back at the demon. "E626 will accompany you, at a respectful distance. The rest of his squad are resting in the house or patrolling the perimeter. How many in your squad, E626?"

"Dylan moved us up to eight, Sir." The creature spoke with almost a lisp, possibly because of the oversized canines pressing against the back of skinless lips.

The subtle reference to the security in place was not lost on Thomas. He would have to be very creative to succeed, and still would not likely survive. Finding this nursery tugged at him, but there didn't seem to be a rush on the recruitment, so perhaps he could get the information and relay it to Kiana or Crow. *I'm considering this a suicide mission.* He nodded, not to the demon directly, and finished his tea. Some time to clear his mind and think would be good.

Bruce headed toward the entryway. "Dinner tonight. A tour of the training area and barracks tomorrow. I promise you won't be disappointed with either."

CHAPTER 25

HADDIE WOKE to the soft jostle of the car as they pulled into a gas station with white awnings over the pumps. Terry chatted from the front seat, and the stale scent of burgers and fries wafted around her. Her throat felt dry. She blinked to clear the blurriness from her eyes. Kiana sat beside her. Mountains and pines spread from the asphalt, and the sun still shone brightly. *I haven't slept that long.* Where was Detective Cooper? She leaned around the edge of her seat and had to grab the armrest to keep her balance. His knee protruded from behind her seat.

"We didn't leave him with the other bodies," Kiana said. Her tone was slightly amused.

"I—" Haddie stopped as her throat scratched.

Kiana motioned to the pocket of the driver's seat where a new water bottle had been stuffed along with a plastic bag and some protein bars. The water had a slight chlorine tinge to it, but Haddie nearly emptied it.

"You've been out a couple hours." Kiana opened her door as they came to a stop. "Bathroom?" She pulled her crutch up from the side of her chair.

Haddie wasn't sure she could stand, but nodded anyway. Terry gave her a goofy smile as he climbed out. They were on their way to New Mexico, evidently. She didn't remember much that happened after she'd been hit with the dart. Crow had been shot. He was climbing out of the driver's door. How?

Cooper leaned up next to her seat. "I could use the bathroom."

Kiana shook her head. "We'll stop on the side of the road; you can pee there."

He snorted. "And if I need to do more than that?"

"I'll buy you a roll." Kiana slammed the door shut.

Haddie fumbled with the seatbelt. *Did they carry me in here?* Her joints hurt more than usual, but she'd used her powers twice today. The tranquilizer had kept her from feeling too much pain. *I must look like crap.* She opened the door, and Kiana had tottered on her crutch to meet her. The petroleum fumes helped clear Haddie's head. The gas station appeared empty, but there were lights on inside. Traffic sounded from nearby, like they were near the highway. I-5?

"Careful, you'll be a little wobbly." Kiana hobbled aside as Terry came around to offer a hand.

Crow watched as Haddie put a foot to the ground, then he headed toward the door of the station. Her knee buckled, then held. Within two steps she'd gotten her footing and let go of Terry's arm. The door to the station opened, and Crow winced as he handed her a key on a plunger. He pointed to her right. "Bathroom's on the side. You need anything?"

Haddie shook her head and held the plunger high at the top where the key hung from a drilled hole. Grimacing, she walked with Kiana.

"Where's my key?" asked Terry.

"Ask for your own plunger, pipsqueak." Crow headed back inside with a snort.

"Thanks, Kong."

Kiana shook her head. "Be glad you got to sleep through the last several hours."

The highway traffic raced by with a dull rumble. If they were on I-5, they were close to California. The hills looked right for that location. Any of the smaller highways wouldn't be this busy. Was a main highway the best choice? Wouldn't the police and FBI be looking there? She glanced at the empty gas station. *Not here.*

They rounded the corner of the building and Haddie looked back at the Highlander where Cooper waited. "Any word from Dad?" she asked Kiana.

"No. We got new burners; yours is in front of your seat, in the pouch. Crow and I both left messages on the gaming sites. Hardest to track. We warned him about the burner, but no response." Kiana tugged at her ear as if worried. "Nothing."

The last word carried the weight Haddie felt.

They couldn't even be sure they were heading to the right place. Terry rarely steered them wrong, but they assumed a lot. For all she knew, Dad could be in a Portland FBI interrogation room. Liz might be able to check on that with an open warrant, but they couldn't contact her.

"How long before we get there?"

"If we shift off driving? A day. Maybe get there midday tomorrow." Kiana gestured toward the door. "Go ahead, you missed the first pee break."

Absently, Haddie opened the door and set the plunger on the floor. They couldn't afford to be wasting time if Dad needed them. It was just as possible that he didn't want any help. He had to know that they'd worry and react. Maybe he figured they wouldn't know how to follow him, which meant he planned something dangerous. If it involved the FBI, they were headed in the wrong direction. *I need to get hold of Liz.* At least Meg and Sam would have taken Rock and Jisoo out of danger. *Had Sam seen me use my power?* Haddie could be pretty sure that Crow had. What would Sam think? Haddie finished, washed her hands, and opened the door. Kiana leaned on her crutch.

"Are you okay?" Haddie jerked a thumb at the small bathroom.

"For a couple weeks now. Worked it out."

Haddie shrugged and strode to the Highlander. Crow pumped gas, and Terry walked toward the side with a large drink and his own plunger key chain. She opened her door and grabbed the plastic bag to get her new cell number. *Newest.* She hadn't had to memorize so many numbers since her high school lockers.

Cooper leaned forward. "So what's the plan? Do you even know where your father is?"

Haddie studied him. *Sad Man.* Even now, he wore a scowl. She wanted to believe the angels. It could, however, just be her overactive imagination. *I saw them. Clearly.* Still, she couldn't just blindly follow what she imagined they believed or thought. Having Liz check on the warrant would be useful. Besides, Haddie needed to make sure Liz was okay.

She grabbed her water bottle and headed for the gas station door. Her face would freak just about anyone out. *Can't be helped.* Crow hadn't bought her a make up kit. Maybe at the next major stop she'd have him pick something up.

A thin man with light brown skin pulled himself up

from his chair when she stepped in. He frowned at the sight of her face.

"Water?" She sloshed the little remaining in the bottle.

"Yes," he pointed toward a sink by the coffee pots.

"Thanks." Haddie smiled and stepped over to fill her water. "You get any cell reception out here? I haven't had bars for miles."

"Uhmm, yeah. Some. It's spotty along the highway."

She capped off her water. "You mind if I send a text?" Despite looking like a walking disease, she smiled and he nodded.

He handed over his phone, pausing only slightly when he saw her hands.

"Thank you." She tilted her head. "It's a work message. I appreciate it."

She texted Liz, "Bunsen burners compromised. 5,417 parts Water and 260 parts Ozone. 24 units. Replace equipment before attempting further activity." Waiting until the message went through, she left the phone on the counter. He would likely disinfect it before touching it again.

"Thank you." She waved her water bottle and headed for the door. Liz wouldn't have a problem with the code. She'd been the one who started their use of molecular formulas. H_2O and O_3 would not be difficult to pull numbers from, and the extra digit would be ignored.

Terry passed with both plungers. "Great idea, aren't they?"

Haddie raised her eyebrows. "You should get them for game night. Livia would love it."

He laughed, then his expression dimmed a little and he headed inside. Haddie understood. Livia and David would both worry, when they might be at risk as well.

The coerced FBI and the Unceasing seemed ruthless. *If Dad is doing something about this, I want to be there.*

Kiana gave Haddie a questioning glance. "Everything okay?"

"Yeah. I sent Liz my new number." Haddie shook her head at the worry. "I was careful."

Crow capped the gas tank. "Everybody ready? It's going to be dark by the time we get to Reno if we don't hurry." He moved stiffly as if favoring his back.

Haddie stopped at her door. "What's in Reno?"

"Wakey, Wakey." He smiled and circled around to the driver's door. "My shift'll be over, and I intend to grab a quick Bloody Mary."

She shrugged and got in the Highlander. It took Liz fewer than five minutes to call. Haddie hit ignore and texted. "Can't talk. I've got Detective Cooper in the car."

"What?" Liz typed.

"He's a willing participant." Haddie didn't want to type all of it. She could call Liz on the next break. "How are you? Any problems since this morning?"

"No. Your warrant is still active. So where are you?"

"Out of town," Haddie texted. "Can you look up Dad's? I want to make sure they haven't found him."

"You lost your Dad?"

Haddie frowned. "Momentarily. We're looking."

"Will do. It'll be a while. They're a little sketchy with me right now. FBI and all."

"Sorry."

"Don't be."

"I'll call when we get somewhere out of earshot."

"Okay. Be careful."

"You too."

Haddie pocketed her phone and leaned back into her

seat. She could still sleep, and probably should. If they were taking shifts driving, she'd want to pitch in. Kiana shouldn't have to drive with a cast on. Picking up her jacket to wad into a pillow, a silver and black box dropped out. She dug it out of her seat where it landed next to her slacks. *A bug.* She held it out in the palm of her hand to Kiana.

Kiana's face visibly darkened as she swiveled in her seat to glare at Cooper. "When?"

Haddie raised her eyebrows. "Cooper, you did this — it's yours?" She pushed around the seatbelt to get a look at him.

Terry's straw sucked at the last of his drink. "What?"

The Highlander began to slow.

Cooper's scowl twisted as he pursed his lips. "I planned to use it on the FBI."

Kiana snorted. "You were going to bug the FBI?"

He tilted his head with a slight shrug. "I was getting nowhere with them. Something has obviously been going on in my city —" He stopped and sighed. "At the park, before we dropped off my SUV."

"So. You were listening when we were inside the house?" Kiana asked.

Crow pulled the Highlander onto the shoulder and skidded to a stop.

Cooper nodded. "I didn't get much through the pocket of a leather jacket. I just got that you're looking for Thomas Dawson, and Crow would rather see me dead or tied up in a basement."

Crow opened the driver's door. "Still time for that. Pee break."

"I just want to understand what's happening. Some of this, I can't accept." Cooper locked his eyes on Haddie's, ignoring Crow who walked around to the back of the Highlander. "Maybe I can be a help, maybe I can't. I do want to help, though." He sounded genuine.

Crow opened the back hatch and unlatched the chair beside Cooper, slapping it down. "C'mon. Let's take that piss."

For the first time since she'd met Detective Cooper, he appeared uncomfortable. Swallowing, he said, "I can hold it."

"Out." Crow reached in and undid the buckle with barely a wince.

Haddie looked at Crow. "Don't hurt him. I might have done the same." She turned to Cooper. "Take a piss. Let us talk this over."

He nodded and awkwardly began climbing out of the back of the Highlander.

Kiana studied Haddie, but spoke to Cooper. "Give Crow the rest of the gear." She waited until the two men had walked away. "Why, Haddie? We'd be better off not taking this risk. He can't be trusted."

"The angels. They said I had to go to Dad with the Sad Man." She jerked her head toward the back.

"What?" Kiana's head dropped forward in momentary defeat.

"Yaass, angels!" Terry started to say more, but Kiana put her hand up to his face without looking.

She took in a deep breath. "Sad Man? When Meg called you out. The same ones — angels?"

Haddie shrugged as Crow returned, leaving Cooper standing by a tree.

"So can I tie 'im up there in the woods?" Crow leaned against the back, seeming to take up the entire hatch.

Haddie shook her head.

Kiana sighed. "Don't ask why Crow, but stuff him back in here and give me the receiver."

Crow handed it in and looked at Haddie. "I don't wanna explain this to your father. He's gonna be fuming as is."

Hopefully. She just wanted him to be okay. She turned and pressed her head back into her seat. Kiana settled herself and stared forward. No one said a word as Cooper climbed back inside, but Crow grunted as he slammed the back shut.

As they merged into traffic and Crow gunned it, Terry began humming The Who's "Behind Blue Eyes" from the front seat.

CHAPTER 26

Thomas stirred restlessly in the lavish yet plain room that he'd been assigned. It smelled of artificial spruce and detergent. Someone had designed the residence with décor in mind that Dylan or Bruce didn't bother displaying. The sun still hadn't risen, but it was close, pushing the stars out of the sky. The heat hadn't come on, but the fake gas fireplace still flickered, and the temperature had dropped, possibly below sixty. The closet had been outfitted with an abundant supply of khaki uniforms that matched those of the trainees at the compound. *How long does he expect me to stay here?* It also lent a subtle hint to his status in the general's eyes.

Dinner had been a lengthy event with an open discussion on the state of world affairs. Bruce coaxed as much as he could from Thomas regarding his viewpoints; not surprisingly, they had similar opinions about politics and governments. Going along with the framed discussion had given Thomas a chance to gauge how long his recruitment dance would last. *I'll likely be dead if he gives up on me.*

Their discussion during games of billiards had been another round when Bruce attempted to pin down more of Thomas's past. There had been no mention of Haddie or Meg.

He paused at the windows that looked out the back of the residence. They were doors actually, but had been secured so that he couldn't open them to exit onto the small, second-floor balcony.

A new demon had replaced E626, but they looked nearly identical. The creature waited in the hall, and others had been visible wandering the grounds outside the mansion, their glowing eyes bright in the darkness.

Thomas took a quick shower, the second since his arrival, and wondered if there were a crew of coerced personnel that serviced the residence. Dylan did not seem like the type to clean, yet the rooms were immaculate. A pre-dawn gray lit the window as he headed downstairs with his demon escort trailing behind. The stairs let out near the sitting room where they'd played billiards, and the gas fireplace there still flickered from the evening before. Their glasses lay where they'd been left on the tables. The billiards table still had two sticks resting on the green felt. *A quiet night, let's see how today goes.*

He opened the door, and cool air breezed in with spicy aromas from the dry plants. The patio had clay tiles and stretched along the back of the building. Thomas left the door open for his escort. *This would be a beautiful place, in other circumstances.* Hills and peaks rose into the gray sky, and dark green brush dotted the landscape. Around the house were tended gardens of ornamental bushes. He raked his hair back and enjoyed the chill. The khakis were just warm enough.

He strolled down the patio to the west where a driveway peeked at its end. Oaks and maples had been planted along the pavement but looked out of place. He stopped a few paces short of the corner where a propane tank dome rose from the bushes. A commercial generator sat beside the building. He'd thought it air conditioning equipment. Thomas turned, looked at the demon, and measured the distance from the tank to the fireplace in the room with the billiards. He could make the ground between disappear, along with part of the tank, and take out at least the center of the mansion. *And me too.*

The ground behind the house rose steeply. If he were up on the ridge, he might survive. *At least I have a plan.* He let out a breath as he walked back toward the demon. The creature stood slightly shorter than E626 and the same height as Thomas. *I need to learn more about the general's plans — and where this nursery is.* Then, he just needed to make sure Bruce was in the house when he acted. Thomas might not make it past the roving security, but surviving the assassination had been secondary all along.

Stepping inside with the intent of foraging some coffee from the kitchen, Thomas heard a door open in the hall and took three long steps in that direction.

"Coffee?" Bruce asked, walking down the hall. There was one door before the corridor opened into another open area. He wore matching fatigues; the tan suit was gone.

Thomas nodded. "Black."

"Same."

Bruce led the way to the kitchen. "Sleep well?" he asked over his shoulder

"Not really."

"Shame, I'll try and wear you out a little today." Bruce spoke amicably, as if they already worked together. He offered a smile as he walked to a coffee pot near the sink. "I thought we'd start at the training grounds after breakfast. Then we'll head into the caverns and check out the barracks."

"Caverns?" Thomas leaned against the counter and crossed a boot over his ankle, acting relaxed.

"This mountain range is full of them. Keeps the troops away from curious eyes. I've got a lot of property here, and it's well patrolled, but the airspace isn't secure." Bruce turned as a door closed somewhere in the house, then checked his watch. "They'll be up to prepare breakfast."

Thomas didn't turn toward the approaching footsteps. *Shoes, not nails.* Were they coerced humans? Dinner had been waiting when Bruce had brought him to the table, and when they came back in from a cigar, the settings had been removed. There hadn't been one sign of serving staff.

The two demons that trailed behind Bruce's assistant were partially clothed. It appeared the clothing grew on them like skin. These had sections that had grown in patches, leaving random areas thinly covered or the rippling muscles still exposed. They did not have the same stature as E626 or his cohorts, and their eyes focused on the trays they carried. The food had been prepared elsewhere and brought in covered serving dishes. Scents of bacon and eggs wafted behind them as they passed, along with their own rank odor. The sight of them and their exposed flesh, along with the mix of scents, did little to stir any appetite. It became clear why the table had been preset for dinner.

Bruce poured two cups of coffee and pointed to the patio outside the kitchen. "Coffee first?" He seemed nonplussed by the creatures, but perhaps sensed Thomas's reaction.

Taking a cup, Thomas led the way. The fresh air

cleaned away the odors. He avoided looking west, toward the drive and the propane tank buried underground. "It's beautiful country out here." The escorting demon stood at the doors behind them.

"Sameedha managed some substantial acquisitions." Bruce sat in one of the wire-framed chairs.

From what Thomas understood, Sameedha had brought rich debutantes into the raves, but it was likely Lady Erica who coerced them and drained their assets. He just nodded and sipped at his coffee.

"We've been well funded for two years now, from multiple sources. Our purchasing focus has been on acquisitions that we can maintain after our initiatory event, and bare liquidity to leverage for the upcoming reactions. What you may find surprising is our communications and telecoms position." Bruce drew in a deep breath. "Assuming a crisis-driven decline, how do you suppose today's society will deal with it?"

"Panic?" asked Thomas.

Bruce smiled grimly, as if disappointed. "Think about what we discussed last night. How ensnared today's adults are with internet media, as opposed to the Great Depression when print and radio were the source of information. If we have a large placement in these technologies, then we will control the information flow. People will not be looking for solutions and certainly not the truth, but they will be looking for someone to blame. Our Unceasing groups will be able to gain a tighter grasp. By the time the infrastructures completely collapse, we will have large sections of prime resources under physical control." He waited, as if for a response. "They will be an ignorant army, that can be assumed, but what better type is there? As long as there is strong leadership and their bellies are full, we can maintain order. The areas we don't choose to control will fall to anarchy and chaos. Later, when we have rebuilt an infrastructure, we can clean up the remnants."

Thomas finished his coffee and placed the mug on the glass table. "Aren't you concerned about nuclear activity when governments lose control of their weapons?"

Bruce smirked. "We're planning on it. Certain areas are too populated for our control."

The sky had lightened to a pale blue, but it would be a while before the sun broke over the Sandia range. Thomas didn't want to die, but this man could not live. Bruce alluded to plans coming up soon and those already in motion. Learning what they were and their principal players would be a great advantage, but there may not be time. *This might not be his main facility. Texas?* Terry had seemed to believe there were connections with properties and Unceasing in that state. *But I'm here now.* Playing a possible recruit would only last so long, and the general wasn't foolish enough to not consider that Thomas might be trying to kill him. The exhibition yesterday had been a response to that concern.

"Breakfast? I'd like to get started early, before it gets too hot. Mid-eighties today." Bruce stood.

Thomas followed with his empty mug. Hopefully, Crow had Haddie in check. Kiana wouldn't become alerted until tonight; he rarely let a day pass without contacting her. *Neither can be sure where I've gone.* If he removed Bruce, then likely the remaining coerced, including the FBI, would be as incapacitated as Josh.

Breakfast proved filling, if not appealing, after witnessing the demon servers. Bruce's assistant waited in the kitchen as they ate and E626 returned to relieve the present demon guard. Being able to distinguish among them disturbed Thomas. *I could end this now.* First, though, he wanted to see those caverns.

CHAPTER 27

Haddie snorted and rose high in her seat to avoid the morning sun that crested in the east directly in front of her. It made driving difficult. They'd cut through some hills along I-40 and through a town before the land flattened enough to let the light blind her. Dry tumbleweeds clung to the sand beside the highway, and clouds streaked across the sky. The air blew cool from the dash, but she still felt grimy in her day-old clothes. She drove with her window cracked to lessen the odor of five people jammed in the Highlander along with all the garbage they'd collected. Crow snored behind her.

She'd slept some during the night, but none of them appeared well rested. She hadn't caught Cooper sleeping yet. At least they were in Arizona and would be to Albuquerque a little after noon. *Soon.* Hopefully Dad was there, and they could find him. Their plan didn't stretch much further than the drive. Crow had called in some help, but hadn't elaborated in front of Cooper.

The angels and all the messages she had believed in the

field with Meg came across as more questionable the longer they drove. Bringing Cooper had made them all on edge, except for Terry. They had to watch what they said, and that left her feeling like they had no plan. They had an address east of Albuquerque in the mountains. *That's it.*

The road inclined, and Haddie flinched. No matter how high she rose, she couldn't avoid the sun. "Damn."

Kiana leaned up from behind. "That's rough."

"Can't see anything."

"You're on the road still."

"Thanks." Haddie shaded her eyes, focusing on the sliver of asphalt over the hood. At least the road was straight.

Terry shifted, curling toward the window.

Cooper spoke from the back, "I'm up for a shift at the wheel."

"Give it a break." Kiana snapped.

"Assuming you're headed straight down I-40, not much along here except for Albuquerque," he said.

They couldn't be sure how much he'd heard with his bug, but they assumed he knew their destination. He played like he didn't know where they were going, though. This had been the first time he'd mentioned the city. *He's getting on my nerves.* He hadn't acted very sad.

Cooper sighed. "I told you, I just want some answers."

"I don't care what you want. Sit back and shut up. Sleep." Kiana had a sharp, exasperated tone.

"I've slept plenty."

Kiana's voice rose sharply. "Don't push me, Cooper. I mean it."

Cooper huffed, Crow stopped snoring, and Terry blinked awake. Haddie focused on the road, but her chest tightened. Kiana would be worried about Dad. They were all stressed from the day before.

Crow swore and grunted. "A little sleep would've been nice."

Terry yawned and blinked against the sun. "Exit coming up. Breakfast?" he asked Haddie.

She nodded, keeping her hand shading her eyes. "Probably best." She glanced up at the mirror. Kiana had moved out of sight and Cooper had leaned back. "Can grab some gas as well."

Breakfast turned out to be a twenty-four-hour Subway, and Crow escorted Cooper to the bathroom and back. They made for an odd looking couple. Cooper hadn't made any attempt to contact his police department or anyone else in the bathroom. The detective's usually neat face had grown coarse with black and gray hairs. Haddie remained standing and drank unsweetened tea when Crow led Cooper back into the Highlander.

Crow nodded his head away from the vehicle and pulled out his phone. "Just got these." There were pictures of a large building surrounded by a small compound. An armored military truck kicked up dust along a hill. A pair of men in camouflage walked along a ravine with sparse brush. "That's all they got 'fore someone shot down the drone. They've got a second that they'll bring in from the north. There's that compound and two buildings, residences, on almost two hundred acres."

"Shot it down?" She breathed in and out. "So, they know we're watching?"

Crow rolled his shoulders, as if stretching bruised muscles. "Hard to know what they think. Drones are pretty common, especially around scenic areas."

"It's dirt and brush."

"The Sandia mountains are a popular hiking spot; this here's just the foothills." He smiled when she glanced up. "You weren't listening to your boy, Terry, ramble on last night."

"I was trying to sleep." How would they know if Dad was even there? She hadn't expected patrols, but Terry had said that it was likely where the Unceasing were training.

Terry popped around the side of the Highlander with a large cup. "I don't ramble, I elucidate." He nodded toward Crow's phone and tilted his head questioningly. "Something relevant?"

Crow scrolled through the pictures on the phone.

Terry stopped him. "Zoom in. There. Those are troops, maybe Unceasing trainees. I should go to the recruiting office and see if I can infiltrate."

"Hold up there. You ain't going in there. We've got eyes getting set up." Crow glanced over to Haddie. "No one's going in until we spot Tempest. Even then, if he doesn't look like he's in a spot, then we don't do nothing 'til we get word."

Haddie raised her eyebrows. She didn't necessarily disagree, to a point. They wouldn't sit around forever. *I won't.* Terry wasn't far from an idea, though. If she went in, and if they had been looking for her, she could bring Cooper's wire and communicate with Crow and Kiana. *Not something I need to mention now.* No one would be happy about that plan.

Terry spoke, his mouth just over his straw as if he were about to take a sip. "We need to get better pictures, then."

Crow grunted. "Workin' on it." He shrugged. "We'll know more by the time we get there."

Cooper started to get out of the SUV; they'd left him inside with the subs and Kiana. "What's the plan?"

"The plan is you —" Crow stopped and motioned Cooper outside, waited until he got close, and leaned in conspiratorially. "Plan is, you stay out here with Terry while I go talk to Kiana in private. Got it?"

Haddie chuckled as Cooper's scowl deepened. She didn't follow Crow though. "We're not just going to trust you easily. You get that, right?"

Terry nodded. "You did bug us. Electronically. Kiana and Crow, you bug in other ways.

"I put myself at risk to get information — to get to the bottom of this." Cooper shook his head. "I'm getting the feeling you don't know much more than I do, and we've got no plan."

He had gotten them out of the park and helped during the attack. *I can't trust him.* She couldn't believe he wouldn't arrest her and Dad if he had a clear chance. The less he knew, the better.

"He's baiting you," Terry said.

Haddie frowned. "Cooper, you already know way more than you should. I'm not sure why I brought you along." *The angels, that's why.* She headed for the car. "Keep him away from me, Terry."

"Got it, Buckaroo."

She climbed in the driver's seat while Kiana looked at the pictures on Crow's phone. Haddie's sub lay in the console. She opened it. Extra pickles and black olives made for an interesting breakfast choice.

Her face tense, Kiana pulled at her earlobe as she looked. "That's it?" She gestured a little harsher than usual. "No sign of Thomas, or even a house?"

"Working on it." Crow shrugged. "Give it time."

"He might not have time." Kiana swallowed and glanced at Haddie. "Sorry."

Haddie wiped her lips with the back of her hand. "I'm worried, too." She forgot sometimes how Kiana might feel. *How would I react if this were David?* He'd be vulnerable. Dad wasn't.

CHAPTER 28

Thomas shifted as the man swung. Pudgy and angry, the soldier extended himself, and Thomas caught him in the kidney with a solid punch. The man grunted and landed on his knees, stirring up reddish dust. He swore as he scrambled to his feet and lost all control, diving at Thomas. The instructor yelled something, but Thomas grabbed an arm and leveraged the man into a roll. Before the soldier could race back toward him, the instructor and one of the other trainees had him restrained. He swore livid threats. *This is no army*. Whatever training Bruce offered the Unceasing, it wasn't enough.

He jerked when Bruce clapped him on the shoulder. "Nice style there. A bit of a mix." He leaned in. "Good job. They see you at an instructor level."

Thomas nodded. The training compound smelled of gunpowder and echoed with target practice. Bruce planned on putting men under his care, nurturing him into a mentor — a common tool when building an army. Thomas had seen it plenty of times, fallen for it himself, and learned to position others in the role. It bound leaders to the cause, no matter how unjust, as well as to the soldiers under their command. The longer Bruce took to attempt these tricks, the more time Thomas had to learn information. So far, no opportunities had shown themselves. Bruce kept his information and communications locked down.

Knocking dust off his fatigues, Thomas followed as they headed inside the range, a remodeled building that might once have been an arena for rodeos or cattle sales. Gunfire echoed inside the metal structure. One end, where targets hung from pulleys, had been lined to absorb bullets. Trainees fired pistols at varying distances, and instructors walked behind them, checking their progress. Near the entrance, an industrial generator chugged, and a group sat at a counter attending monitors. Thomas nodded toward them.

Bruce glanced over. "Road surveillance. They also work with the armored teams, setting up scenarios and monitoring responses." He spoke loudly, over the gunfire, and headed toward a side door. "Our initial salvage will start with Albuquerque, Amarillo, and Oklahoma City. We'll set up provisioning logistics and draw troops in along the corridor. Food, medicine, and vaccines will be available for soldiers and their families. Texas has been primed to fall in quickly, and we'll move out from there. Communications will be key in recruitment. All my installations have stores of propane or natural gas and generators."

They stepped into the sun and strode toward the back of the building. The ground rose into brush and scattered pines. The sounds of armored transports growled as they walked into the wilds past a small utility building. E626 and Bruce's assistant followed a few steps behind, and a road led toward the peaks of a house in the east.

Thomas pointed toward the building.

"Barracks," Bruce said. "For the trainees. They live on property for periods of sixty days. I hire any of the decent prospects from here or the other two training facilities. The rest either return at later dates for more training or are settled into cities with direct orders. We call them sleepers, and they like the role."

"What will they do there?" Thomas asked.

Bruce studied him for a moment and shrugged. "Disrupt. They know what to look for and will act at those points."

Thomas stopped at a ridge beside Bruce. In a gully below, a group of trainees moved toward a mock police line with plastic shields and armored vehicles. The bottled liquid they threw and the guns they fired did no harm, but an instructor stood on a small platform with a man at a communication array. The trainees moved in a uniform attack targeted at a single point in the double line of officers. The instructor noted close gunfire and the police dropped, weakening their line. When enough liquid covered the armored transport, a red light flashed, and the police nearby evacuated their positions. The attackers pressed into the line, disrupted it, and an unseen signal stopped the fighting.

Bruce turned toward the compound without comment. "The training here is primarily focused on boosting morale and weeding through the prospects. The same with one of our Texas centers. If we continue these discussions, we'll take a look at a more serious bootcamp later, maybe in a couple days."

"Where's that?"

Smiling, Bruce gestured southeast. "Texas."

"Big place."

"It is."

Thomas wouldn't be getting that location from Bruce

anytime soon. *I need to know where that nursery is.* His descendants and relatives of Sameedha and the others were being held there. If he could get that location to Kiana and Crow, then any sacrifice would be worth it. The day had already turned hot as the sun rose over the eastern peaks.

The information he'd learned so far had been disclosed to show the strength of Bruce's hand. Everything, except this facility, lacked details. Already, Bruce dismissed the training after Thomas had come to the conclusion of its limited merit, intended to lead into a conversation of the more intense training. How long would these disclosures last? Their next stop Bruce had alluded to as both the barracks and the caverns; obviously he hadn't meant the house to the east. Were the barracks for the demons? *Likely.*

"We are going to meet up with Dylan. He's got a lot of the more technical information for any questions you might have." He jerked a thumb toward E626. "I'll initially engage them as shock troops. That will be their preliminary use until I establish a powerbase. Eventually, as I move outward, there will be some clusters of resistance — small martial groups that form cohesive territories. I project them to come from the more rural areas throughout the Rockies and perhaps the northeast and Canada. The worst will likely be in South America, but by the time we get down there, I'll have solid industries functioning here. Air superiority and fuel will be the key resources by that time."

Bruce pushed too hard. His plans weren't as solid as he led Thomas to believe. What does he need me for? That might be key in getting more information. They reached the armored transport that had brought them from the house that morning. "So, what's my role in all this? Surely you don't need me just to wrestle with your newbies."

The question stopped Bruce. "First and foremost, brotherhood. We are from outside this world. How far have you seen into your ancestors?" His eyes tightened, seeming hungry for the information.

Haddie, from her descriptions, had to witness some of Thomas's regrets and failures. However, he didn't want to think of the monstrous uses of their power he'd seen at the hands of any ancestor. "Hard to tell." He took a step toward the stairs of the vehicle. "Brotherhood? Is that what you call kidnapping my descendants and killing the rest?" He turned to catch Bruce's face tighten. Thomas smiled grimly and climbed inside ahead of the others.

Bruce followed and let the demon and Stanton climb inside behind him, close the back hatch, and settle before he spoke. "I am serious. We are connected in a way other humans are not. You will see this in time. That brotherhood is important to me. Dylan and I are the last functioning Noveilm that I know of. And I believe I would know otherwise. We need to resurrect our position as protectors of this world." He looked down at his hands, speckled with purpura. "We can talk about this tonight with your aquavit and a cigar."

Thomas nodded, not wanting to aggravate the man any further, for the moment. They were headed toward the house and veered right onto a dirt trail. The path led toward a ravine that climbed up the high ridge east of the house. Ahead, three demons waited, dressed in the same fatigues as E626 with the sleeves torn off. The road had been cut into the slopes, leaving window-height walls. A dark shadow or opening lay beyond. The guards stood at a strange, curved barricade and waited until Bruce leaned forward to be seen before they carried the metal frame off the road. Even in the sun, he could make out their glowing orange eyes.

The driver turned on the lights and headed toward the opening. A dark corridor led into the mountain. Sturdy braces and a level floor gave the sense of a road or train tunnel, with junctions for pedestrians or smaller vehicles. They descended quickly. Then Thomas could make out the lights. *Too many*. Through the stone he could make out the glow of the demons' eyes. He stopped looking forward and focused on the lights as they curved into an open cavern. His heart began to race. Bruce smiled, just watching Thomas's expression.

The driver turned, and the headlights shone on metal beams that braced the ceiling in giant arcs forming poles where they came together. The multitude of demons blocked the view across the cave, but he could judge its immense size. More than a hundred glowing eyes shone from the barracks.

CHAPTER 29

Bruce studied Thomas; his reaction would be key. He had to see the futility. *I hold the upper hand.* It would have been easier if the daughter or the child could be found. As expected, Tempest had a soft spot for his own relatives. He would cling to the idea of saving them. *Until I can show him a better world.*

Thomas didn't move, even as Stanton opened the back hatch.

"Impressive, isn't it?" asked Bruce.

"Surprising." Thomas blinked and turned to follow Stanton. "How long have you been building this force?"

Bruce climbed out behind them. "Twenty-six months, since the first viable E class specimen." A fair boast, but not all of these were E class. *I'm not sure how to interpret his response.* How long had Thomas lived? He had an uncanny ability to remain unreadable. More and more relied on getting his daughter. Bruce refrained from taking too deep a breath and telegraphing any tension.

Thomas walked directly into the barracks, despite his obvious repulsion of E626 and his squad. "I thought everything started this month." He stopped at the first arching pillar and the troops nearby noticed them. Rows of double-bunks were lined between poles in a neat grid. The soldiers rested or cleaned, but some ate, and only those on duty tended to their weapons. They had been warned about the guest.

Bruce was forced to follow. "Our initial attack this month is merely setting the stage for what will follow. We'll use it to spread suspicion so that later events will distance allies and make new agreements unlikely. It has the added effect of weakening the United States."

Dylan came down the hall that led from the house, a narrow corridor to the back left of the barracks.

Bruce stepped up beside Thomas. "I hope to have ten companies by the time we need to use them."

"These caverns will hold that much?"

"Much more. We've had to move our Boise storage here." The loss of Barbara had been a blow. Araki had little use, but Barbara had been formidable in logistics. Later, they would have been crucial in breaching lines. *It's having lost Erica that hurts the most.* Even adding Thomas to Bruce's arsenal wouldn't make up for the loss of those she controlled or the future assets that had been planned. "Dylan's here if you have any questions about the troops." He guessed that Thomas would be curious. Their duration and survivability were unparalleled by any humans.

Dylan's lips were tight, and his eyebrows furrowed slightly as he approached. *He doesn't approve of the visit.* Despite Bruce's suggestion, Dylan wore his casual zippered sweatshirt instead of fatigues. "General, Sir."

Thomas turned at the greeting and studied Dylan. A blunt animosity had developed in their interactions, much of it stemming from Dylan's resistance.

I need to control this situation. Bruce took a deep breath and bellowed, "Sergeant E209, have your men fall in." The soldier jumped from his bunk and barked to the others. Select specimens separated from bunks as the squad raced to form a double row two paces away. They adjusted their fatigues and then snapped into position. The rest of the room continued on without much regard. "What do you think of my men?"

Thomas wiped his hair back and nodded appreciatively. "Well trained. Impressive."

He'd want to know their weaknesses. *I would.* Hopefully, later, he'd be concerned with their strengths. "Feel free to question Dylan," Bruce said.

"How are they created?" Thomas asked, turning his side to the squad.

Dylan frowned. "I manipulate the DNA and some of the early mass of an embryo. The General determined that I operate on a molecular level."

Thomas glanced at one of the soldiers. "So, they're grown, like in a petri dish?"

"No. Born. We found it best to manipulate inside a live host."

"A pregnant woman?" Thomas's tone rose. He appeared to find the process disturbing.

Bruce interrupted, "They are unaware. We remove the specimen before full term; they are modified to grow quickly. The hosts believe they have miscarried."

Thomas turned to him. "And where do you find these women? Are they volunteers?"

"Unwed mothers seeking help are easy to find. In the end, we help them move on with their lives." *Most.* Some didn't survive the pregnancy, but Thomas didn't need to know that.

Still, Thomas frowned. His pity was disappointing. Society had created the problem of discarded mothers and children. *I'm just using them.* Dylan pursed his lips in a sour face. *This isn't going well.* He had hoped to awe Thomas with the potential weapons the soldiers presented, not get mired in an ethical debate.

Stanton nodded discreetly, holding the tablet at his chest. They'd received another message from the team in Eugene. So far, they'd bungled the capture of the woman. Hopefully, they'd rectified that. It would make things easier if he had a little leverage.

"Dylan, explain the variations on the skin that you created." Bruce nodded to Stanton and stepped away.

"The skin and clothes are grown as part of a loose epidural layer, easily shed for movement. That, along with retractable nails and teeth, were developed so that we could implant our soldiers into public areas before activating them." Dylan gestured to his own teeth. "Retract." The squad complied. Dylan continued, explaining the ratios to human strength, as he'd been coached earlier. He was more prone to action than thought.

Stanton held out the tablet and activated a message from the team tasked with procuring Hadhira Dawson. "Target presumed out of range. Also missing, known associates Terrence Lipton and Detective Dale Cooper. An APB is out on Detective Cooper county-wide." The FBI had a nationwide alert out on her, but it appeared she'd gone underground. *I need her in hand.* His jaw tightened, and he glanced over at Thomas. The man might not be swayed on his own accord. *I need to delay until she surfaces.* Why was the detective missing? Perhaps she'd killed him. Some of the FBI were missing since yesterday.

Bruce sent an acknowledgment and headed back toward Thomas and Dylan.

Where would she be hiding? He wasn't about to activate more resources until he had a viable target. Already, they'd lost men on a bungled attempt. There were more than enough men in Eugene to search for one woman.

"Two hearts," Dylan answered.

Thomas turned as Bruce returned. His expression grim, but otherwise unreadable, he said, "Formidable soldiers." The tone flat, it almost seemed as though he said what was expected.

"Squad, escort," Bruce said to the troops. He turned right to lead them across what he'd labeled the parade grounds, a wide unsupported cave with a natural ledge at the back. He motioned to the driver to follow them. The squad stalked alongside and behind. "We use parts of the cavern for storage. More so, lately."

"Certainly secure," Thomas said.

Bruce nodded. The man remained almost glib in the face of the operations. *I'm not sure he'll budge*. The damage the man had caused already extended projected timelines. The loss of Erica crippled crucial placements. "One last bit of the cavern to tour, and we'll head back and freshen up for lunch."

The parade grounds ended in an archway carved big enough for a semi to bring in loads. Bulbs flickered on as they sensed motion, and the dull thuds of the large lights echoed down the exit. The strange grinding echo met them as they entered. It had started months ago, but engineers had found nothing. He motioned for the vehicle to wait. "Squad, released." Without any fanfare, the soldiers turned and headed back to the barracks. The display had been wasted on Thomas.

Dylan raised his eyebrows, and Bruce nodded him away as well, leaving Stanton and E626.

Thomas scanned the tunnel, peering down the exit. "What's that noise?"

The echo was dull but pervasive, like wind rushing through. "Best our engineers came up with was water movement deep under the rock."

"Unlikely." Thomas furrowed his eyebrows and wiped back his hair. "Strange."

To their left, crates and piles hid in the shadow until Bruce walked over and flicked on the lights. "This is the armory."

A side cave stretched deep and away from the tunnel. Neat stacks of crates ran west in rows. The new surface-to-air missiles had been brought as contingencies after they'd lost control of key positions at local airbases. He led Thomas in to read the labeling. Certainly, a military man would be impressed with the amount of armament in this one cave.

Thomas pointed to the south wall. "Rather close to the barracks, isn't it?"

Bruce's jaw tightened, but he forced a smile. "As you said, the area's secure." *Damnable man.*

CHAPTER 30

HADDIE SAT BEHIND CROW, resuming her original position beside Kiana. They'd reached Albuquerque, and her chest tightened as they drove through the city. *Where are you, Dad?* He hadn't left a message on their usual gaming site, so she'd begun checking some of the games they'd used previously. The conversation in the Highlander had quieted when they reached the city traffic. Her thoughts were on their next steps, and no one wanted to discuss them in front of Cooper. She and Terry had resorted to their phones. Crow had turned the radio to seventies rock music.

They would have to stop soon to discuss their final plans, and Haddie needed to refill her water. Her stomach had soured from the stress and snack food. The scent of bagged popcorn lingered. I-40 ran thick with traffic; she'd grown used to empty lanes. A sharp ridge of dark mountains stretched out to the east.

They hadn't come up with much of a plan during their gas station breaks. She and Crow would scout the property from the north. Kiana would watch Cooper at a hotel room with Terry, who would be handling communications. Crow had been reluctant to have the other investigators connect with Terry, but had agreed. The heat wafted off the desert, distorting the horizon. *I need to hit the bathroom before hiking.* She had asked Liz to get with David and let him know she was okay. He had to be worrying.

Terry turned to Haddie and lifted his phone. "All matching encrypted packet traffic is going through New Mexico since yesterday afternoon. I'd bet money that big boss is there." He cringed when he looked past her to Cooper. "Sorry." Quieter, he said, "Still think we should send me to the recruitment office."

Haddie didn't know if Terry was getting the drone images yet, and she was more interested in those. The couple hundred acre ranch in Coyote Canyon felt like the right place to find Dad. The patrolling security and compound looked military, exactly the place she imagined she would find a megalomaniac trying to start the apocalypse. *I just need to make sure Dad's there.* Dad had to have a plan.

Crow pulled the Highlander onto an exit and Haddie tucked away her phone. Buildings and desert were scattered around them, and the mountains consumed all of the eastern horizon. As they turned onto a road, it appeared as though the city had ended, butted against desert.

Terry pointed to the hotel at the corner. "I won't starve." Breakfast houses and fast-food restaurant signs cluttered the roadside.

Crow snorted and pulled through the intersection on the green light. The gas station sat opposite the hotel where the others would wait. She wrapped her hair in a knot, unable to feel at ease. *I'm close.* The hills she could see might be where they'd be headed.

As Crow went inside to pay, Haddie dumped their

backseat trash and waited for Kiana to get out. Terry needed two trips before he'd cleaned out the front of the Highlander. "You guys go first. I'll wait here until Crow comes out."

The scent of dust and exhaust hung in the heat. The sun roasted exposed skin and Haddie squinted. A hat might be a good plan for hiking.

Kiana finally spoke after they walked to the back to use the bathroom. "You okay?"

Haddie drew in a breath. "Yeah. Nervous, I guess."

"Don't go past the boundaries we set up. You've got the hunting app, so you'll know where the property lines are. We've picked the best spots to zoom in on the building. Don't improvise. Don't overreact. This is just reconnaissance."

"Like Boise."

Kiana chuckled. "Hopefully not."

Haddie filled her water bottle in the bathroom and strode out, ready to get moving. She wished she hadn't brought up Boise. Her chest felt like her ribs tightened. *Relax*. Breathing deeply in and out, she wandered through the convenience store looking for nuts or protein bars.

Two large officers approached the glass door. One of the men had a gray bushy mustache and the younger man was clean shaven.

Haddie almost dropped her water bottle. Shaking, she knelt down to study the hot and fiery peanuts at the bottom of the rack. *They're just here for coffee*. The lady at the counter greeted them, and Haddie tracked them across store by their responses. She stood up, walked to the front window, and headed for the door, forcing her grimace into a smile for the employee.

Terry, leading Cooper, opened the door. "Did you —"

He stopped mid-sentence and ogled the two officers in the back.

For a moment Haddie, Terry, and Cooper clustered at the doorway, then Terry backed up. Awkward and staring, he turned to follow Haddie toward Crow at the gas pump. Cooper blew out a sigh, but trailed behind them. Kiana hadn't come out of the bathroom yet, so they couldn't leave.

Haddie opened the car door and hissed at Cooper. "In the back." She chanced a glance over her shoulder toward the store, but the glass reflected too much light for her to see either the officers or Kiana.

Cooper complied and slid past her while Terry moved over to Crow, who acted as though nothing were amiss. He leaned his palm against the back of the SUV while he pumped with the other hand. His beard hid much of his features, but his eyes were tight. Terry awkwardly explained the situation in a whisper. "I saw," said Crow through gritted teeth in his otherwise calm expression.

Kiana hobbled out the door. She'd planned on buying snacks for the room, but she had none. The broad smile she had plastered on her face dropped as she headed toward them.

If the officers had seen Terry's awkward entrance and retreat, they would surely suspect their odd group. What would they do? Run the plate? Question them? Haddie's heart fluttered as she moved around the pump. Terry clustered close to Crow at the back of the SUV.

Kiana had a few steps remaining to reach the pumps when the officers stepped out of the store. The gray mustached man stood with his coffee in his left hand and studied them. The younger man passed by, then stopped when his partner didn't follow. If they asked for ID, Haddie and Kiana were both in trouble. Cooper's gun was in the glove box with the insurance and registration. Crow rattled the nozzle back into the pump and studied the screen. Time crawled, and Haddie froze as the two men stepped toward them.

The back door to the Highlander opened and Cooper stepped out. He waved a wallet at Terry. "Found it. C'mon." He had his badge pinned back on his chest.

Terry jerked, as if he'd been asleep.

Cooper strolled toward the two officers with a smile. "Afternoon."

CHAPTER 31

DALE PAUSED as the two patrolmen stopped. His ankle still burned, and he stunk from wearing the same shirt for thirty-six hours. The drive had been difficult. *I'm not learning anything.* He hoped that once they reached Thomas Dawson that more information would be forthcoming. If they were all taken into custody, he would learn nothing.

Terry had made the officers suspicious. *Civilians are idiots.* If Dale wanted to find out what Haddie was up to, he'd have to get them out of this.

"Where you headed?" asked the officer with the gray mustache.

"San Pedro this afternoon and then white-water in Taos tomorrow." Dale tilted his head. "Something wrong?"

The officer tapped his chest and nodded to Cooper's detective badge. "Where are you out of?"

Cooper looked down. "Shit. Oregon. I threw on the shirt this morning and never noticed. Sorry." He pulled the star off and then quickly produced ID. "We've been non-stop."

Terry still hadn't made a move to follow. It would go a

long way in convincing beat officers that there was nothing going on if everyone just acted natural. Crow and Haddie had moved to the other side of the SUV and Kiana hobbled to the door.

The older officer looked over Dale's ID, then nodded. "Be careful." Either the department had kept the search to a county level, or these two hadn't seen the need to commit his name to memory. The FBI could raise an alert, but those in Eugene were more likely to be focused on Haddie rather than him. The man switched the coffee to his right hand and took a sip.

"At my age, I have to." Dale resumed his walk toward the store. The officers walked to their car parked by the ice, and Terry finally ran out from the gas pumps to follow.

Inside smelled like hot dogs and stale beer. Dale stopped at the first aisle and picked through the beef jerky, keeping an eye on the squad car. The officers had gotten inside but made no show of leaving yet. If they were still suspicious, they would have asked the others for ID.

The bell on the door rang as Terry slunk in. He wiped hair out of his face and scampered beside Dale. "What did you say to them?"

"That we were here to go hiking, then rafting."

"They bought it?"

"I'm a fellow officer, why wouldn't they?"

Terry stared at the jerky for a while and finally nodded. "Thanks. I need to piss."

Dale sighed. "You should take care of that." He walked to the register and paid for his beef jerky. *This is my best chance to find out what Thomas is up to.* Haddie and Kiana obviously thought the man had gotten himself into trouble. Stuck in a hotel room wouldn't get him as much information as investigating with Crow and Haddie, though Terry's slips had given Dale the strongest clues yet. Crow had some people in the area doing reconnaissance, but as of yet, Thomas had not been confirmed to be at the location. *This is why I hate working on a task force.* Too many opinions and not enough solid direction.

When he left the store with Terry a few minutes later, the patrol car idled by the ice box. Kiana, Crow, and Haddie had piled into the Highlander. Dale went around to Haddie's side to get in.

"What did you say to them?" Haddie asked, her tone sharp and aggressive.

As he climbed in the back, he repeated the assurances he'd given Terry. Haddie didn't appear comforted.

Terry climbed and swore. "Sorry. I totally freaked out when I saw them."

Crow shifted into drive and exited the gas station slowly. "I'm going to hit a store before we go to the hotel. I don't want them to see where y'all are staying."

As they drove, Haddie sighed audibly and turned. "Thank you," she said.

Dale smoothed his mustache. He'd acted on his own behalf, primarily. Whatever had happened in the park hadn't been natural. If that was Haddie, which he still did not accept, then he needed to understand how such a thing could be possible. None of this came close to making rational sense. There had to be an answer.

"I want to help," he said. "I want to understand. Your father is in trouble, but what trouble?"

Haddie studied him for a moment. "I wonder if I was supposed to bring you because of the gas station, or something else."

"What?"

She shook her head and turned away. "Terry, do you have the photos now?"

"Yeah, I was just looking." He handed his phone to her when she reached for it.

Haddie scrolled through images and stopped, showing Dale the screen.

It was a fuzzy picture of four men standing behind a military armored vehicle. Two tall men in full fatigues, a smaller man in a blue shirt with a tablet, and the last with sunburn who looked like paramilitary with the sleeves torn off a pair of fatigues. *Not much information.*

Haddie pointed at one of the tall men. "We think that's Dad." Her finger moved to point at the sunburned man. "That's a demon."

CHAPTER 32

KIANA ABSENTLY RUBBED her ear and threw another pillow at the headboard. The air conditioner clattered at the front window, and a slight scent of mildew carried with the cool air. She climbed onto the bed and set her good leg out straight, then lifted the cast up to join it. The damnable crutch she left leaned against the wall beside the end table — a reminder of her uselessness. *Thomas needs me, and here I am.* Crow and Haddie had taken Cooper with them. Either Meg's angels had rubbed off on Haddie or the episode at the gas station had convinced her.

Terry had set himself up at the desk of the hotel room with a liter drink and a tablet that Crow had purchased in Arizona. He, at least, would have something to do.

Why would Thomas have done this? He must have believed he acted to stop something worse from happening. It could be to protect Haddie. Kiana fought a resentment that he would be willing to sacrifice what she had with him for anything, including his daughter. *I've never had children, though.* There had been a time when she'd considered it, but the army had never left her with enough time for family. There had been one soldier in Bosnia for whom she'd started to feel possibilities, then she'd been sent to hell — Afghanistan. During this morning's drive, the desert had been a reminder. *Thomas*. That had been him standing near the uniformed demon, she was sure.

"I've got some data from the San Francisco tablet analysis. It might help us track outgoing packets."

Kiana blinked and sighed. "What's the difference?"

Terry turned to ask, "The difference in the packet encryption, or from what we were tracking?" He grinned. "I started to go full geek on you, then realized you probably don't care about that stuff."

"I don't. So there's one type going into the tablet, and another coming out."

"Yes, which means we can have some analysis on where he, assuming the male from the photo, is sending instructions. Like New York or someplace. Then we'd know more about his plans."

I don't care about his plans at this point. "Sounds good." She swallowed. "Any more surveillance photos?"

Terry returned to his tablet. "Naw. They've lost three drones and only have some stationary cameras up. Place looks dry."

"Is there any increased activity on the stationary cameras? Extra patrols?" Three drones taken down would cause her to beef up security. It also meant they had at least one sharpshooter.

"The saved videos are motion activated, so let me check recording times."

She scratched under her cast. Meg had worked hours on painting the rough plaster. They were mostly flowers, interspersed with a few brightly colored foxes and puppies. Living with the girl and Sam had lightened Kiana's life. It would mean nothing without Thomas, though. *We need to find him.*

Haddie shouldn't have brought Cooper. He couldn't be trusted. Listening in on their conversation proved that he had his own agenda. Kiana could remember when she first saw Haddie's power. She hadn't accepted what she'd seen with her own eyes, and there had been fear as well. It still didn't make sense, but none of what she'd seen had. *It just is.* Cooper probably tried to reconcile with that. Once he did, would his reaction be to bring Haddie to his superiors, or move on?

Crow would keep an eye on him, but a betrayal at this point could be dangerous – for everyone. Meg and Haddie believed in their angels, though the description sounded far from being angelic. Kiana couldn't dismiss it considering everything she'd seen, but bringing Cooper sounded like a bad idea, no matter how you looked at it. He'd helped with the patrolmen. It should have ended there. They were going to have enough difficulty infiltrating and extracting Thomas as it was.

"No increased activity," Terry said. "Seems quiet, actually."

What the hell, Thomas. Did you even consider me when you did this?

CHAPTER 33

Haddie walked behind Crow and jumped as her phone vibrated. The hillside, which looked barren from a distance, had dried weeds covering the ground and scrubby pines growing like brush. They blocked the horizon, except the higher peaks, and forced them to wind their way uphill. Spice and earth scented the arid land. They had slowed and formed a line once they'd stepped off the road. Surprisingly, she had decent reception.

Liz texted, "David is missing."

Haddie stumbled, kicking a cloud of dust into the air. Could he be working out of town? "What?" Her heart began to race.

"I checked the police logs, because his phone went to voicemail and his office hadn't heard from him today. A patrol found his car last night in a parking lot at a gym on 11th."

A cold shiver ran up Haddie's back. Is this my fault? Had the Unceasing kidnapped David? Her hand shook.

"Everything okay?" Cooper said from behind her.

She'd come to a stop, staring at Liz's words. Her water

bottle swung at her belt with a dull ring of metal against her leg. "No," she whispered.

Crow turned to stand in front of her. "What's wrong?"

Haddie shook her head, wanting to reply to Liz, but she couldn't think of what to type. She could only imagine David at the gym with men forcing him into some car at gunpoint. David hadn't grown up fighting, or even trained like she had. His father was an attorney, and his mother worked as a CFO. They had lived in an affluent suburb of Seattle where he'd gone to private school. Rough men and guns were not something he ever expected in his life. *I did this.*

Crow touched her hand holding the phone, and it helped stop the trembling.

"David, my boyfriend." She swallowed, suddenly feeling the sun and heat. "He's missing."

"You think these people took him?" Crow asked.

She nodded. What was she supposed to do? "Can you have some of your or Dad's people look for him? Investigate? Find him?" she asked, each question became more desperate.

Crow pulled out his phone. "Full name and address?"

"David Crowley." Haddie rattled off his home and work addresses, then his license plate and car make and model before Crow raised his hand and shook his head.

"That's good. They'll dig everything up." He typed and she watched him send the message.

It changed nothing. Someone had taken David because of her, she was sure. Inside, she became hollow. More than ever, she wanted Dad to be with her. *I'm supposed to be saving him.*

She texted Liz, "Please keep looking."

"I am."

Haddie glanced back at Cooper; if he were in Eugene, she'd beg him to find David. Instead, they were standing in scraggly brush hoping to find Dad. Crow watched her and she nodded quickly. As they resumed their walk, she fought tears and lost. Her feet felt like lead weights.

The slope of the hills rose and fell, hidden behind dry brush and short pines. A glimpse of the next ridge would pop up before the angle would shift and they climbed sideways down loose sand and scraggly plants. Numb, Haddie trailed behind Crow without thought. They'd punched her in the gut, and she couldn't recover.

"Careful here," said Crow. He pointed toward two short pines. "We're coming up on the point Kiana picked out for us. Check in with Terry to see if he has anything for us."

Haddie pulled out her phone and couldn't help but see the last text, Liz's promise to continue looking for David. *I need to get Dad out of here, then we can find David.* She blew out a breath and texted Terry, "Any updates?"

Terry replied faster than she could have typed. "Biff is making good time. We are on stationary cameras until they get more drones. No increased activity, Buckaroo. You good?"

Haddie froze. *I'm not good.* "Okay. About to reach our first view." Liz and Crow already had people looking for David. Terry didn't need another focus.

"Let me know."

Crow grunted as he crouched and then knelt close to a thick pine, pulling out one of the electronic monoculars. They both wore the long-sleeved brown shirts and gray khaki shorts he'd bought along their way. Cooper had ended up with a gray T-shirt from the grocery store with a cartoon rabbit on it. He hadn't complained, even when Terry had started joking about it.

Haddie crawled on her hands and knees in hot sand to get beside Crow. The ground dropped in a steep slope. In the valley, a beige mansion with flat and peaked roofs stretched in an island of green landscaping. A nearby ridge blocked the west end of it. The grounds and building looked lavish. From what little she could see, nothing moved outside.

"Nothing." Crow handed her the monocular.

Haddie zoomed in on the windows of the second floor and the tops of a few on the first. Brush and the angle of the slope killed most of their view. Kiana had warned her there wouldn't be much visible. Maybe there was a better spot where they could see more. Kiana had used elevation maps, but that didn't account for trees and brush.

They had hoped to determine whether there were guards or military and if Dad were in the building. Either could be likely with as little as they could see. They needed to get closer. From the plants, it appeared as if a ridge rose close to the house. Over the roofs, the driveway and front gardens were more visible than the back of the house.

"What do we do?" Haddie asked.

"Sit it out. I told you we might be stuck in the same place for a while. Jus' relax and take a load off."

Cooper spoke from close behind them. "Might want to rethink that. We've got a patrol coming from the southwest that will cut us off from your car."

"Damn," Crow cursed and scrambled backward.

Haddie followed as her phone buzzed in her pocket. While Crow and Cooper searched around the hillsides, she checked her phone and saw a message from Terry. "Demons headed to your location. Evacuate."

Crow growled. "They're headed toward us. Get down Haddie, head north, and circle back toward the car."

"Terry says we have demons headed this way."

"The two coming at us ain't demons, I don't believe, but still, get out of here."

Hot, still air hung around her. She didn't rise and try to see the two guards, but she didn't leave, either.

Crow dove toward the ground with an audible groan.

Automatic gunfire rattled in the quiet desert. Bullets tore green lint from the tree where he'd been crouched.

Cooper, the closest of the three of them, returned fire.

Haddie huddled behind a pine. Through dry branches, she could see them. The two soldiers had rifles. *Not coerced.* From the sounds of the shots, they'd cover this area easily. *Someone would be hit.* These were part of the people who took David.

"Stop," she yelled angrily.

Cooper caught one of the men in the chest. Blood sprayed before her tone rang.

Both men faded.

She sucked in a breath and jerked back. Pain crawled along her jaw.

Crow stared at her. His eyebrows furrowed, as if trying to understand.

Her skin exploded in fiery pain and her knees wobbled. She grabbed a handful of pine needles on a thin branch. The world turned silent.

"What . . ." Crow began.

Haddie's first vision blackened the bright sunlight and brought her to a humid night. Frogs croaked behind her. To her right, a fire burned, hidden in tree trunks and tall grass. Ahead, a metal barrel glinted with the firelight, and she shot where the body would be. Gunfire returned, more than she expected. The forest speckled with muzzle flashes. Dad's voice yelled out as he fired in return. Half of the sparks disappeared.

Day burst in and lit the sky again. She lay soaking in mud and the stench of death. The battle sounded around her. Her side burned with fire. *I've been shot.* A shadow loomed. Turning, she heard the tank heading toward her. Dad shouted, and his tone rang out. The metal vanished.

Twilight gripped the sky. An explosion sprayed mud and small points of pain dotted across her leg. She'd been running, and fell. Barbed wire and barricades stuck out of the sand and grass. Soldiers ran in pandemonium. Some screamed. A long-handled grenade landed beside her face. She'd promised not to use her powers. Yelling, the explosive faded.

Haddie rolled against prickly branches that highlighted the pain ravaging her skin. The New Mexico day appeared brighter than her visions. She'd slid, as any sense of direction had disappeared.

Crow grumbled something unintelligible.

Cooper stood with his back to her, searching between trees. His head and shoulders rose and fell, and she imagined the brush and stubby trees he was trying to look past.

She winced and pushed tender palms into hot sand. Branches and pungent pine needles plucked at her hair. *We need to run.* Someone would have heard the gunshots. The sounds of her visions and the rattle of the automatic rifle mixed in her memory. *Get up.* Somewhere behind, a branch snapped. Haddie yanked forward, losing strands of her hair to the tree.

Cooper turned and fired over her head.

Haddie covered her face and rolled to the side. Dirt and needles stuck against her lips. Looped through her belt with a carabiner, her water bottle twisted under her. As if an animal rampaged, limbs snapped and raging guttural noise sounded. There was more than one.

Cooper's muzzle flashed.

A shape darkened the sky over Haddie for a second.

Cooper let out a grunt as it hit him. *Demons.* She glimpsed orange, glowing eyes. Sand rained down on her. A second thud came as they hit the ground, and the ground vibrated.

She pushed backward and flailed as the ground gave way to a slope.

Crow screamed.

Haddie's leg thrashed to keep balance. Still, she slid in soft sand. *Grab something.*

A red skinless arm lifted Crow by the elbow. An audible snap jarred Haddie. Crow shrieked as his arm bent the wrong way.

Her slide downhill spun her sideways. The creature stood between two short pines. It wore an army uniform with the sleeves cut off. Standing taller than her, it dangled Crow off the ground. The big man's face grimaced in agony.

Haddie screamed in anger. The tone rang in the hot air. Crow dropped as the demon disappeared.

She spun with the grinding sand that seemed to scrape off her searing skin. Brush and sand blended as she toppled, then it faded with the blue sky as her visions set in.

PART 4

You have only begun to learn your power; with my help,
you could learn the true aspects of your skill.

CHAPTER 34

Thomas poked a cucumber in his salad. He ate with Dylan at the round table of the sitting room where the arched windows looked out on the foothills. Despite the dining area off the kitchen, Bruce favored this room for meals. Dylan acted indifferently, and Thomas only interacted with the man when Bruce left them alone. *I'll need to decide soon.* This evening, he'd have the opportunity to open a hole from the pressurized gas tank outside into the house where the fireplace could ignite it.

Bruce had walked away with Stanton to deal with a message on their tablet, leaving Dylan with Thomas. E626 stood far enough back from the meal that his reek couldn't overcome the scent of a rib roast.

Thomas hung his fork in the air. "So, why the absence of skin?" He gestured toward the demon.

"They have skin." Dylan spoke as he chewed. "Thin and translucent, thicker on their palms and feet." He swallowed and motioned for E626 to approach, then poked a thumb between the muscles and sinews. A thin layer resisted. "Part of an effect from the genetics that give them superior regenerative abilities."

Thomas put down his fork. "How regenerative?"

Dylan smirked. "They've taken multiple shots and survived. One to the brain or heart is usually fatal. With their enhanced agility and strength, you might only get one shot."

Thomas would have to act this evening. Crow would only be able to keep Haddie back for a couple days, and Terry had already highlighted this place. If he could leave Bruce inside during dinner and take a walk outside, he might be able to survive. He still hadn't determined where Bruce had stashed the children who were descendants of those who had powers. Supposedly young, like Meg, they could be sequestered anywhere. Even if he had a week, Thomas might not be able to pry that information from his hosts.

Bruce still hadn't returned from the foyer where he'd gone with his assistant. Depending on what he had planned for the afternoon, Thomas might be able to search the house for an office. So far, the escorting demons hadn't restricted his movement. Any clue to the nursery's whereabouts might change his plans.

Thomas reached for his glass. "Have you tried incubating your soldiers with our genes?" He gestured between them, indicating people with powers, those that Bruce called Noveilm.

"Not yet." Dylan took another bite of his steak.

Is he avoiding this topic? Could they have exactly that plan? Was that the intended use of the nursery? He picked up his drink and a bead of condensation rolled off his glass and splashed against his fatigues. *Give it a shot.* "Are they too young?"

"Yes, though we could harvest eggs." Dylan spoke as he ate, then looked suspicious, and grabbed his own beverage.

He's been coached to stay off this subject. Thomas resisted looking toward the entry to check on Bruce. "That would require medical facilities. It would make sense to keep them in a clinical environment." If Thomas could get that information to Terry, the others might be able to find the children. They were probably at another property owned by Bruce's holdings.

Dylan shrugged and drank.

Bruce strolled back in. "I'm going to have to attend to some things while you two finish up." His expression stiff, he seemed disturbed. "Dylan, perhaps some billiards." The comment came with a smile, but there seemed a hint of a command to the suggestion.

Dylan's eyebrows furrowed, then he nodded. "Sounds like fun."

Thomas doubted either of them relished more time with the other. He'd likely be able to excuse himself from the activity.

Bruce strode toward the hall where Thomas guessed an underground entrance lay. Between Bruce's arrival and the servant's activities, it seemed likely. *What has Bruce upset?* Thomas swallowed, hoping he hadn't misjudged Haddie. He had planned on Crow keeping her safe.

The door closed in the hall with a faint echo.

Picking his fork back up, Thomas kept his focus on his plate. His only plan relied on Bruce being in the building with a fire lit. If Haddie, or anyone, disturbed that, he might have to consider secondary plans. He possibly could attempt a casual search, but if Haddie were here, they would tighten security. He should be able to spot any increased patrols from the upper windows. All bets were off if she were captured. Something had concerned Bruce. *I need to get rid of Dylan and do some recon.*

CHAPTER 35

Haddie rested, or hid, nestled in the pile where she'd found herself after her visions. The pine at her shoulder smelled spicy and sweet. *Where did I land?* She'd slid downhill, toward the property they were supposed to be stealthily observing. Her skin burned worse down the side that had dug into the sand, but she didn't move. The memory of the visions still disoriented her. A truck revved somewhere nearby, and it echoed against the hills. Thick branches shaded her head and face. The ground angled downward in a steep slope.

Thirsty, she could feel her water bottle pressed against her stomach. *They could still be looking for me.* Crow was hurt, or worse. *No gunfire.* Was Cooper dead? Maybe Crow too? I've got to check on them.

Careful not to shift, she lifted her hand to the tree. Tender nerves touched sap and rough bark. She could tighten her grip if she started sliding. Her hair clung in branches and tucked under her shoulder. *I lost my phone.* It had been in her hand on the ridge above. The camouflaged bandanna she'd tied around her hair had fallen off in the tumble. Lifting her head, she searched, careful not to move too fast.

Through the branches, she had a view of the house, or might, if she could get in a better position where the other brush didn't block her view. Below her, the slope dropped out of sight, reappearing in a dry gully with a trail.

She stretched her neck to see the house. One main floor window arched behind a firepit on a patio with a small garden. *Where are you, Dad?* Holding onto the trunk, she inched upward until branches blocked her head. Needles clung to her dusted hair.

If the same people who had Dad kidnapped David, would they bring him here? Her heart began to race as she studied the house. *And what will I do?* Crow and Cooper might be dead. *They spotted us, somehow.* That patrol and those demons had zeroed right in on them.

Someone spoke below her in a deep, guttural voice. Haddie froze, eyes panning the edge of the slope. They might know exactly where she was and be climbing to her now. She yanked strands of hair that had been stuck to the tree and spun her head to search around her.

Toward the house, a figure ran along the trail, a demon dressed in the gray-green fatigues. Pinned over its shoulder by one arm, it looked like Cooper bounced, unconscious. The image was bizarre and unreal. Instead of a fireman's carry with the torso to the back, his legs hung behind the creature. Its path would lead them just under her position.

Haddie flushed, surprised to feel some guilt. He had pushed his way into this with them, but she'd allowed it, after the angels.

The demon continued until it passed the slope where she couldn't see into the ravine. A guttural exchange followed, and she imagined there were demons below her.

The scraping footsteps padded below her and then disappeared. The slope appeared to end to her left, rising up in a sharp incline, then leveled out higher above. *An entrance?* Her heart fluttered. *Were they holding Dad there? In a cave?*

Haddie adjusted her hold and slid down to her elbows, cringing as sand threatened to roll off the edge. With her right knee propped against the tree, she crawled forward. The slope didn't drop like a cliff. A steep edge led to a flat section. In the gully, at least one demon stood with a red, fleshy head visible. It guarded the trail a good distance from her. The top of a pine in front of her gave some sense of depth. *I could get down there — with a rope.* She lay, glancing between the demon and the treetop. How much noise would she make climbing down? Her joints already felt like she'd jumped off a cliff.

Making it to the ledge where it looked level, she might have a better idea. She also might not be able to get back up. What if Dad were inside? It meant leaving Crow up on the ridge. If he lived, he could make it to the SUV. She'd gotten rid of the demon, and the other had carried Cooper away. *I might be able to help Cooper and find Dad.*

Taking in a deep breath, she dragged her leg along the tree and crawled headfirst down the slope.

There were two demons guarding the entrance, but they watched the house. Their backs to her, they wore the same military fatigues, but carried no weapons. The distant truck revved, and the sound echoed up the ravine.

The entrance carved into the side of the hill showed steel supports in sections forming an arch. The opposite wall of the ravine had been cut into a sharp drop. The trail had shallow ruts from vehicles. Her dust-covered hair rolled in front of her, bristling with green pine needles. *I need to do this.* Haddie held her breath as she let go of the tree with her toe and pulled toward the ledge.

Angled down, she edged her left knee closer to the ravine and kept her eyes on the guards. They stood in front of a spiked metal barrier that spread from one side of the cut edge of the ravine to the other.

Placing her palm on the edge for leverage, she sidled to bring her knees onto it. The pine in front hadn't grown very tall, somehow escaping the excavation in a shallow of the ravine.

The dirt under Haddie's hand crumbled away. *Damn.* She pitched backward, and the slope above flashed as she fell. The blue sky hung for a moment before she landed hip first behind the tree. The black maw of a tunnel waited at her feet, but she took too long to recover. The ledge above poured sand in a tan waterfall behind her head. *They had to have heard that.*

Wincing, she pushed to sit up and swiveled. The tree blocked one of the guards, but the other remained in place, staring at the road leading to the back of the house. How had they not heard her? Careful not to make any additional sound, she climbed to her feet, her eyes riveted on the guards. Sand sloughed off her back and legs.

Each step sounded loud and grating as she crab-walked toward the entrance. She stepped into the cool shadow, focused on them. A few steps inside, she squinted down the tunnel, black as pitch. She couldn't make out any shapes within the darkness. Now what? It had to go somewhere. The demon had carried Cooper inside.

The air reeked, and a sound like rushing water or wind echoed inside. Her eyes finally adjusted from the outside light. A few lengths of rocky walls and steel supports showed before a dead black swallowed all light. She'd left

Crow alone, all in the hopes that Dad might be inside. Her only choice was to continue. Her back and joints ached, overcoming the tender skin after using her powers. Once again, she'd gone from a simple plan of surveillance to digging into places she probably shouldn't. What was she supposed to do? Any plan would have entailed coming to get Dad out. *Now, I have two men to rescue.*

CHAPTER 36

DALE JOLTED awake and tasted blood in his mouth. He lay bent over a shoulder, and the soldier reeked. They were in the dark, walking toward a distant light. A dull roar, like wind, echoed around them. Pushing with both hands against the man's chest, he couldn't break the grip pinning his hips. A skinless arm with black-tipped nails slapped into Dale's face. It wasn't hard enough to be a punch, but it dizzied him, and fleshy bare feet became his blurry focus. They stepped on stone with a shuffling echo. *I'm in a cave.* He remembered the creature that had leaped impossibly uphill to slam into him. *I put two shots into its chest.* A bullet hole frayed the soldier's fatigues with only a hint of blood.

This is one of Haddie's demons. Another impossibility. She was right. *This can't be.* She had made two FBI agents vanish. Harold Holmes and his brother were gone. Whatever Thomas and Haddie were up against might be bigger than Dale could imagine.

Industrial lights thudded on overhead, cutting the darkness and highlighting smooth gray rock. They traveled along a trail where tire tracks left imprints in the dust of the stone floor. Crates piled to his right. *Underground storage?* He had seen the aerial images of the compound located south of here.

They would want to interrogate him. Had Crow and Haddie survived? The first blow to his forehead had knocked Dale unconscious. *The strength in this creature.* How had it been created?

He'd lost his gun. The arm pinning him pressed against an empty holster.

They walked through an arch with steel supports into a brighter section of the cave. It stunk like warm meat. Guttural voices spoke off to his right. Were there more of these creatures?

Moving away from the noise, the demon approached a short ledge and began shifting Dale like a rag doll. The world spun and Dale blinked against the lights in the ceiling. The creature placed him on stone and stared at him with eyes that were too large. It had no eyelids. Oversized canine teeth extended from the bottom jaw. Exposed muscles wrapped from the hairless head under the collar of the military fatigues. *This isn't right.* It certainly wasn't human. *A mutant.* Had they created some gruesome super-soldier? What was it waiting for?

There were more creatures milling about in a large room with bunks. Dozens from the look of it. Next to the entrance, a dark tunnel sloped upward into blackness. These caves served as barracks as well as storage. *And jail.*

A deep stench hung in the air. His jailer stunk. Neither of them moved. Dale could try and run back the way they came, past the crates, but he'd been unconscious and didn't know where the tunnel went. Not to mention the mutant seemed to be more agile, and likely faster, than him.

They stood long enough that the lights turned off in the corridor where he'd been brought in. Motion sensor. *I won't be sneaking out of here.* It wouldn't be likely he could bluff his way out of his situation, but he'd try. They hadn't killed him outright.

"I'm Detective Cooper. Homicide."

If it understood him, it gave no indication. The large, unblinking eyes focused on his, but it might not be very intelligent. Those in the barracks engaged in tasks that any soldier might be assigned.

Deep in the barracks, a door opened and exposed a square of light and a silhouette. After a moment, the figure resolved into a soldier, a human, who walked from the far end toward Dale. Tall, he walked with an authoritative swagger. Trailing behind him was a smaller man stepping quickly to keep up.

Dale rubbed his mustache. He'd have to play along as best he could and avoid giving them too much information. He might not survive the interrogation, especially if he had no further use to them.

The soldier had a solid build and stood at least six feet high. He walked to where Dale waited and held out his hand. "ID."

Dale nodded and pulled out his wallet. "Detective Cooper. Homicide, Eugene, Oregon."

The smaller man stood behind, expressionless. He cradled an electronic tablet. The man in charge looked through the identification and then the contents of the wallet.

Dale swallowed and said, "I'm tracking Thomas Dawson. He has a warrant out for his arrest."

"Remove your clothes."

Dale paused. He'd expected a rebuke for being out of

his jurisdiction, or some other argument. Perhaps the soldier had a more military interrogation in mind.

The leader motioned to the creature. "Or, he can do it for you."

Drawing a deep breath, Dale began untying his shoes. *This man doesn't care that I'm an officer*. He started to reiterate his focus on Thomas Dawson, but held back. Let the soldier lead the questions. They would likely be in regard to Crow and Haddie; they'd obviously been spotted – the patrol and demons had been on them too quickly. *He's going to want answers*. And when he gets them?

The bullet wound in his ankle had swollen red, and dried blood flaked off.

There was no reason not to implicate Haddie and Crow, except to delay the man. They'd likely all been spotted anyway. The soldier probably had concerns there were more than just the three of them. They likely didn't know about Kiana and Terry. There would be no reason to mention them. *Alluding to them might keep me alive.* Standing on the ledge, he removed his pants.

The leader motioned to his underwear. Fighting frustration, Dale complied. The cave was a lot cooler than when he'd been brought in. He finished and held his hands clasped in front of himself.

"Where is Hadhira Dawson?" the soldier asked.

Dale shook his head. "At the moment, I don't know."

"Who was with you on the ridge?"

"Crow. Haddie I brought, hoping we could talk her father into surrendering."

The man's jaw tightened. "Who else knows that the three of you are here?"

"My communication team in Eugene." Dale drew in a tight breath.

“What are their names?”

“No. We need to discuss the situation.”

The leader smirked. “Hmm.” He dragged it out as if humming, and it quickly became annoying, like he was mocking.

Infuriating.

Adrenaline pumping, Dale wanted nothing more than to tear the man apart.

CHAPTER 37

HADDIE CREPT along the last part of the tunnel before it opened with a steel arch and dimly lit carved walls. The sound of rushing water grew stronger as she progressed, as did the dull ringing of someone's powers, but the angry screaming was loudest. *Someone sounds hysterical.* She couldn't make out the words. There was still a small side tunnel she could backtrack to, once she peeked around the corner to see what had caused the ruckus. The voice wasn't Dad's, but it could have been Cooper's. *If he were maniacally enraged.* A burnt smell clung to the air, though it had turned cooler underground. The light from the entrance shone against the first curve; no one had followed her in.

After drinking as much as she could, she'd left her water bottle behind. It made a dull noise, but in the silence, she heard every scuff of her shoes. It didn't matter now, with all the noise ahead. *What is going on?*

At the corner she took a deep breath, twirled her dirty hair tight to the back of her neck, and pressed her face to the rock, peering around the edge.

Cooper, struggling in the grip of a red-fleshed demon in

uniform, screamed a tirade. *Nude.* What had they done to him? He swore and threatened, only a word or two of which she could make out. Something about demons and killing. The target of his anger was a tall man in a camouflage uniform who stood with his head titled, listening. Another smaller, indifferent man stood behind, undaunted by the madness. The taller man paid attention, even leaning forward as if trying to discern the words.

That's Bruce. She recognized the man — out of place without a suit, but that was Bruce Palmer. Her mind separated the sounds. The ringing was his power. Her chest tightened. This was the man who tried to recruit Dad? Who'd killed Meg's family? The mastermind behind Lady Erica?

She'd sat down and had lunch with him. The image of him smiling at a Chinese restaurant didn't mesh with what she saw now.

What's his power? Pissing Cooper off?

It didn't matter. She could use her power and end this all while he focused on Cooper. It might save Dad. *Murder.* Haddie swallowed. Could she? She'd killed a man with a hammer when Dad had been coerced. Josh would never be the same because of Bruce. What would Sam say? *The greater good.* To save Dad, she could do this. Even Cooper didn't deserve whatever Bruce was doing to him.

One of the experiments Liz had wanted to try was to test Haddie's power over distance. *I should have agreed.* Bruce stood about half a city block from her. *How close do I need to be?* Steel girders arched across the opening to the lit cavern where Cooper ranted. Poking her head out a little farther, she searched the cave between one arch and the next. Square stacks rose in the darkness. She could sneak through there, out of sight, and come up to the next arch. It would cut the distance in half.

The sound of rushing water, or wind, echoed strongest here. She couldn't pin it to a wall; it came from everywhere. The air shifted, not as cool as it had been before. Hair pinned in her fist, she stepped forward, slipped around the corner, and pressed against the wall. Side-stepping, she moved until the edge of the opposite arch blocked her from view. *I can do this.*

Cooper's raving sounded ragged now. His throat was squeaking out threats. He mentioned her, and her strange powers, cursing her. He didn't seem to like Bruce either, though he didn't have a name to fix his hate onto.

Drawing a deep breath, Haddie started to cross the cave. Even in the darkness, she walked so far from the demon that she could barely make out the glow of its eyes.

An odd thud sounded above, a buzz, and then a bright ceiling light flooded the area around her. Wooden crates formed a wall to her right. A second light followed, then a third, leaving her standing exposed in the middle of the cavern.

Cooper's voice croaked into silence and a man bellowed orders. It could have been Bruce's.

The area beyond the crates looked closed in. She'd be trapped if she went that way. Her only escape would be back up the tunnel to where the other demons guarded the entrance. She could destroy them if needed. Cooper would be left with Bruce. *Dad isn't here.* Where was he?

Did they have David?

Haddie ran for the entrance to the tunnel leading out. Bruce stood apart from Cooper and his demon. The little man had turned his face up, but with no expression. She spun and growled at Bruce. *I've got to try.*

Her power rang out in the air. It dulled, striking his protection. It rebounded like never before. A physical impact that caused her to falter. Bruce grinned, then opened his mouth. She heard his tone ring out. Bringing up her defenses in time, it pressed on her as strong as Sameedha's had.

I can't fight this. Maybe she could find Dad, and together they could take Bruce down. Stumbling, she made it through the arch and turned left toward the opening. Soldiers followed. There were too many for her to consider defending against. Bruce's power followed her, a pressure against her defenses. She hoped it would lessen when she reached the opening and the guards. *If I make it that far.* Running, she could hear pursuers reach the corner, nails scratching on stone. She could turn and use her power, but then she'd lose momentum, and there had been too many. Intent required her to know what she wanted to vanish.

They were too fast. She spun at the last moment and managed a squawk. Her tone rang out and one of dozens of demons, the closest, disappeared mid jump. The pain tore across her skin like needles and glass. A second demon slammed into her, and a new pain wracked her elbow and the back of her skull as she hit stone.

Wide horrifying eyes, stretched facial muscles, and teeth were the last things she saw before the visions hit.

The first brought her to a dark house where men attacked Dad and his family in the middle of the night. Shapes and shadows, and the panic that comes from being awakened to danger. The second took her to a sunny forest where Dad protected a young son from a pair of men with rifles. The last happened on a muddy street, under a yellow-flamed gas lamp when a man burst from an alley and plunged a knife into Dad's side.

The memory of the pain lingered when she returned to the pressure of the demon pinning her to the ground.

Bruce jogged up the tunnel. Demons spread out around her. He slowed with a broad smile on his face. "You have no idea what a pleasure it is to see you again, Haddie."

The creature's foul odor hung in her nose, she ached, and her skin felt shredded. She'd failed. There wasn't enough left in her to fight all of them. Clenching her jaw, she pushed at the demon. "Get this thing off me."

CHAPTER 38

Bruce studied Hadhira Dawson, a large woman whose hair was coated with dirt and debris. Her face tightened into a fierce expression as she struggled against his soldier. *This is a warrior.* A hostage for the moment, he hoped he could turn her to his cause. Having two supporters who could shift time would be immensely useful. Getting her to help might be more difficult than convincing her father. *Thomas has been around long enough to want a better world.* With New York only days away, Bruce didn't have much time.

"Can I let you up?" asked Bruce.

"To hell with you."

He smiled. Even surrounded by his forces, she didn't show fear.

Soldiers waited attentively around her, their dull smell, like that of a meat packing plant, hung in the corridor despite the breeze. The unusual rushing sound that echoed in the walls grew louder with only her grunts to compare.

Thomas could be manipulated more easily now, and it

wouldn't look like Bruce had gone back on his word. Hadhira had attacked first. Would she follow if the father joined? Barbara had resisted at first, but eventually she'd fallen into line. Bruce still had Hadhira's boyfriend as hostage, though he could discard the man once he'd assessed her disposition and willingness. *This is turning out to be a promising day.* He'd begun to consider he'd have to give up on Thomas.

"Let her up," he said.

Hadhira scrambled up as his soldier obeyed. She wore all camouflage. His cameras had picked up three intruders on the north ridge. The third would likely be dead, but he'd have the body recovered. He guessed he'd lost some of his own in the action, but well worth it. *A prize on my doorstep. In Eugene, all this time.*

"Bring her." He motioned to the soldiers, and two of them took her arms. She could attack them, but there were more. Being relatively young in the use of her powers, he doubted she could keep it up very long. However, he hated to lose troops. How powerful was she? He would sedate her if she became too difficult. First, he would try and calm her.

She had come with the detective. How had they discerned that Thomas would be here? Why were they working together? Bruce might be able to open a dialog if he promised that her father was safe and here of his own free will. *I'm going to have to be careful.*

"Where is Dad? What have you done with him?"

Bruce didn't turn back to address her. "Your father is our guest. He contacted me. Why are *you* here?"

He turned the corner where the motion sensor lights still shone on the armory. His men had filled in from the barracks. They were drawn toward violence, but could restrain themselves. Beyond in the parade grounds, the detective stood in a small semicircle of soldiers.

Hadhira spoke up after a moment. “Are you bringing me to him?”

CHAPTER 39

THOMAS STEPPED TO THE WINDOW. A faint tone had rung beyond his hearing, like someone had used a power. It could have been Bruce. The general had been concerned about something. Surprisingly, demons were searching the hills behind the house. *Something is going on.* Thomas leaned against the warm glass to see farther to each side. Eight demon soldiers patrolled the small section in his view.

Haddie? If so, then possibly Kiana and Crow were here. They might have guessed where he was. Terry had been on Bruce's trail.

Thomas had excused himself from Dylan with a request for a nap; the man had been relieved if anything. E626 guarded the hall outside. He had planned to take a walk around the house checking rooms and the door that might lead down to the barracks. His demon guards hadn't restricted his movements, though they made sure to keep him in sight unless he was in his bedroom and bathroom.

His jaw tightened, and he wiped back his hair. Who else besides Haddie could create a stir? Bruce would let him know if there were any other players, but there would be somc indication.

Dammit, Haddie. It had to be her. How could Crow have let her try something? Kiana should know better. Thomas couldn't sit and do nothing.

He turned from the window and strode to the door, stopping before his hand reached the knob. If he destroyed the demon, Dylan might hear his tone. Thomas would be committing to an action that would break the uneasy treaty he'd reached with Bruce.

Hell. He pinned back his hair with both hands and paced the room. Haddie could be in trouble, or it could be a wayward demon that concerned Bruce. *I don't know anything.* He entered the bathroom and went to the small windows. They were locked, like the door to the balcony. The farthest would open to the roof's edge, though not over the roof directly. Escaping out a window wouldn't be as inflammatory as destroying one of the demons, but it still might have negative consequences. The lock was simple.

"To the devil," Thomas said, heading back to the bedroom for an iron poker. After quietly closing and locking the bathroom door, he pried against the window lock, slowly ripping out screws and bending metal with the pressure. It didn't make much noise, and after a minute he climbed out the window backward.

If any of the searching patrols noticed him, he couldn't tell. Sitting on the sill of the window, he grasped the stone framing and pulled his weight higher to get a foot up. Once he had both feet firmly on the ledge, he gauged the distance to the roof before jumping. He slid on the tiles. Flattening on the slope, his palms dragged him to a stop with his boots dangling over the edge. With a slow, careful shift of his knee, he rose to crawl.

The roof sloped to a peak over the back sitting room and then to a higher summit along the spine of the building. The incline over his bedroom rose the steepest. Thomas stood and walked carefully toward the highest crest, gaining a view of the hills in front of the estate. There were demon soldiers there as well. Perhaps they had lost Haddie, or he'd made an error slipping out of his room.

Flat roofs covered the east end of the building with large air conditioning units mounted in the middle. He'd be less visible there. One section of the building rose above the closest roof with windows and an access door. It didn't seem likely that Dylan would choose that view. *I can hope.* The pitch above the bedrooms dropped to the flat section, but he couldn't see how high the drop was. Easing himself feet first, he crawled on his backside to the ledge.

A good five feet. He pushed his heels off the roof, spun, and slapped his hands on the tiles as he dropped. He slowed enough that he tapped the wall with his boots and landed with only a slight grunt onto the flat roof. The scent of hot asphalt hung in stagnant air.

CHAPTER 40

HADDIE FOLLOWED Bruce down the corridor, escorted by the gruesome wide-eyed demons. The sound of rushing air or water persisted, and the air stunk of the creatures and burnt gunpowder. *Where is Dad?* She couldn't trust that he was okay. She'd make them take her to him. They headed back toward where Cooper had been held captive. *Naked.* What was that about?

The demon soldiers spread throughout the caverns, attentive but not aggressive. They had captured her; they didn't need to attack. *What do I do now?*

The lights that she'd triggered were still on. The cave had piles of crates with lettering that made her imagine munitions. Some of the complex seemed natural, though the floors had been ground smooth and flat, except the ledge where they'd pinned Cooper. Natural stone rose up about half her height and randomly jutted into the larger cavern. The sounds faded, but the stench of the demons didn't. The creatures crowded the room, even thicker in a large opening to her right. At the far end, another unlit exit dug into the stone.

There were too many demons around her, and Bruce wouldn't give her an opportunity to get away. Cooper's face formed an angry scowl.

Bruce walked toward the rising stone where they had Cooper.

"Are we going to see my dad?" Haddie asked.

They paused in front of Cooper.

"Search her."

One of the demons stepped forward and patted her down, almost human-like. The stench stiffened her, and she raised her arms to quicken the process. Luckily, she didn't have her phone. Her last communication with Kiana had been something like "we're in place."

When the demon stepped away, Haddie stared down Bruce. The tall man had a couple inches on her and most of the demons. "Dad?"

"First, we'll talk." Striding the last few steps, he gestured to the ledge where Cooper stood. "Have a seat."

Haddie stopped at the edge and crossed her arms with her eyebrows raised. "First, we'll see my dad."

Bruce motioned for her to join Cooper. It was tempting, considering none of the demons stood up there. Haddie raised her chin, unmoving. He grinned as if mildly amused. "Get up there — or I'll have one of my men put you up there."

He would. Haddie tightened her jaw and climbed up, conscious of Cooper's lack of clothing. Bruce tried to make them feel powerless. Trapped, she couldn't disagree. What did Bruce plan? She didn't sit; instead, she stood beside Cooper. "Is Dad okay?"

"Thomas? He's relaxing — playing a game of pool with one of my people."

Doubtful. "Why are you afraid to let us see each other?"

Bruce ignored her jibe. "Other than the police officer, who did you come here with? Uninvited."

"Crow. Your demons killed him." She hoped Crow had survived and her comment would close the conversation. Bruce had no way to know about Kiana and Terry, or Biff. Would her friends follow her? Her stomach tied in a cold knot, thinking of them risking themselves. They might.

"Who else?"

Haddie paused. What did she hope to gain from this conversation? *To see Dad.* "Don't you think I would have brought everyone I could to save Dad?" If she had brought reserves, Bruce would be on the alert. If they'd come alone, he might relax. He wouldn't kill her. *I'm an asset, like Dad.* She swallowed and glanced at Cooper.

Bruce's eyes flitted to Cooper. What had been discussed before she'd arrived? Had Cooper outed Kiana and Terry?

"Yes. And we found you three. How many more are there?" Relaxed, Bruce held his hands in front of himself.

"Just us three." He couldn't know about Kiana and Terry; otherwise, he wouldn't ask. Would he?

Again, he looked to Cooper. Haddie forced herself not to follow suit.

Bruce nodded. "Very well." He tilted his head and studied her. "How did you find us here?"

Haddie couldn't tell him the truth. It would implicate Terry.

"Bring me to Dad, and I'll tell you." She could make up a lie by then that would protect Terry.

"Hmm." His tone rang out in the air, echoing in the cavern.

Haddie squeaked and her tone rung in protection; she barely realized she reacted. What was his power?

Bruce smiled. "Interesting." His tone remained as a threat.

She wouldn't be able to attack while she protected herself.

His attendant in the dark suit stepped up and showed Bruce the tablet. Immediately, his expression darkened. "Did you and your father plan this?"

What was Dad doing? Did he know Bruce held her captive? A glimmer of hope rose in her chest. Her eyes flicked in the dark recesses of the tunnel, expecting to see Dad.

"Plan what?" she asked.

He studied her with a scowl that matched Cooper's. Glowering, he shook his head. "I've got to go handle your father." He turned to his demon soldiers. "If she uses her power, kill the detective and knock her unconscious. Don't let them escape."

CHAPTER 41

Kiana absently rubbed her ear, listening to Terry chatter about data encryption. The midday sun taxed the air conditioner, and somewhere inside the machine she could hear dripping. Uncomfortable in the bed, she had few options except to sit quietly and worry about people she cared about. *They need me.* She didn't trust Cooper, even if he had helped at the gas station. Thomas and Haddie always got neck deep into trouble, and this time, all she could do was wait in the hotel room with a crutch.

Biff would arrive soon; he'd stopped to pick up some food. She barely knew him, more from stories than the little interaction they'd had since Thomas had left Eugene and his past life.

She couldn't imagine what Thomas had planned. Whatever she did guess made her squirm from apprehension. As a father, his thoughts would be to protect Haddie. In Kiana's relationship with him, she cared about Haddie, but not to the point where he should sacrifice himself on a suicide mission. Heading into an armed camp alone didn't leave him a lot of options. Did he think Haddie would just sit idly by and not go help?

"What do you think?" asked Terry.

"What? I'm sorry."

"The one tower is the only location close enough to the house to provide cell service. If we disable it, then we might blind them somewhat. If they're using a satellite backup, though, it wouldn't matter." Terry sipped at his drink. "But, it would mess with Haddie's phone and Crow's people, as well."

"Then, no. But how?" She took in a breath, focusing on his response.

He chuckled. "I was saying – that my friend can initiate a diagnostic that'll knock connection off for fifteen to twenty minutes."

"Not now, but it's good to know." Kiana wanted to text Haddie or Crow to check on their situation, but even with their cells on vibrate, they'd agreed to leave it to them to initiate.

"I figured. Just wanted you to know a new option." He shrugged. "Crow's people haven't had much luck. Their fixed cameras haven't shown any activity, but they are positioned pretty far out. Haddie and Crow should be getting a better view by now."

Kiana drew in a tight breath. She worried that her coordinates might have been too close to the property line. It was the only way to get a good view of the house with the terrain around it. Aerial had proved difficult, and Crow's people still hadn't gotten more drones in the air.

She jumped as a knock rapped at the door. Terry glanced back, and she motioned with her head for him to answer and pointed at her eyes for him to see who it was.

Her phone buzzed with a text from Biff. "Here."

Kiana sighed. "It's Biff."

Terry opened the door and the warm air flooded in. Desert dust replaced the room's musty scent.

Biff, his hair styled up off his face, smiled and shoved a bag at Terry. "Snacks, as requested. Good seeing you again, Terry." He wore a light-blue, short-sleeved, button-down shirt and dark brown work pants. Carrying another bag, he stepped in and closed the door. He smirked at Kiana lying on the bed. "Should have brought bon-bons. Where's the crew?" He'd shaved the beard since the last time she'd seen him, leaving only the trimmed mustache.

"They're out trying to get a visual on Thomas." It had been three hours, with only one text when they'd left the SUV.

Biff's grin turned somber. "You're sure he's here?"

Kiana glanced at Terry. "We think his target is here."

Terry worked on a bag of peanuts. "The Boss Man's here, for sure."

Dropping a bag beside Kiana, Biff sat on the opposite edge. "What is T doing?" he asked.

"I don't know." *He should have told me.* It had to be dangerous, to act without letting anyone know. Now Haddie was there — with no word from anyone.

Biff raised both hands in the air. "So what are we doing?"

"Waiting," she answered with a tone surprisingly bitter. "We aren't to contact them unless we get new information from Crow's people — and —" She motioned to Terry.

He glanced back at his screen with a mouthful of peanuts. "Nothin'."

Biff shook his head. "They were leaving over three hours ago. I think this deserves a break in the silence.

They'd have their phones on mute or vibrate." He tilted his head forward, eyebrows raised questioningly. "Yeah?"

She took in a deep breath. She'd been tempted, and with Biff's urging it wasn't hard to pick up her phone. Typing "Ok?" she messaged both Crow and Haddie.

The three of them fell silent, leaving only the grinding of the air conditioner and an occasional drip. A minute went by before Terry crumpled up an empty plastic bag and tossed it into the garbage can.

Biff sighed. "So, we wait."

Kiana laid the phone by her side and nodded. She could imagine them hiding in the brush, not wanting to move to check their phones — or worse. Cooper had been a bad idea all around, but Haddie and Meg's angels had supposedly helped with Lady Erica. All of it sounded bizarre. It didn't fit with her lifetime of experience in the military and the FBI.

Terry typed on his tablet, snorting. "The Unceasing have announced that they will be putting up a candidate for the Florida governor's race."

Kiana took a deep breath. "I thought they expect the world to end soon."

"Seems like they still do." His chair creaked as he turned around. "Not sure Florida would notice."

Biff chuckled, but his jaw remained tense. He leaned back and threw a knee up on the bed.

Terry's tablet beeped and he spun to check it.

"What?" Kiana asked.

"A video clip." He stood and came to her side of the bed, holding the tablet so they could both see.

Biff shifted behind her, jostling the mattress.

Trees bristled at the bottom of the image, with the house in the center and mountains rising up behind. The video zoomed in on the mansion, and it stretched across the screen. A pair of soldiers walked across the driveway, heading to the bottom right. In the upper left, a dark figure climbed down an embankment. Two ruddy-faced guards stood in front of a cave opening.

"That's Haddie," Kiana said.

The dark figure had light hair, if not Haddie's stark white. She slid off the edge and landed behind the guards. Kiana winced, but the soldiers didn't move. In a moment, Haddie stood up and crept into the darkness of the cave entrance. The video continued panning across the massive building. *Where are you, Thomas?*

Terry sucked in a breath as the clip ended. "There's patrols around the house. The investigator thought this might be one of our people. Should I tell them it's Haddie?"

Kiana shook her head. "Just have them hold that position and let us know if there's any other activity." The house appeared unoccupied. Was the base underground? *Haddie, what are you doing?* Perhaps Thomas was in the cave as well. There were more soldiers than they'd seen so far.

Kiana's phone vibrated, and she jumped. Terry spun in his chair. Biff peered at her as she picked it up.

Crow had sent a single word. "Help."

CHAPTER 42

Haddie stood tense in front of their audience of gruesome wide-eyed demons. They weren't all the same, but they were more human than any she'd seen outside the compound. *What is Dad up to?* She couldn't trust Bruce. Perhaps Dad had taken her distraction as an opportunity to escape.

The demon soldiers were thick in the cavern in front of her. Others piled in the room ahead, where she could make out supporting beams over bunks. The armory lights had turned off, but she could see the glow of demon eyes from where they waited. Would they truly kill Cooper if she tried something? *What do I do now?*

"You know him?" Cooper asked. His tone remained calm though he scowled at their guards.

"Yes." Did it matter if she told him? "Bruce. Client of Andrea's. I'm guessing he was just trying to find out what he could about Harold Holmes."

"Military?"

She wasn't about to mention Dad's letter. "I imagine so."

"He —" Cooper's voice faltered. "He made me angry."

An odd statement. "Well —"

Cooper turned and searched her eyes. "Can you make someone furious . . . with your powers?" His tone sounded unsure and didn't match his expression. There was a desperation to his question.

She shook her head. *The screaming I heard.* "No. Is that what he did to you?"

He drooped and blew out a breath, as if shaking off a thought. "I guess. I'm not sure I understand." He motioned to the demons. "But, all this. I don't understand any of it."

"Bruce is planning a war." She didn't need to mention the letter. The Unceasing website had more than enough information.

"You and Thomas, are you trying to stop that?"

That hadn't been the direct plan. She'd wanted to know what they were up to, and Dad had been focused on keeping Meg safe. "It's worked out that way." They actually didn't have much of an understanding of what Bruce planned. It felt like a war, considering the comments from the Unceasing.

"And the FBI are helping him?" Cooper tilted his head. "Were."

"I think only a few are coerced."

He paused for a moment. They stood in front of Bruce's unmoving army. There was almost no sound in the cavern.

Bruce had been concerned. Had Dad done something?

"I think they were going to torture me." He motioned down his nude body. "You interrupted that. Thank you."

"We're not out of this yet."

He lowered his voice. "Can't you just . . . do your thing?" He nudged his head toward the closest demon.

Haddie scoffed. There were dozens spread out in just

the cavern they stood in. More dotted the armory, and far more packed the barracks. Liz would have loved the opportunity to experiment. How many demons could Haddie make disappear? If she failed, in the slightest, Cooper would be dead. She had the sense these demons took their orders literally.

She shook her head. "You did hear what he said."

Cooper nodded a bit too emphatically. "Yeah. But I imagine I'm dead no matter what. I won't live long unless we get out of here."

The dark tunnel to their left might lead out. Cooper could escape through it. Bruce had headed into the barracks where a small corridor opened in the far back. *There's too many.* The closest demons had disturbingly human forms and stood attentively watching her. Some in the barracks appeared misshapen, but large and dangerous. If her powers couldn't handle this many, they'd kill Cooper and attack her.

If Dad did distract Bruce, now would be the time to try anything.

"If I try," Haddie said, "Then you've got to run." She tilted her head left, toward the tunnel.

He studied her, not agreeing.

"I've never tried anything like this before. It might not work . . . the way I expect. They'll attack me, but kill you." She'd seen the lesser demons in action before. They wouldn't hesitate. Violence seemed in their nature. These likely were barely restrained even now.

The demon in front of them said nothing. Staring with lidless eyes, it could probably hear them. Did it wait for her to act? Sharp canine teeth rested against the muscles of its upper lip. She wouldn't flinch at making it disappear, no matter how intelligent it acted.

"I don't see a better option," said Cooper. "I just wish I had my gun."

The creatures had no weapons, except for their claws and teeth. Haddie shivered, imagining them ripping Cooper apart.

"I can't." She shook her head. Dad might have a plan, or a better one than getting Cooper killed. *Or not. He doesn't even know I'm here.* If she did nothing, it might be worse for Dad and Cooper. Bruce likely would kill Cooper, and hostage her against Dad. *What do I do?*

"You need to try," Cooper said.

Every option could lead to failure. *I have to try something — we can't just stand here waiting.*

Haddie took a deep breath. They'd kill Cooper. *That much I know.* "I can't," she repeated.

CHAPTER 43

Kiana climbed out of Biff's truck, barely using her crutch. The hot, afternoon sun beat on the sand, and pine scented the stagnant air. They'd driven past the Highlander through the dirt and dust to the ridge she'd told Crow and Haddie would be the best vantage. *This is on me.* Crow had responded once more when she'd asked if he were near that location. She kept her Glock 19 loose in her right hand.

Biff followed a trail into the short trees and brush. He crouched and peeked about each tree. He'd been quick to offer a rescue in his rental.

She followed slower, scanning the surrounding brush for signs of Crow. Her outlandish, colored cast seemed imprudent amid the dull grays and greens. She'd lost Haddie into some underground entrance. Thomas still evaded them. *Where is Cooper?* Once they found Crow, she didn't want to leave the others behind. *Not when I'm this close.*

Crow's rough, dry voice called from her left. "Hey."

"Biff," she called. Limping toward Crow, she saw the trail he'd left dragging himself in the sand.

His arm twisted inside a bloody sleeve that he'd bound with cord. He had one knee up and kept the other leg out straight.

"What happened?" she asked. He stunk with more than just blood.

"Your demons. I don't think I really believed." He nodded as Biff arrived. "Tore my damn arm out of its socket, bone's pokin' out my elbow." He snorted and coughed. "And I twisted my damn ankle." Locking eyes with Kiana, he grimaced. "They took Cooper. Don't know what happened to Haddie. I passed out. I think they just left me. Just . . . disappeared."

Vanished. Did Haddie use her ability? They needed to get Crow to a hospital. The goo on his uniform could be the demon that attacked him, if Haddie had used her powers. "Let's get you in the truck."

"Whiskey?"

"After the hospital." She looked at Biff. "You got this?"

Biff nodded. "One way or another." He grabbed onto Crow with both arms and managed to pull him standing. "Terry was right. I should have brought a forklift."

Crow coughed, almost a laugh. "They were out here lookin', but never found me."

Biff climbed under Crow's good arm and turned toward the truck.

Kiana shivered, watching the arm flap. Crow winced and his eyes rolled, but he didn't make a sound.

They all stopped as a vehicle sounded to the north.

Kiana hobbled over to a tree where she could see their truck. "Get down." She dropped under the branches and waited as the rumbling engine grew close. A large engine, it whined as it took the last ridge and skidded to a stop in a cloud of dust. An MRAP. She'd driven them before. Two soldiers peered from their seats at Biff's truck and scanned the area. How had they located them so quickly? There had to be equipment, possibly cameras, up here. *I sent Haddie right into a trap.* Crow was hurt, Cooper captured, and Haddie somewhere inside this hell hole. *Where are* you, *Thomas?*

Two men exited the MRAP and searched Biff's rental truck with AR-47s at the ready. *Padded uniforms. Kevlar.* Someone outfitted this operation well.

Kiana waited until they followed the tracks leading to her before she fired.

The first went down with a shot just left of his nose. The second guard crouched and fired wildly into the bushes. She took him in the temple over his left eyebrow.

"Biff?" she yelled.

"We're good. That was quick."

She stood, leaning heavily on her crutch, and winced at the pain of her full weight on the cast. She might end up with surgery. "Leave Crow for a second. You need to use their equipment and call in before we get more troops up here." She just needed a delay. The uniforms had name tags. "Muffle the com. Call in with the name on the uniform, tell them you downed two intruders. All clear. Use the other tag and state that he's been wounded and you are bringing him in. It should keep reinforcements from heading out immediately."

That MRAP could take a lot of punishment. She wanted to drive it into the compound and hunt for Thomas. Kiana shook her head. She balanced, hopped, and limped toward Crow sitting in the sand. His color looked wrong, but he managed a smile.

Biff made the call with a cocky voice as if auditioning

for a TV movie and she winced. Hopefully, the dispatch officer taking the call didn't know the soldier.

As Biff jogged back toward them, Kiana turned to Crow. "We're not going to have much time to get you out of here."

He frowned. "You're not stayin', are you?"

I want to. "I don't think it would help."

Biff ran up with a lopsided grin. "They bought it."

"Just to be sure, let's get out of here." Kiana moved back to give him room. She scanned around them, but the ridge rose between them and the house. The mountains climbed farther beyond to the east in dark shades.

As they stood again, she held out her hand. "I'll drive the Highlander." They'd passed it on their way up.

Crow dug into his pocket with his good arm. "What if Haddie needs it?"

"She went in some tunnel. We've got her on video. Does she have keys?" Kiana glanced back toward the MRAP.

Crow frowned and shook his head. "Nope."

Kiana swallowed. *I don't like leaving anyone here either.* But she couldn't limp into the enemy's compound with her Glock 19 and demand they release all prisoners. This had been planned as a recon.

Her phone vibrated and she sucked in a breath as she juggled the keys and her crutch, hoping it was Haddie.

Terry texted, "I've got eyes on T."

CHAPTER 44

HADDIE FOUGHT desperation as she stared at the motionless demons. She'd almost become accustomed to their stench. Those less than human-like in the barracks moved about in some activities; she could see the glow of their eyes shifting through the wall or when they came to the opening to look at her. *Am I just going to wait here?* Cooper had pushed for her to use her power, but had seemed to let it go.

How could these creatures just stand here entirely motionless? She would have sat on the ledge, but it would feel like she'd given up. The only option she had might kill Cooper. She'd never liked him, though he had helped her get out of Eugene. Why had the angels wanted him to come? *The cops at the gas station?* There had to be more than that. Could it be that simple? Or would he have something more to offer?

"What do we do?" she asked.

He shifted his bare feet, scuffling on the stone. One of his ankles had an ugly pink sore. She focused on his face. It had to be uncomfortable to stand naked, but she wasn't about to offer any clothes.

"I don't see that we have any real resources, except your abilities." His lips tightened. "Which you don't believe are sufficient. However, completely effective or not, they might be our only choice. I understand you might not have used them on quite this many." He cocked his head discreetly at the demons. "But you took out two FBI agents. Is there a limit?"

She glanced from one gruesome face to the next. *Is he trying to goad me into this?* What were her limits? Dad had taken on groups of enemy soldiers. *None this big.* Was it just intent? *Hell, Liz would really love this. I should have experimented more with her.* "I'm not going to risk them killing you. There might be a better chance. What if they try to move us somewhere?"

"I don't get the feeling that this man is that sloppy. He won't give us a chance. I'll likely be interrogated and killed right here." He took in a deep breath. "You won't know your limits unless you try. If that's what's holding you back, then this isn't the time to worry about it."

"When would be a better time?" she asked. *Afterward?* While they were knocking her out and killing him wouldn't be a better time. "I'm not risking you."

"I'm asking to be risked." He sighed. "I expect I'll be shot soon and buried out here in these hills. I'd rather go out trying, but I won't make much of a dent without you."

She imagined Crow dangling with his broken arm. The demon soldiers had moved too quickly. Haddie shivered. "I can't."

"Okay. What if just jump off here and attack the one right in front of us? Would you react?"

She nodded. "Probably." *I would.*

"And I'd die rather quickly, just to get you to act."

Likely. "Don't." Her pulse raced and her eyes flitted sideways to make sure he wasn't moving.

"I will unless you take action first. Same results, perhaps. However, it could work, and I'd get to live."

"Don't," she repeated. She hadn't really known Cooper. In the past day, he'd surprised her in ways that she hadn't expected. At the moment, he terrified her.

Cooper took a step.

Haddie heart flipped. "Please."

The demon closest to them appeared to tense. It would have heard at least part of their conversation. Did it react because Cooper might attack? Or her? All too human eyes watched Cooper. They would kill him before she could react. "Okay," Haddie said.

He drew in a long breath. "I'm ready."

She focused on the eyes spread out before her. *Intention.* She spread her focus across three caves. Jaw tight and heart racing she screamed, "Go to hell."

The tone rang in the air and the demon before them faded, as did the one behind. The timing lagged but just at the edge of her perception.

Three more.

Four more.

Her ability centered on her and spread out in a wave. The first tingles of pain washed down the side of her face. Pressure built in her skull and the outer edge of her power hit three demons, but only partially vaporized them. Their organs and bone exposed, they stood frozen, surely dead, but not gone. *I've failed.* They'll kill us both.

Around the cavern and beyond, the orange glows hung motionless.

The demons couldn't move, as if stopped in time. Her

skin crackled with purpura along her neck and wrists. Her head would explode soon, but she didn't stop the tone. It held the demons at bay. Joints burned. She didn't dare move. Time seemed to have stopped, at least around the demons.

Cooper's head twisted toward her. "More."

She didn't have more. *I can't hold this forever.* When she stopped, they would attack. There were no sticky smudges on the floor. *How far back in time am I sending them?* Perhaps she'd pushed too hard, in the wrong way. *I don't know what I'm doing.*

"More," he yelled.

Dozens, maybe hundreds of grotesque demons remained, affected, but not gone. Pain threatened to topple her. She would let go at some point. Bruce would come back and shoot her. She'd failed. They wouldn't survive. The air reeked anew. Even the insides of her nose seemed to shred with purpura. *I can't.* Cooper would surely die.

The bright lights dimmed.

No.

The visions were coming.

CHAPTER 45

Bruce stood at the window facing the back of the house; he messaged on the tablet held before him. The staff had left the sharp scent of disinfectant in the room. Dylan had moved to the roof with his men hoping to spot Thomas. Stanton stood impassive, his eyes bright with Lady Erica's powers. If she had lived, it all would have been easier. *Thomas would have had no defense.* More troops would have to be drawn from the barracks. There'd been an incursion on the perimeter again, and drones spotted. *I'll need to get out of here.* How had Thomas planned all this?

Two assets or two hostages? With New York only days away, Bruce didn't have the leisure to indulge Thomas or his daughter. They'd have to make quick choices whether to join him or die.

"Anything?" messaged Bruce.

Dylan responded immediately, "We might have something. Spotter noted movement heading north toward the training compound."

"Alert them. Subdue and capture." They'd lose a few

men, but Thomas didn't have control of his powers well enough to take them all on. Hopefully, none of them would shoot. *If I lose Thomas, I still have Hadhira.*

"Already ordered."

Dylan could manage things here. He'd been trained.

Bruce switched to message the barracks. "Send a squad to the training compound." He might have to nullify some of the new recruits, but he couldn't let Thomas escape. He sighed. "Second squad to northwest perimeter." The people Thomas had brought seemed to use the access roads there.

He contacted his pilots. "Ready the helicopter. Three." Bruce wasn't confident that he'd be able to take down Thomas alive, but he had to try. At least the man didn't have a weapon. A trained fighter in his compound would quickly turn into a massacre and rout. Perhaps, Thomas planned on getting weapons there.

I could go up with Dylan. Bruce walked over to the fireplace and lit it. It certainly wasn't cool enough to warrant a fire, but the rolling flames eased him. Thomas had been a dream, the one plan that had started all the others. The Noveilm united. *Here to save the world.* That seemed unlikely at the moment. *I* had *joined them under my command.* He would again. The blood had been saved in his little orphanage. Dylan had eggs to work with as well.

The tablet buzzed and he spun.

"Confirmed," messaged Dylan. "Armed. Rifle and grenade belt."

Bruce's finger hung over the screen.

"We have a shot. He's climbing a ridge. Thirty seconds."

Grenades. Thomas would go for the helicopter. He wouldn't need a grenade. There could be more of his troops testing the perimeter now. *Maybe he wanted me to catch the ones in the northwest.*

Bruce had the daughter. *One asset.*

"Take the shot."

CHAPTER 46

THOMAS DUG his boots into the stiff dirt and worked up the incline. A whiff of gunpowder mixed with pine. The regular tap-tap of the training compound's range set a clear sense of direction. Initially, he'd just been trying to keep out of sight of the demon patrols outside the house; now he had a target. *Hopefully, they won't be looking for me.* The odds were slim that he could get access to their communication center, but he didn't have a lot of options. If Haddie breached the compound, he couldn't let Bruce get a hold of her. A hostage situation would change all the dynamics. *I'm not ready to make that choice.*

Once he got out of sight from the house, his chances of success would go up. *Still not good.*

The gunfire ahead slowed, ceasing. One vehicle rumbled at the compound and a second raced parallel to Thomas in the west. He'd managed to avoid all the patrols he'd seen so far. The first pair he'd taken out for their weapons, far enough from the house that Dylan might not have heard the tone of his power.

Unseen, the western vehicle whined and changed direction. *Hell, toward me.* They threatened to find him climbing up the ridge. Thomas dove for the shelter of a pine.

A single bullet thudded into the dirt. It couldn't have come from the patrol; they hadn't come over the western crest yet.

A second bullet tore through the branches of the tree a hand's width from his face. *Sniper.* They would pin him here for the patrol to pick up. The soldier would have to exit the vehicle to attack. *Or capture.* Bruce likely had standing orders to take Thomas alive; that would give him some advantage.

The sniper's third shot splintered the trunk just above his head and left the scent of pine in the air.

A troop carrier raced toward him, billowing dust and riding the slant at a sharp angle. He couldn't hide from them and keep the cover of the tree. His jaw tightened, rekindling the pain from using his powers a few minutes prior. *Where the hell are you, Haddie?* He'd reacted, leaving the estate. It had been a gamble.

The beige troop carrier skidded to a stop in front of his tree, and the distinct sound of the fourth bullet ricocheted off metal.

Thomas slid back in the sand, readying the AK-47 he'd taken.

The truck sat at a sharp angle, so when the passenger door flung open, he saw the beads in Kiana's hair as she leaned over from the driver's side. They locked eyes before the door swung closed again. *Then, Haddie is here.*

Thomas scrambled up. *How'd she secure one of Bruce's vehicles?* Probably the same way he'd gotten the guns, ambushed Bruce's guards. Fumes pumped from under the frame, and he welcomed the smell. A rumble from the training camp told him one of the other troop carriers headed toward them. Yanking open the passenger door, he jumped in with a smile.

"Hold on," Kiana yelled and punched the truck into motion, heading toward the top of the ridge. Her lips curled at the edge in an expression that meant she was enjoying herself. "Glad you're okay."

"Me too." Thomas slammed the door and braced himself. "There's a vehicle coming up the other side." He managed to point out the front window in the last direction he'd heard the engine.

"Got it."

A bullet rang off metal in the back. "You shouldn't have risked coming out here," he said.

"Wouldn't have to if you could have thought this through." As she crested the ridge, she yanked them east and skidded down the incline until the tires caught. The other vehicle slowed halfway up the hill.

Thomas could hope it would cause a moment of confusion, long enough for them to get a lead. "Where's Haddie?" he asked.

"Underground somewhere." Kiana focused on the terrain ahead. "We saw her go in a cave entrance. Visuals have been spotty."

Hell. The barracks with all the demons. "Why did she go there?"

Kiana managed a shrug. "Don't know. Do you know the layout? Where to?"

Thomas wiped back his hair. He couldn't leave Haddie there. They would have captured her. His hopes of assassinating Bruce diminished; he had to focus on getting his daughter.

"I need a place to drop you off – I'm going in there." He eyed the ridge ahead and the mountains beyond. If they turned around and headed west, he'd have to come back through with them alerted. They had RPGs.

"We," she said.

"I'm not risking you."

"True. I'm risking me." Kiana followed the ridge east as it dropped toward the road. "Where to?"

He might lose both of them. Kiana had proved as stubborn as Haddie and himself. Trying to find a safe spot to drop off Kiana would allow them to entrench. Bruce had already mobilized. *I don't like this.*

His chest tight, Thomas shook his head once before speaking. "There's a company of demons inside the caverns. Bruce's army."

"Sounds dangerous. Can I go first?" She smiled, as if she'd made a joke.

"Behind the house — just before it." He pointed downhill. "Take the road, there's a dirt trail up a ravine."

He hung on as she veered to the ridge and wove between two trees. "Where's Crow?" Thomas asked.

Her face tightened. "Biff's taking him to the hospital. His arm's twisted out of the socket. Demon."

"Biff?"

"Long story. Crow had him come out to us after he had trouble with goons and skipped out of Eugene, probably this Bruce you mentioned. I take it he's the leader?"

They skidded as she met the pavement and turned sharply to follow it. Heat wavered off the hill ahead.

"Yeah. He's got a power that makes people rage," Thomas said.

"Hmmm. Like you, Biff, and Crow?"

A bullet clanged the side of the carrier. Thomas could see the house, at least the tips of the roof. The shooter would have a clear view when they got close to the ravine. "Be careful. They might have snipers on the house."

"Caliber?"

"Heavy." He tapped the bulletproof windshield. "Might pierce."

Kiana wove erratically down the road. "Cooper's here too, maybe captive."

Thomas jerked his head toward her. "Detective Cooper? What the hell?" *Haddie.* What had she been up to?

"Yep. Angels said to bring him." She smiled again.

"Why are you happy?" he asked.

"Because you're alive, Putz."

A bullet ricocheted off the hood.

He'd left them in the dark, and Kiana deserved better. Guilt flushed on his cheeks. If he'd died killing Bruce, she never would have known what happened. *Should have guessed that Haddie would have kept at it. And Kiana.* "How'd you find me?"

"Terry. Traced packets here and ownership back to an Indian company."

Figures. "He's not here." Thomas frowned.

"Nah. We left him at the hotel in Albuquerque. He's monitoring the people Crow brought in. He's the one who found you scrambling out in plain sight." Her tone turned somber. "What were you planning, Thomas?"

"Stopping Bruce." He gestured ahead. "Turn right on the path."

The house stretched ahead. Was Bruce there? Or in the caverns with Haddie?

The window beside Kiana cracked with a thud. Spider webs crawled from the bottom front up six inches. A little higher and the bullet might have gone through and hit her.

She'd barely flinched. With her jaw set, she tugged the steering wheel tight and took the corner, leaving the rear of the vehicle to the house.

The path led toward the ravine that carved into the eastern slope. Bruce's three demons raised their rifles, but didn't point, as if they hadn't gotten word that Thomas was in the carrier. *That bodes well. If I can keep ahead of their communications, we might have a chance.*

The shadow of the opening lay beyond the guards. Their curved barricade sat blocking the road. He could hear Haddie's tone, distant but ahead. His pulse raced. *She's alive. In trouble from the sound of it.*

"Thomas?" Kiana didn't slow down, barreling at the demons. The road, cut from the earth, corralled them in.

"Keep aiming for the tunnel. I got this." He leaned forward and growled.

CHAPTER 47

HADDIE CLENCHED her teeth at the pain, only vaguely aware of Cooper holding her shoulders. Half-disintegrated demons leaned on the stone floor a few yards from her ledge. *How long can I do this?* The moment she let go, the intact demons farther back would rush them.

Imperceptible on first glance, they had moved. The remains of the closest were falling. She hadn't completely stopped them in time. Two demons close to the edge of the arch into the barrack had been touching each other when she first yelled. Now, they separated slightly as the soldier behind moved around the first. *It's not holding.* They were moving.

I've failed. Cooper would die. Through a parched throat, she managed to speak. "Run."

"I'm not leaving."

He'd held her when the first vision came. She'd carried the tone throughout the first incursion of a memory from Dad's past. Since then, another vision had seeped in and left her blind to the demons and the cavern. Another felt imminent.

Pain rippled across her skin, as if she'd been flayed. Pressure pounded against her skull. They wouldn't have to knock her unconscious, she'd get there on her own. *I can't keep this up.* She would only delay the inevitable. Then, they'd kill Cooper.

She wet her lips. "Run."

Cooper said nothing, and didn't move.

Lights flickered in the tunnel to the left. Bruce? She swayed, almost letting go of her tone. Maybe more soldiers. Headlights shone on them.

"Too late," Cooper said. He had a resigned tone, as if a store had closed early. The angels and Meg had called him the Sad Man.

One of the large vehicles charged toward them going too fast and left fiery sparks in its wake.

Bright beads on brown skin, Kiana wore a smirk as she drove toward them. She took the corner squealing tires and plowed into half a demon in her path.

How had she gotten a military truck? The back was open, bouncing across stone and shooting fiery trails.

Dad!

He hung on the back edge of the vehicle with his left hand and fired an automatic rifle with his right. Gunfire echoed in the cavern as he began shooting suspended demons. "Get in," he yelled.

Bullets sank into the flesh of the closer soldiers. As the metal entered, her power seemed to slow their trajectory, leaving only a shiny wet hole with no accompanying blood or reaction.

Cooper jumped off the ledge.

Haddie's tone wavered, and motion rippled across the demons. She flinched at Dad's gunfire. The room smelled of fumes and gunpowder. Her knees sagged.

Her tone failed.

If Cooper hadn't been there, she would have fallen off the stone ledge. He caught her. Her right hand flopping loose, he propped her onto his shoulder. "Damn, you're heavy."

Growls and pained grunts sounded as the world turned a dizzy gray. Cooper shifted and her view swung along gray rock. The sounds of mayhem and death dulled. Her surroundings darkened as if she were about to enter a vision.

Her heartbeat slowed, and time drifted in the enclosing cocoon until she barely felt herself dropped onto the warm metal floor of the vehicle. A hand grabbed the back of her head before it hit. Someone moved over her, possibly Cooper. Distant yelling and gunfire faded at the edge of her hearing.

I'm passing out. They'd never make it out of the caverns.

The ceiling above her lit with a dot of light. She sucked in a breath as it grew quickly, as if dropping from high above. In moments, it sped toward her, taking up the expanse of the roof. Her hands rose protectively. Through the bright light, she could see an endless tunnel stretching back to a distant pinpoint.

Angel. Light curved off the edges, lighting the metal at its edge with feathered incandescence. Thin, engraved ribbons wound up and back down the corridor at a lightning speed. For the first time, Haddie sensed a presence at the opening.

Peace sank into her like warm sunlight on skin. *We'll be okay*. The pain in her skin vanished. She took a deep inhale and energy coursed through her.

A melody of tones rang in her ears.

Tears formed in her eyes at the emotions flooding through her. She yearned to hear every note.

Time stretched before the music echoed and faded.

Sounds rushed in of gunfire and Kiana yelling. The truck rumbled across the cavern, bouncing Haddie on the metal floor. Bodies thudded on the outside of the truck, and nails scraped on metal.

As quickly as it arrived, the angel sped off, dwindling to a point of light and winking out her sight.

Haddie braced herself and looked past Dad firing out the back.

They're too close. A horde of demon soldiers packed the cavern, and the headlights of a vehicle shone behind them. More dropped in from the sides, and some scratched against the vehicle. Sparks splashed from the metal stairs dangling behind the truck. A sickening thud sounded from the front. Kiana drove over them, the bumps never slowing the military vehicle. Dad fired, dropping some of their pursuers behind them, but more pressed closer in a tangle of running and leaping flesh and uniform. *Too many.*

"Hold on," Kiana yelled from the front, "curve!"

They were heading out the direction Haddie had come in. Lights thudded above in the section they rode through. Crates towered on the right side.

Cooper reached past Haddie to a belt Dad had draped across his shoulder and back. Smooth, round hand grenades hung off the green fabric. Grabbing one, Cooper yanked it off.

Dad turned wide-eyed and yelled, "No! Armory!"

Cooper pulled the pin and lobbed the grenade over the horde.

"There's munitions." Dad fired close range into the forehead of a demon as its head appeared. It had been crawling on the side of the truck.

Dad's voice turned to a growl. "We won't make it out."

As Kiana took the corner, Haddie slammed to the side. Cooper bounced off the wall and fell beside her.

Dad swung one-handed and swore. "Punch it. The explosion will take everything down."

Recovering herself, Haddie sat up and looked to the side of the corridor at the rock wall between them and crates of explosive about to go off. *I just slowed time.* It hadn't been intentional, but it had worked on the demons. She'd pushed a firing bullet back in time.

Nails scratching on stone, the soldiers slid around the corner, leaping toward them.

It's got to work. Haddie drew in a quick breath and cried, "No."

The wall beside her, and the demons following, faded away.

No. She almost stopped her tone. *Not what I intended.*

Bright bubbling fire and smoke flashed into existence slamming toward them from the side. It hit an invisible wall where it vaporized. Behind her line, the explosion raged, but the edge disappeared when it hit her powers.

The ceiling cracked above them, and stones wedged loose from crevices and dropped to the ground. The truck swerved and bounced as the rock floor shook, but Haddie kept the firestorm blocked. The opening she'd created lay below them at the end of the tunnel, glowing a haunting red.

Pain crept across her skin; like heat on a burn, it brought back the memories of what she'd just gone through in the caverns. The demon army would have to be destroyed in the maelstrom rocking the hillside. If Kiana didn't get them out soon, they'd be buried as well.

Sunlight lit the shaking walls on each side of them. Her tone wavered and broke. In a gust of orange, flame burst from the bottom of the corridor and blew burnt gunpowder and acrid chemical fumes into the truck.

Dad turned from the heat that engulfed them.

Haddie's world turned white. A young man grappled with another on a muddy, sunlit street. A girl in a dull tan dress ran from between two wooden buildings, screaming. Haddie looked up from the ground where she lay, bleeding from a painful wound in her chest. She raised a gloved hand toward the girl, her daughter, and yelled at the two brutish men following her.

The vision darkened into a smoky, fire-filled night that reminded her of the plight outside her body and imagination. Soldiers in bright blue uniforms rode toward her through the smoke. She moved to clear the way, but the closest swung with a sword that glittered red, reflecting the burning town. Dad's voice swore before the blade reached his chest.

The last vision found her pinned under a massive bear. Her side already burned from claws, and weight crushed her legs. Spewing foul breath, the animal opened a wide maw and dove for her face. Dad's voice barely groaned.

She returned to the bouncing truck with her hands pushing to keep the beast away.

The last of the tunnel lit brightly around them. They were near the exit. Dad held on with a grimace. The ceiling behind them broke off in huge chunks and clouds of dust. Cracks webbed across stone walls to the sides before they burst clear.

Kiana yelled from the front. "Hold on!"

The truck slammed into something with a dull thud, jarring, but roaring forward. Whatever they hit next threw the front of the vehicle into the air.

Haddie flew out the back with Dad. Flailing, she spun back toward the cave mouth. Dust poured toward her.

At the stairs below them, the truck came to a sharp halt. Cooper let out a grunt.

She hit the dirt harder than she expected. Her skin already crawled with burning pain, but scrapes ripped across her face and hands. Her hips felt like they locked as she skidded on rocky ground.

The cave behind her collapsed. Dust poured into her mouth and eyes. It had a weight to it that rested on her like a blanket. Shoving her face to the ground, dry soil stuck to her lips. Her stiff hair fell forward to cover her. The ground rumbled as the caverns collapsed. Grinding stone shrieked in the air. The scent of fire and chemicals lingered in her nose.

Haddie jumped when Dad's hand brushed against her side. "We've got to keep moving." He found her arm and pulled. His boots scraped as he stood.

Her eyes burned and gritted with dust; she blinked, but couldn't keep them open. Blind, she let him lead her.

Cooper swore, his echoed voice likely coming from inside the truck.

Kiana coughed, and her tone was strained. "Thomas, we've got a problem."

CHAPTER 48

Thomas walked Haddie around the side of the troop carrier, blinking and looking back at the hill. The caverns continued to collapse. *We should be out of danger.* Dust rose off the hillside, and dimples were already forming. He kept the AK-47 ready, pointed toward the raised front of the vehicle. *Where are the guards?* Kiana sounded worried, but she hadn't come out of the transport.

The tires had gone over the barricade, but sharp spikes had flipped on impact and lifted the carriage up. He couldn't smell gas. Cooper, and perhaps Kiana, moved inside. *We still have a long way to get safe.*

The driver's seat sat empty. "Kiana?"

Her voice sounded behind him in the dust cloud. "Doors wedged. Coming around."

One of the spikes bent the metal at the base of the carrier.

"Where are the guards?"

"Underneath." She coughed. "We've got trouble on the house. Roof."

The ground shook and the hill groaned. A section

pulled in trees and brush with a sucking noise. He guessed that they stood on solid ground, but he couldn't be sure. *We need to keep moving.*

What had worried Kiana? He stepped over the spiked barricade and saw the limp hand of a demon. She'd pinned them.

Dust clouded his vision, but he could see the shape of the house ahead. The hill had been cut to accommodate the road, so he had a narrow view. There were demons patrolling somewhere. *And a sniper on the roof.* Thomas stopped, holding Haddie from climbing after him.

Soldiers scattered across the roof, their weapons ready and pointed in their direction. It would be hard to miss the smoke, dust, and collapsing hillside. He made out Dylan's large form, watching a man who knelt beside him, almost out of sight.

Snipers would pick them out easily if he led them down the road. The carved sides didn't offer many options. Demons would be there soon.

Any chance of stopping Bruce or finding the kidnapped children was gone. Whatever the man planned for New York would still happen. He couldn't blame Haddie for trying. *I could have handled this better.* A little time spent smoothing things over with Haddie and Kiana would have given him more opportunity with Bruce. The opening wouldn't happen again.

The man beside Dylan stood. He held an RPG and turned it directly toward Thomas and the troop carrier. *We're pinned.* Dylan crossed his arms, and he looked smug even at a distance. More men with weapons were lining up along the edge of the roof.

Thomas didn't have a clear view of the grounds. The tank that he'd planned on targeting lay buried on the far right. Half of that end of the building was hidden behind a slope.

Thomas completed a mental image of the building in his mind.

Haddie tapped at his shoulder. "Dad?"

Hope someone left a pilot light on. He swore in a throaty growl, and his tone rang in the air. Imagining a slice across the tank and building, he hoped the gas would exit into the house before igniting.

Dylan and the other soldiers looked aside, but the man with the RPG stayed focused.

The explosion billowed out the windows of the house. The RPG fired, then the roofs and walls flew off in sections.

"Get away from the truck!" The dull roar of the exploding building covered his voice. He pushed Haddie back. The first burning of his purpura traced along the side of his face.

The fiery trail of the rocket launcher flashed through smoke and debris. Too late, they were penned in.

"Dad?"

The smoke trail of the weapon separated from the billowing smoke and soared toward them.

They would have been doomed, with or without his actions. Dylan wouldn't make it. The man's body had been thrown back toward the middle of the roof. *Nothing would survive that.* A second explosion, deeper, rocked the ground under Thomas. Charred remnants vaulted into the air, and smoke covered the grounds where the house had stood.

"What's going on, Thomas?" Kiana asked.

Her voice trailed off as the visions hit him. He lost the moment's panic in a maelstrom of violent acts by his predecessors. His stomach threatened to rebel as he returned to the present.

The missile skimmed over their heads, narrowly missing. The smoke trail hung close enough to almost touch. His head whipped to watch it hit the hillside behind them. The detonation blew shrubs and sand into a plume. Cooper swore close behind. *We're alive, for the moment.*

They had a short opportunity to get out. The demon patrols would still be looking, but there was a lot to distract them. His body ached and resisted, but he stepped forward. The hill had stopped rumbling, though smoke poured through a hole on the slope.

The training ground and more men waited to the south, Albuquerque to the west. "We're heading northwest. Grab weapons — we still have demons to deal with." He glanced back at Haddie; her eyes watered but were open. "Keep sharp."

Maneuvering her cast, Kiana followed with her pistol ready. "We've got a vehicle on the northwest perimeter. Crow's. I got the keys."

The dust from the collapsed caverns still clouded around them. The house burned red under a blanket of black smoke that slowly rolled over the folds of the hillside. The trail they stood on meandered toward the estate, and they would have to travel along it to navigate around a steep northern slope before they could turn northwest.

Had Bruce evacuated? Thomas couldn't see clearly to the southwest where the training compound lay. *I hope he doesn't send his trainees.* Sheer volume would overcome their inexperience. Thomas wouldn't be able to make good time with Kiana in a cast.

Haddie looked about to collapse from exhaustion. She'd kept the armory explosion from killing them, pushing part of it back into time. She'd shown more ability with her powers than he ever had. *Now she is paying for my attempt.* Keeping her out of danger had been his plan.

Cooper stepped over the barricade, covered in dust. At least he'd found an AK-47 in the carrier. *Where the hell were his clothes?*

"Call out if you see movement. Fire on anything." Thomas pointed downslope toward the smoke. "Our best path lies just north of the building, then we'll look at the terrain there." *Kiana's not going to do well on the slopes, even with her crutch.*

Acrid smoke wafted up to them within the first couple minutes of walking down the trail. The early afternoon sun hung ahead of them, and the heat had sweat beading on his sides. The slope to the north curved too steeply for Kiana's cast.

A demon scampered into sight, high on the same hillside. It spotted them and bound downhill as a second red face popped up behind it.

"Demon!" Thomas crouched and fired a single bullet, his magazine empty. "Devil in hell." He ejected it and reached for the spare wedged in his belt. *It's gone.* He must have lost it when he fell out of the troop carrier.

Kiana fired a single 9mm shot, and the creature lurched mid-jump. She repositioned, but Cooper fired before the second demon had fully crested the ridge.

Haddie tapped his shoulder, "Dad?" She pointed behind them to a pair of demons coming down the slope from the east.

He spun and scanned the area where the smoke cloaked the path ahead. "Cooper, on your six. Fire while you move." He tugged on Kiana's arm. "Keep moving."

The first demon rolled into a dry runoff on their right; Kiana had taken it down with a head shot at twenty yards or more. At least an ex-FBI and a detective would have good aim. *We're still likely outnumbered.* How many of the demon patrols had been near the house when it exploded?

He forced Kiana to keep moving into the thickening smoke while letting Cooper finish off the pair that followed. An engine rumbled to the south, but far enough away that they wouldn't have to worry about it immediately. Haddie looked haggard but alert. Kiana kept a good pace, despite the cast.

Nails could be heard scraping in the denser smoke, and Thomas stopped. Fewer than ten yards ahead, the demon burst into sight with a torn uniform and a shredded right arm. Most soldiers would have been incapacitated. The creature adjusted as it spotted them and loped in their direction.

Thomas flinched as Kiana's shot came close to his ear. As the demon spun to the side from Kiana's bullet, Cooper fired, and the creature dropped to the dirt.

The smoke carried the stench of burning plastic. Creeping forward, the slopes and hills disappeared around them. The flames from the burning structures to their left broke through in dull red. Thomas focused past the ringing in his ears, but heard nothing except the distant vehicle. It headed in their direction.

He'd hoped to get a bearing of the passage northwest by now. Gauging the sun, he veered slightly north. The smoke would not disperse. The uneven ground inclined to their right. He had tried to keep to a flat trail where Kiana could move easier. The haze hung so thick that Thomas could barely find Cooper at the back of their group.

When they finally passed north of the burning buildings and the smoke thinned enough to see the hills, they'd already eased up an incline. The ridge to the north would be a difficult climb for Kiana. *We can get her up there.* Thomas rested his hand on her arm and gestured uphill.

His jaw clenched in sudden anger. His cheeks flushed in rage. Bruce's tone rang around them in the swirling smoke.

PART 5

Join us, I implore you.

CHAPTER 49

Haddie gritted her teeth, and her protective tone rang out. The reek of smoke wrenched her stomach. *Where is he?* It had to be Bruce. The power had hit her with rage before she reacted.

Dad's face grimaced and his hands clenched into fists. She refocused her tone and tried to spread it over their group. The man's power seeped in. Anger boiled inside, and justified or not, it threatened to overcome her. *I can't fight this.*

Her face hard and eyes bright, Kiana looked at Haddie. For a moment, it looked as if she might attack, then she limped past.

Bruce stood to the west, on the ridge that bordered the house. Haddie recognized his tall shape and uniform. His suited attendant hovered close behind. Three dark figures waited beside one of the beige armored transports, demons from their shape and ruddy color.

Dad shook his head, trying to fight Bruce's power. He needed to learn how to protect himself, instead of leaving it all on her. She pushed harder, trying to keep the thoughts at bay.

Kiana's pistol cracked, and Haddie jerked around to find a demon tumbling downslope from the right. Two more shapes followed in the smoke behind. Kiana pulled the trigger again, and a desolate click followed.

"Thomas?" Kiana called out. She dropped the pistol and grabbed Cooper's rifle from his hands as he stood shocked and swaying.

Bruce pinned them. His demons would come in while they stood. They couldn't retreat toward the house, and the steep slope to their right only left them the option to go toward Bruce. *All I can do is hold him off.*

Roughly, Dad pushed past Haddie and growled at the oncoming demons. His tone rang sharp in the air. Smoke eddied where their bodies had been.

Kiana pulled up the rifle and aimed at Bruce.

Bruce's power pressed against them all, seeming to grow in strength.

Haddie watched Kiana. She'd once been on a range with Dad when he'd shot a rifle; the target had been half the distance, and he hadn't made all the shots.

Kiana fired.

Bruce didn't even jump. His attendant shifted, and the three demons lurched and began running up to him.

Dad slumped to one knee, likely as the visions hit him. Whatever he'd done to the house would have taken a lot out of him. If Bruce's power didn't roil her blood, she'd want to sit.

Kiana fired again.

Haddie jerked her focus back to the hill. Bruce staggered, and his power snapped off.

For a third time, Kiana fired.

One of the demons lurched, but the other two swarmed Bruce. His attendant joined and they began moving him back toward their vehicle.

Haddie panted as she let go of her tone, and Kiana brought down the rifle.

"Thomas?" Kiana asked.

He nodded. "I'm okay. Did you kill him?"

She leaned down awkwardly, wedging her rifle into the sand for support. "Chest. Lung or shoulder. Wrong side." Her hand lingered at his neck, but she didn't touch him.

"We need to stop him . . . New York . . . No." He coughed. "We need to keep moving. Northwest." Dad swayed, barely able to maintain his position.

Haddie slipped to his side, cringing as she reached under his arm to help him up. *Sorry, Dad.* She knew what her fingers felt like on his skin. He tensed, but lifted with her.

Bruce's armored truck spewed dust as it tore off the hill heading south. They'd lost him. What was this about New York? *Dad hates letting him get away as much as I do.* They were lucky to be alive. Dozens or hundreds of demons were destroyed in the cave-in. Smoke plumed into the sky from the burning mansion, and a smaller tendril rose from the hill to the east.

A distant siren sounded from the south. It stopped and sounded two short bursts. A signal? Dad turned with a frown, but said nothing.

Kiana limped on the opposite side of Dad, rifle at the ready and scanning the hills, her crutch forgotten. "What happened, Thomas?" She shook her head. "Why did you come here?"

"I wanted to stop him." He walked on his own, unsteady and in pace with Kiana's limp.

"How did you find him?"

"The letter."

Haddie raised her eyebrows, then glanced back at Cooper. He listened to them. Nude and covered in dust, he maintained a scowl and a sense of presence that gave no indication of embarrassment. He wasn't that bad of a guy, overall. *What would he do now?* The Eugene police would wonder where he'd been for the past two days.

They climbed a steep incline, and Haddie watched the crest nervously. Smoke from fire had filled the area below them, highlighting the vale that the estate had been built into.

"I'm sorry." Dad smoothed dusty hair.

Haddie glanced over, but he spoke to Kiana. What did he apologize about? Attempting suicide?

"For being an idiot?" Kiana asked.

"Yes. For being rash and not letting you know what I was doing." Dad shook his head. "It was unfair."

"It was," Kiana agreed.

Haddie blinked, feeling chilled. *What about my feelings?* She'd nearly lost her dad. She frowned and fought tears.

"You, too," he said to her. "Sorry. I was selfish and absorbed."

She started when he spoke. Caught up in her self-pity, she hadn't seen him turn.

"I understand." She'd put herself at risk without telling anyone. It hadn't been fair to them. *Did I ever apologize to anyone?* David.

Haddie stiffened. *I have to find him.* Stumbling, she

looked back at the smoking ruins of the house. "Dad. Did Bruce have any other hostages? Prisoners?"

He shrugged. "I don't think so. None he told me about."

Her stomach churned. She remembered Liz's last phone number, hopefully. Surely David would have shown up by now. "Anyone have a phone? I lost mine."

CHAPTER 50

Dale followed the others, grateful for the slow pace and any shady spot in the sand where he didn't burn his feet any worse than they already were. He'd seriously considered getting them to stop at one of the mutants that Kiana had shot. After standing around naked, he'd settle for a pair of pants and socks, no matter whose. Shoes, if they fit. The afternoon sun had baked the sand blistering hot. Embarrassment bubbled up as Kiana glanced back to check on him. They would crest the ridge in another minute of climbing.

We might actually make it out of here. The man Kiana had shot, Bruce, consumed his thoughts. He'd been able to bring Dale to a humiliating and uncontrollable rage. No one should have that power. Haddie and Thomas he could almost accept, especially as they had saved his life.

Haddie finished her call with a friend back in Eugene. "Dad, we need my phone."

"Where?" Thomas asked.

Kiana pointed in the direction they headed. "If it's at the spot I sent you, then right past this ridge."

Thomas nodded. "We'll look, but I don't want to take long."

Dale cleared his throat. "My gun's up there too. I've got a good idea where, once we get to the spot." If no one had taken it.

"Good idea." Thomas naturally took control as if he'd been military at some point. It hadn't been in his records. The man looked like a biker and had connections in various motorcycle clubs in Eugene. A mechanic.

Haddie had shifted to near hysteria over her missing boyfriend. She'd regained some of her strength and moved quickly to the front. With all that had been thrown at them in Eugene between the ambush and the FBI, Dale might be in trouble.

Kiana acted much like she had during the ride here, calm and even-keeled. Her eyes roved across the terrain around them, but there hadn't been any sign of another mutant.

"I'm going to have to go after Bruce again. I can't let him continue. I believe he will try to bring society down." Thomas spoke to Kiana. "How did you find us, exactly?"

"Terry. He found a way to track communications."

Thomas tilted his head. "Tell him to keep tracking."

Kiana dialed as she limped. "Terry? Can you keep your ears on that tracing you're doing? We lost the leader here. He's been shot, though."

They reached the ridge, and Haddie sprinted toward an area to the right that looked familiar.

"Terry says it looks like an evacuation out of the southern compound."

Dale stopped and turned as the other two looked south.

He couldn't see anything with the smoke that covered the sky. Fires still burned at the ground. He'd come to get answers to questions about Thomas and Haddie, and instead, he had more. *I've torched my life*. His bullets would be found in the bodies or at the scene of the ambush. How could he explain any of it?

My career is over. Did it matter? There was a madman who bred mutants with plans to destroy the world, a military man with resources and abilities that defied belief. From the stories, there were more working for him. Men like Harold Holmes. How many more people were out there like Thomas and Haddie?

"C'mon." Thomas growled. "I don't want to be in the open when the authorities show up."

Neither do I, thought Dale.

CHAPTER 51

HADDIE'S HEART POUNDED, worse since she could do nothing about David. The acrid smoke from Bruce's burning house did little to quench her panic. *What if David had been inside?* She couldn't believe that. Her muscles tightened, rebelling with her aching joints and the sun searing sensitive skin. The four of them were beaten and nearly unarmed. Kiana had probably damaged her leg; the doctor had been adamant about keeping weight off it.

She flinched at every movement in the brush and swaying branches of the trees, but they hadn't seen a demon since Bruce had fled. *I hope he dies.* If he healed as quickly as herself and Dad, he might not. Another part of her wanted to chase him down and find out whether he took David.

She found the area where they'd been attacked. Tire tracks crisscrossed the sand. Someone else had been up here afterward. Haddie pushed through pine branches, and their scent tinged the smoke. The edge where she had slid off that morning sloped sharply down to disappear into the disaster below.

They could replace her phone, but borrowing Kiana's until then added to Haddie's sense of helplessness. It was foolish, but she wanted to be able to talk with Liz at any moment. When her friend went to David's after work, especially. *We need to get back to Eugene.* Would the FBI still be looking for her, and now even Cooper?

She found Cooper's gun wedged in a branch near the base of a tree. He'd just separated from Kiana and Dad and scanned the ground.

"Got your gun," she said and held it up, pinched between her fingers.

He pressed through the brush, and she focused on his eyes. *We need to find him some pants.*

"Thanks. Find your phone?"

She shook her head and turned around to continue her search and avoid looking at him. "Kiana, can you call my phone?" She'd left it on vibrate.

"We need to hurry, Haddie." Dad's voice sounded dry and harsh.

He's right. They couldn't be sure the demons weren't still out here. And she needed to get back to Eugene.

The brush to her left vibrated. "Got it!" she yelled.

She jogged back to Dad and Kiana, keeping ahead of Cooper. Dad looked worn; purpura darkened his face. I must be a mess too. Her white hair hung in odd brown strands, and her clothing had turned a dark tan with dust. It only took a couple minutes before they found the trail she'd come in on. The roof of the Highlander peeked between stubby pines.

"Terry's at a hotel room?" Dad asked.

"Close by."

"I need you to get Haddie out of here. I'm going to stay

with Biff and make sure Crow's okay, unless Terry comes up with something right away."

Kiana snorted and shook her head. "Not leaving your side."

"Okay." Dad rubbed his hair back. "Haddie, you take the Highlander back, drop off Terry and Cooper. Then get with . . ." He glanced back at Cooper. "Rock."

"Cooper helped us get out of Eugene. He might not be welcome back."

Dad nodded. "I appreciate that; however, he doesn't get near Rock."

Cooper coughed. "I've met Sam before, and now Meg."

"That's nice. Stay away." Dad held out his hand to Kiana. "Keys, I hope. I'm in no mood to hot-wire."

If Bruce had David, she might be going with Dad. *I'm not giving up on him.* David had a very organized life. He wouldn't leave his car at a gym, or not answer a message. "I'm finding David, Dad. Even if that means going after Bruce with you."

Kiana handed Crow's keys to Dad. "That makes three of us."

"Four," Cooper said. "If you'd trust me."

Dad glared at all of them. "I'm in no mood." The SUV beeped as he unlocked it. "Devil take me. Haddie, see if there's a damned towel or blanket in the back for the detective."

"Ex," Cooper said.

"Whatever." Dad opened the driver's door.

Haddie rode in the back with Cooper, who wore a green wool blanket wrapped around his waist. She rolled her phone in her hands. Liz would be off work in half an hour.

Kiana called Biff on speaker phone.

"How's Crow?" Dad asked.

"Good to hear your voice, T. He's in surgery. Man, he was mangled. Whatcha need?"

"Can you stay with Crow?"

"Yeah, as far as the nurse on duty understands, I'm his brother, since Mom remarried after she got pregnant with me after having an affair with his dad's boss. They didn't ask a lot of questions after that. And, you know I'm a charmer."

"Jerk," Haddie chuckled from the back.

"Love you, too, Haddie." Biff used his crooning tone.

"Keep me updated. Thanks." Dad's hand paused over the console.

"Will do, T. Bye."

Dad tapped the console and ended the call. They drove in silence. Haddie still couldn't shake the image of the demon dangling the large man in the air. She couldn't fully blame the creature for its vicious nature; Bruce had been responsible for that. The raves and all the coerced were his fault as well. How could a man believe in an idea enough to warrant all these deaths? What did he plan in New York? Maybe they'd stopped his scheme.

The car began to ripen as they drove into the outskirts of the city; Kiana had the air conditioner at maximum. Albuquerque reminded her of the area where Dad — now Biff — had the garage, rural but busy.

A few people stopped and noticed them on their way into the hotel, but the parking lot wasn't crowded. *I need a shower*. Everyone needed fresh clothes and a bath. No one stopped them heading to the room. The trail of smoke coming out of the hills to the east seemed small.

Terry jumped as Kiana opened the door. "You look like crap." He smiled and let out a long breath. "So, what happened? I mean, I know you're still looking for Boss Man, but like, what happened?" His eyebrows raised and he moved a strand a hair out of his eyes as Cooper walked past him toward the clothes he'd left behind. "I was feeling left out of the party, but . . . What did I miss?"

Dad just shook his head and helped Kiana to the bed.

Haddie motioned to Terry's drink. "Bruce had an army of demons. They were nearly human."

"Had?" He handed her the cup.

"We blew up the caverns they were hiding in." She grimaced at the sweet and sour soda. *I need a shower.*

"Caverns. Too cool. So, like a gas main or dynamite?" Excited, Terry's eyes glittered. "How does one destroy a demon's lair?"

Dad walked past them toward the bathroom. "Cooper threw a damned grenade into an armory."

Cooper watched them, clothes in hand. "I didn't know it was an armory. There were a bunch of mutants — demons — chasing us."

"How did you survive?"

Haddie tilted her head and shrugged. "I did my thing, and pushed the explosion back in time. At least, our side of the blast." She touched her stiff, dirty hair and dropped her hand. "I also found out I can slow time, sort of."

Dad came out of the bathroom with two plastic cups of water for himself and Kiana. "Is that what you were doing? I meant to ask, but we got busy."

"I tried to make the army of demons disappear." Her cheeks warmed. Saying it sounded stupid. "But only a few of them did; the rest just stopped moving."

Terry whistled. "Wait till Liz hears."

Haddie nodded. "I know, right? Anyway, afterward I thought I was going to die. Like I had nothing left. Then the angel came in through the roof of the military truck, and I felt like it saved me, gave me power." She pursed her lips. "I wouldn't have been able to stop the explosion if they hadn't come."

"You glowed." Cooper said.

"What?" Haddie asked.

"Like a blue glow on your skin. Both when you stopped the demons, when I thought you were unconscious, and again, when you held back the blast." Cooper swallowed and looked away, as if he hadn't meant to tell her.

Haddie had seen it when others used their power, but when the angel visited as well?

Terry waved his hand near Haddie's face. "So, you blew up the lair, got graced with an angel, and glowed blue."

"When we got out, Dad blew up their house. That was your gas line."

"Damn. What's up with that, T?"

Dad glared at Haddie. "We need to get Haddie out of here."

Terry spread out his hands. "Have some pity. I've been stuck here answering the phones while you got to go out . . . and play in the dirt."

"Thank you for that. They had men on the roof of the house." Dad sighed. "The man who created the demons was there. One of his people had an RPG aimed on us. I didn't have much of a choice."

With a nod, Terry seemed to appreciate the notice of his part in the day. He turned to Cooper standing in his towel. "And where are your clothes, Dude?"

Cooper tightened his scowl, which looked a little less fearsome now that stubble covered his cheeks. "One of the demons captured me."

"For your clothes?"

Haddie chuckled. "Leave him be, Terry." She pointed

to the bathroom. "Who's first in the shower? Dad? Because you'll need to help Kiana."

Dad nodded and moved to pull Kiana up. Seeing them together made Haddie think of David; she checked her phone and was able to subdue her panic to a queasy uneasiness.

Haddie patted Terry's shoulder. "Think you could run out for some unsweetened iced tea?"

"Me?" He smiled. "Why, because I don't have an FBI warrant, and I'm wearing more than a blankie?"

"Exactly. We'll need to get on the road soon. Dad and Kiana will be staying here. I need to check on David, and then . . ."

"Don't tell me where you'll be."

Haddie raised her eyebrows. "Why not?"

He drew in a breath. "I'm going back to Eugene. I can't leave Livia. If the FBI tortures information out of me, I'd rather not tell them anything useful." A smirk formed to one side of his lips. "I'll keep up a blog. Every day at noon. If I ever don't post, you'll know they've got me."

She rolled her eyes and dropped onto the bed. "Wake me when it's my turn."

In three hours, she stood with Cooper and Terry at the door giving Kiana a hug. "Keep him from doing anything crazy."

Kiana laughed. "Right. Be careful."

Haddie wanted to find David; the rest she'd deal with as it showed up. "I will." She faced Dad. "Not going to run off, are you?"

"Sorry about that." He pulled her gently to him and held the back of her head. "I love you, Haddie."

"Love you, too, Dad."

CHAPTER 52

LATE THE NEXT EVENING, Haddie drove through eastern Oregon toward Eugene. The Highlander stunk of fast food. Stars speckled the sky between clouds. *What if Bruce has David in Texas?* Liz had checked David's apartment each day while she was gone. Tuesday, two days ago, Haddie had woken up with him; now she didn't know where he was. The goons who went after Biff could have him, or the remaining coerced FBI. Her muscles knotted across her shoulders from sleeping in the back seat and the stress.

Cooper snored quietly behind her while Terry nursed a drink from their last stop. The radio played K-pop low on the front speakers. They'd all slept heavily over the past twenty hours, but she'd learned more about Cooper driving overnight with him. He *was* a sad man.

"How are you going to find David?" Terry asked.

I don't know. It terrified her. "Any ideas?"

"I could check with the police, say that I'm a worried friend."

Haddie grabbed her hair and began twisting it into a

knot. "Liz already did. They've just put out a BOLO. They're not serious yet."

Terry stared at the highway, lips pursed on his straw. "I've got people looking for the encrypted packets, but it sounds like Bruce might be quiet for a day or two."

Back to Texas, probably. Maybe he bled out. She drew in a breath. What would his people do with hostages then? "I've got to find him . . . David."

Cooper yawned. "Follow the money. If Bruce hired someone instead of using his own soldiers."

Terry pulled out his phone and twisted in his seat. "Not bad, for a cop."

"Ex."

Haddie glanced in the mirror. She hadn't been able to figure out what Cooper planned. He said he couldn't go back to the police force. He'd left bullets during the ambush at the hillside house, and once he left the scene, the police would no longer consider it a good shooting. *So, what am I supposed to do with him?*

"Kamal said he'll do it." Terry grimaced. "Forget that name, Cooper."

"What name?"

"Right. My friend will look into transfers from the different bank accounts owned by Bruce's Indian company and send me anything near the west coast of the US."

Cooper snorted. "Hackers? Nice friends."

They passed the signs for Odell Lake, and she remembered meeting there with Dad to see the letter for the first time. Meg had pointed out the angels. The two of them were hidden nearby with Rock, Louis, and Sam's menagerie. Haddie didn't intend to let Cooper get a hint of their location. He'd helped, and she trusted him, but not that much.

This road had good memories from her childhood. She'd ridden on the back of Dad's bike through the woods and hills. It had a calming effect, if she didn't think about David.

They'd made it to the bridge that cut through the Dexter Reserve, the point where she knew she was just outside of Eugene, when Terry's phone buzzed. She took a deep breath as he checked it and began texting back and forth.

They were past the reserve when Terry spoke. "He's got a payment Tuesday to a bar in Eugene. Four grand."

"What bar?" asked Cooper.

"The Cask."

"I know the owner. Mack Jones. He's got a record, but he's been off our radar for a few years. His brother, Hank, has a continuing sheet of strong-arm robberies. We only made one stick a few years back, but we've suspected him on a number of others. He could be your man. Used to run with Louis Mattes."

The man who attacked her in the park. "Used to?"

"Louis Mattes died from gunshot wounds while you and your father were in a bar, the night your dog got shot."

"You followed us?"

"Two patrolmen in an unmarked car. Thomas, specifically. I was looking for Louis Mattes."

Haddie huffed. "Whatever. Where can we find Hank Jones?" Her emotions whirled between anger and worry over David. "Do you have any idea?"

"Yes. The brothers have a family farm off South Bertelsen. South of where it connects with Bailey Hill Road."

Unconsciously, she sped up. "And you know where their house is? How do you remember that?"

"I remember everything." His tone had a sad note to it.

Most of the weeknight traffic through Eugene had settled, and her only obstacles were the stoplights. She calmed herself enough not to speed and risk getting stopped. Liz had hoped she'd come to her house directly, probably for a blood sample. That would wait.

"Terry, you want me to drop you off first?" She didn't want to stop, not now that they had a lead.

"I'm with you, though I don't know how much I can help." Terry appeared to pull in his elbows tight to his sides, as if trying to compress smaller.

Haddie drove and felt her chest tighten. *I don't want to put Terry at risk.* She couldn't help but race toward what she hoped was David, either. Bruce could have already moved him, but she had to find out. The payment to the bar seemed too good a lead to ignore, and time might be short.

"Just wait in the car," she said. "I'll leave the keys. If you see something from the road you can call me and warn us. If things go bad, we might need to get out of there quickly."

Terry nodded. "That sounds like a good plan." He offered an apologetic grin. "Hopefully, you find him."

Trucks and cars still bustled down Bailey Hill Road when she turned left onto it. More residential than business, traffic moved in agonizing knots. Developments gave way to bigger yards and older houses as they headed to the southern edge of Eugene. Farmlands began to stretch between buildings long before they came to the stop sign at South Bertelsen.

"How far?" Haddie asked.

"Five minutes." Cooper's gun clicked. "Six bullets. You'll take your next right."

Trees thickened around the road after she turned beside a local bar and market. The road wound west before

Cooper turned them left onto a side road and had her pull to the side.

"We'll cut through the woods here. There's a barn that I've always suspected of being a chop shop at times." He closed the door quietly. "It seems the best place to start looking."

Terry stepped out and walked toward the driver's door. "I can't see anything from here." There were no streetlights, and clouds hid even the stars. The only lights were from a house on the opposite side of the road, deep in the woods.

Cooper nodded toward the trees on the right side of the road. "Keep an eye there, or on any cars going down that drive behind us." He gestured Haddie to follow and whispered, "Try to keep your head on tight. The people here will shoot, whether or not they have David. Don't assume facts not in evidence. This is just a recon, until it isn't."

Haddie winced as she stepped onto a large branch and it snapped. Through the trees it didn't seem as if there were any buildings, or farm. Even when they reached the edge, it took her a second before her eyes adjusted and she recognized a large field between them and a squat building to the west. *No lights*. Beyond, she saw small glimmers that could have been the windows of a house. Trees dotted the field, blocking a clear view.

Farther to the south might have been a farm. Ahead of her, scraggly shrubs and high grass grew between them and the blocky silhouette of the building. Cooper crouched as they approached, and she did the same. The windows she could see were pitch black.

Cooper, like Dad, had skill at breaking into buildings; he found an open window and climbed in without a sound. Standing inside, he waved her toward a side door and let her in.

As he opened a steel door, the building, shaped like a barn or garage, had the sharp odor of oil and gas. Her eyes adjusted while Cooper moved to side cabinets and opened them. The skeletons of two cars took up the back end, and junk was piled on the sides and hung from rafters. *David isn't here.* Cooper continued to open doors, and she moved to the opposite side to do the same. Staring into a small locker with shelves and parts, she imagined Cooper was looking for a body, not a hostage. Her chest hollowed and her skin chilled. *David's not dead.* He couldn't be.

CHAPTER 53

HADDIE TREMBLED as she opened the next locker. "David's not in here. We need to check the house."

"Shh." Cooper had reached the bay doors and headed to her side. Voice sharp but quiet, he spoke. "I'm going to check. Keep your head on tight. We can't risk having to pull back before we've cleared every option."

Her face flushed. Clamping her jaw, she resisted responding with a rebuke. He treated her like a child. Keeping her voice low and calm, she said, "David is not dead."

They finished quickly in silence, then Cooper led them back outside. There were two houses visible from the side of the barn. One was directly south, and the other blocked by trees where Cooper pointed.

Cars drove by on the road to the north, lighting up a thicker stand of trees. Following, she crossed a paved driveway, and they entered the copse that trailed along the dried, broken asphalt. It hid the house and masked their approach. His path led them to the side of the house where she could see a dark van with rust and a smaller black coupe. A porch wrapped around the side facing them, and lights inside leaked through curtains. A small second-story gable window was dark, as was the garage that jutted from the front of the house.

He motioned for her to follow, and they used the woods to circle around the house. The back of the house had dimmer windows and the blue light of a television, but the curtains were closed. Obviously, someone was in there. How did Cooper plan on searching the house?

Silently, Cooper gestured toward another building beyond the house. A larger garage with bay doors sat at the end of the drive. *Does he think David is in the other building?* It made sense.

The trees led to the back side of the garage where lights lit a wall and workbench and shone through a window. A storage shed helped give them some cover, and they crept across dry grass.

Haddie had just passed the corner of the outbuilding when two bright motion lights glared down on Cooper. He froze between the window and her when a silhouetted face appeared in the glass.

"Back." He walked backward toward her, as if hoping he hadn't been spotted.

The face jerked away, and a muffled voice yelled inside.

Haddie dropped back beside the trees, but the lights illuminated deep into the woods.

A door burst open from back of the garage.

Two shots fired, but Cooper blocked her.

Dogs barked from inside the house. *How many people were there?*

She didn't see the body of the man collapsed in the doorway until her back pressed against a tree. "Be careful,

David could be in there." Haddie glanced from the house to the open door of the garage. "I should check."

Gunshots fired from the far corner of the garage. A canopy on metal poles shadowed the area, but Cooper returned fire. He moved back for the protection of the shed. "Get back." He fired another shot.

The thin metal of the shed shrieked as a bullet ripped through. Haddie pressed against a pungent pine, and a branch tickled her neck.

The back door of the house opened. All she could make out was a beam of light across the backyard. The barking got louder as two dogs raced out onto the grass. *I can't hurt dogs*. They started to approach with growls, but seemed hesitant with the gunfire.

Cooper fired another shot, this one into the garage. The window shattered and a muzzle flashed from inside.

"No!" Haddie shouted. "David could be in there."

A second gunshot came from inside, illuminating the man standing far against the wall. He had a dark mustache, and a red baseball cap shaded his eyes. She couldn't chance a gunfight between Cooper and the man. "No." Haddie growled and her tone rang in the air.

The man vanished, and her skin begin to prickle around her cheeks.

A round man stepped behind the dogs. Bathed in yellow light from inside the house, he fired. A tree behind her thudded with his bullet.

Cooper turned and returned the shot.

"Don't hit . . ." Haddie groaned as her skin burned from using her power.

Cooper fired a last shot. The dogs reacted strangely to Haddie's power; they had lain on the grass. The man spun to the ground as the visions took Haddie.

She'd dug so far into Dad's past that she'd reached another war. He seemed alone in these, but obviously fought soldiers with old guns. The last vision left her in despair from a slaughtered family that her dad had stumbled upon in the night. She barely recognized the transition back to the darkness of Hank Jones's farm. The gunfire had stopped.

The dogs lay attentive in the grass, whining but focused on her and Cooper.

Cooper tucked his gun away. "I'm out."

The garage and the house were eerily quiet. Haddie shifted away from the tree and winced at the throbbing ache in her hips. "We need to look for David."

"There could be more of them."

Four men seemed enough for a gang. "I'm going inside." She gestured to where the man lay in the doorway. The lights were bright inside. Through the window she could see as far back as the bay doors and the small door between them.

Cooper shook his head and motioned for her to wait. Crouched, he crept for the door. Haddie followed, her eyes focused on the window. The room looked empty except for miscellaneous junk hanging from the ceiling and piled at the end of a worktable.

The small door was open.

Cooper reached the man's body and leaned down for his gun as a van door squealed open in the front. Bent over the corpse, he blocked her path to the garage. "They're trying to leave." Haddie raced around the corner with the overhang. A man's body lay face down in the shadow.

"Wait!" Cooper yelled behind her. "Damn it."

Haddie had already jumped over the dead man's legs and dodged around a rusted Honda Civic on blocks. Lights that had not been on before lit the drive. She hit the front corner of the garage at a full run and skidded on the drive as a man turned from the van.

David, gagged and tied, sat against the back wall inside the vehicle. A pale man with a broad nose turned. His hand swung up with a gun. Haddie could see David's eyes, wide and white. He leaned forward as she came to a halt. Haddie stood five steps from the weapon.

The gun fired and the muzzle flashed.

"No!" she growled.

CHAPTER 54

DALE REACHED THE CORNER, only to press back against the garage at the gunshot. He'd glimpsed Haddie's back, but not the gunman. Gritting his teeth, he jumped around Haddie to take aim.

The beat-up van was parked in the driveway, its side door open. He could smell the gunpowder, but the only person he could see was inside the van, tied up. *David Crowley, I presume.* Had she done her thing on the shooter? The boyfriend struggled to work his way out of the van.

Haddie dropped to her knees and slapped her palms on the driveway.

Evidently, she had made the shooter disappear.

Dale shivered. No matter how many times he witnessed their powers, he couldn't accept it. They and all the others they mentioned, including Bruce, were — wrong. They didn't belong.

He kept the gun at his side as David reached the edge of the van. The man's feet had been tied too close to get any farther than that, and his hands were tight behind his back. Orange duct tape with a design had been wrapped around his face, covering his mouth, but he was trying to say something.

The dogs were still about, though they acted strangely, and there could be others in the house.

"Are you okay?" he asked Haddie as she sagged, her forehead nearly touching the asphalt.

He looked down and noticed his own right hip, his slacks wet with blood. Metal from the shed, or a bullet, had torn through the top of his buttocks. Enough to bleed, but it hadn't seemed to reach any muscle. He could walk just fine. *That nerd kid will still make a joke over it.*

Police response could be slow to reach the edges of Eugene, unless a random patrol was nearby. They had to get out of here. Haddie looked like she was going through whatever happened afterward. That left freeing the boyfriend.

No knife. Let's see what kind of knots we have.

Dale strode toward David and the van.

CHAPTER 55

HADDIE PULLED out of her visions as Cooper stepped away from her and approached the van. "David." Her throat dry, she spoke in little more than a croak.

Cooper glanced around before tucking his gun in his belt and kneeling to work on David's bound ankles. Were they safe? The scent of gunpowder and rot lingered against the growing scent of a storm. It would rain soon.

David watched Haddie, his eyes still wide. He wore his gym sneakers and the black sweats from after a workout. His usually combed brown hair bunched up and stuck in orange tape wrapped over his mouth and head. His chin and jaw appeared fuzzy, perhaps from two days of stubble. *He's alive.* They needed to escape.

She'd just killed his kidnapper in front of him, using her power. The deaths in Albuquerque had haunted her during the drive, but she'd tucked them to the side in her worry over David. Now, she felt an odd sense of shame. What would he think of her?

Her knees burned at the joints, but she had to get up.

The pebbles in the asphalt poked like needles as she leaned forward to get a foot underneath herself.

"Have Terry drive forward down the road to get even with us. He'll see this house, these lights, from the road." Cooper had loosened the knot and unwound the cord binding David's ankles.

Haddie stopped trying to stand and dug into her pocket with skin that burned as if it had been flayed. She wanted to hold David. What if he rejected her? What if he thought she were some kind of monster?

She texted, having to fix mistakes as thick fingers resisted. "Drive forward. You'll see the house we're at. Flood lights."

"You got it, Buckaroo. You found David." He didn't ask, just assumed.

"Yes." She looked over her shoulder, toward where she believed the road lay in the east. The car's lights trailed southward, but much farther away than she expected. In the darkness, she had to guess there was an open field between them.

Stumbling, she managed to get up as Cooper had David standing and worked on the knots on his wrists. "Is he okay?" Her stomach knotted, and she wobbled as she walked toward him.

"From his knuckles, I'd say he got a punch in." Cooper loosened an end of cord and David wriggled his hands free of the loops.

He dug at the duct tape covered in Halloween pumpkins. His eyes were wide, as if in panic, but he shifted away when Cooper tried to help.

By the time Haddie reached him, David gave up on finding the end of the tape and ripped it down to his neck.

Random hairs pulled out and created a fringe at the top of the tape.

"What happened to him?" he asked. His tone sounded almost hysterical. "I saw him fall apart — just disappear."

Her heart sank, and she faltered, looking down at the stain on the asphalt.

David stepped up to her, as if to hug her, when he lifted her chin up. "Your face. They talked about you being captured. Are you okay?"

Part of her wanted to lie. Let him always wonder where the man had gone. *No, it had tortured Liz.* Haddie had to tell him. "It happens when I use my ability."

Cooper pushed them both. "We need to get to the car. Now. Can you run?"

Haddie looked toward the road where Terry waited. David didn't understand, but she didn't have time to explain. She wanted to stop and hold him, to work through this and have him still want her. However, she turned and started to briskly stumble east. Her knees complained, but with David beside her, she managed a clumsy jog. The short lawn ended in an overgrown field after a dozen steps.

"I don't understand," David said. "What ability?"

She wanted to be holding his hands, looking in his face as she told him. Instead, she spoke between ragged breaths. "I made him disappear. I had to. He would have shot me."

"He fired." David said, as if remembering.

A chill crawled up her spine. *He's going to think I'm horrible.* The ground dipped, and Haddie stumbled but caught herself. The rain smelled close. A siren whined from somewhere distant. The police were on their way. At least David was safe, even if he ended up hating her.

"How could you have done that? He — he vaporized."

David pulled at the ring of tape dangling at his neck, trying to stretch it.

"I don't know how it happens. There's a tone that I make." As if on cue, the siren wailed closer to the north. She glanced in that direction but couldn't see any lights. They would make it to Terry.

David remained quiet.

Haddie swallowed panic that threatened to lock her chest. *I'm going to lose him.* Ahead, she made out the Highlander, a dull reflection among trees. They'd get somewhere safe and discuss this. Terry and Liz had accepted her.

She swiveled to look back and saw Cooper limping as he ran. Had he been hit? They couldn't go to a hospital if he had. *We might have to.*

Another dip in the field sent Haddie sprawling forward. She slammed into the dirt face first and sputtered as she rolled to the side. As she pushed up on her palms, David and Cooper each grabbed an arm and pulled her up.

"Are you okay?" David asked, but he removed his hands as she stood.

She nodded and wanted that touch again. His touch.

Cooper jogged off in a limp. "Come on."

Haddie walked briskly, picking her way through what she could see. David stayed with her. The sirens shrieked louder, and the blue lights flickered against trees.

"I really don't understand," David said. He too, looked down at his feet.

A heavy drop of rain splashed off her shoulder. "I'm sorry. I never wanted this. I never wanted you to see it. I don't want it to end us." Her throat thickened and she couldn't say anything more without a sob escaping.

David cleared his throat. "It . . ." He didn't finish his statement.

Say "It won't," she thought.

He stayed silent, eyes on his feet. More raindrops splashed around them. Far behind them, the siren and lights wound down the driveway toward the bodies.

She imagined David wouldn't be able to accept any of it. His life had always been grounded. Even her random disappearances had been too much for him. He would leave her.

The storm opened up, pounding the world into gray.

Tears streamed from Haddie's eyes.

CHAPTER 56

As SHE REACHED THE HIGHLANDER, Haddie wiped her face and pulled her hair back in a wet knot. Cooper climbed into the back and left the door open. David followed him, leaving her the front passenger seat next to Terry. She would have rather had the back with David. *Perhaps he doesn't want to be near me*. Her balance seemed off, and the back of her throat ached. The car stank of stale food from their trip.

Terry studied her. "I heard gunshots."

She nodded. "It didn't go well."

"We need to turn around. This is a dead end," Cooper said.

Haddie adjusted, more to glance at David than anything. Eyes glazed, he stared out his window into the rain, his orange collar still hanging loose.

"Did you get hit?" she asked Cooper.

Cooper shrugged. "Grazed is more like it. A couple stitches." His scowl deepened. She imagined he just realized he wouldn't be heading into a hospital or even an emergency clinic.

Liz might be able to help, if it truly was a scratch. Otherwise, Haddie could hit up Dad for his contacts. Her eyes flicked back to David, but he didn't turn.

Terry started the engine. "Back the way we came?"

"Turn left at the intersection rather than right," Cooper said.

"Then Liz's." Haddie winced and dug for her phone in wet pockets. "She might be able to help Cooper." She held her breath, fearful that David would ask to be dropped at his place and run away from her.

Terry nodded and pulled a tight turn to head back down the street. More blue lights flashed at the end of the road, but the police car darted down the drive.

"Shouldn't we be going to the police station?" asked David. "Aren't you the police, Detective Cooper?"

"Was. If there wasn't a warrant out for me before, there will be after they identify the bullets from tonight."

Terry crept to the intersection and took the turn without stopping once it was clear there were no more lights coming. The rain left a narrow band of visibility along the winding road, and they drove in silence.

David obviously couldn't handle her situation. He'd locked down once he fully realized what she'd been explaining — what she was. *I can't blame him.* It hurt, but he was safe. This had all been because of her; it might not be over. Would Bruce come after David again? Terry? Liz?

Terry planned on going back to his life, despite the FBI. She'd tried to talk him out of it along the ride, but he wouldn't budge. What would David choose?

Rock, Sam, and Meg were safe at least.

Haddie texted Liz. "We found David. He knows. I had to use my power. Cooper has been hit. Grazed he says, needs stitches."

"Great." Liz's text came quickly despite the late hour. "Detective Cooper? I can handle a couple stitches. How is David?"

Swallowing a lump in her throat, Haddie stared into the rain before responding. "Not sure. You tell me when we get there."

"Ok."

When they reached Liz's, Haddie had worked up an argument for David as to why he should leave his life and stay with her. Wherever she ended up. Dad would help. He had money and connections to get them new IDs. She took a deep breath and opened her door into the storm. *David won't do it.*

Terry led the way, and Liz opened the downstairs door. She wore an oversized black shirt with a white, skeletal bat on it. The sharp scent of antiseptic hung in the air.

As Cooper stepped in behind Haddie, Liz nodded. "Detective Cooper."

"Not anymore." He scowled and stepped past Haddie.

Liz gave David a hug, though he barely responded. "We were worried about you. Are you okay?"

He nodded, but didn't reply. The orange collar hung loose from his hair. Still, he avoided looking directly at Haddie. She'd never seen him with this much stubble. His wrists were red and swollen. Liz pulled back and gave him a quizzical look. She patted his shoulder and motioned toward the black couch.

Terry asked, "Scissors?"

"Bathroom." Liz locked eyes with Haddie for a second. She smiled. "Blood?"

I am not up for her probing. "No."

"Bring me a demon head?" she asked.

"No."

"No souvenirs." Liz gave her a hug and turned to Cooper. "Where?"

He motioned to his hip, marking the torn pants. "I'm guessing about an inch, maybe two."

"Drop 'em," Liz said.

Cooper scowled deeper and turned his hands palms up. "Here, in the middle of the living room?"

Haddie blushed. Liz had no idea what Cooper had gone through during the escape. Later, they could laugh about it.

Liz shrugged. "Kitchen then. Haddie? Assistance?"

The smell of antiseptic grew stronger as they entered the kitchen. From the equipment, towels, and gauze piled on the counter, it was obvious she intended to work there anyway.

Terry murmured from the other room, and Haddie felt her ears straining, though she couldn't make out any words.

"Tell me about Albuquerque." As she spoke, Liz exposed a wound smaller than Haddie expected. "White towel and alcohol." She knelt in front of Cooper.

Haddie explained in the same manner as always when they went through the circumstances. She'd mention something and Liz would interrupt with a side question or return to some earlier point. If nothing else, it made the procedure pass and kept Cooper engaged as he added his own comments at points.

When they reached the rescue of David, Liz shrugged at the point where Haddie used her ability in front of him. "Not much choice there."

"No."

Terry and David talked quietly in the other room. She ached to hear their conversation and assumed it was about her.

Liz spread the bandage across Cooper's hip. "What now?" she asked.

"I'm not sure about David, but Terry wants to go back to Livia."

"Detective Cooper, what about you?" Liz asked.

He sighed. "Ex-detective. Call me Dale. I can't go back. I've killed several men, all in a clean shoot, but I didn't stay for the investigations. They'd arrest me on sight."

Liz motioned for tape. "So, Dale, where do you go?"

He glanced at Haddie. "No idea."

She paused with tape in hand. "I'm sorry, but you can't come with me. I'll see if Dad has any thoughts." She planned to go to Rock next, and no matter how much she trusted Cooper now, he couldn't get near Sam and Meg. "I can drop you off somewhere. I'm sorry." She did owe him, but protecting her people was more important.

Liz pursed her lips and pushed a loose strand out of her face. "I can put you up for a couple days, for helping Haddie."

"I wouldn't say no," Cooper said.

Haddie raised her eyebrows. She hadn't expected Liz to make that offer, but it would take away some of her guilt. Maybe Dad would have a more permanent solution. "Are you sure, Liz?" she asked.

"Yeah, no problem. C'mon, help me find him some pants. I've got sweats that'll fit." Liz stood and glanced down. "Like knickers."

Cooper said nothing as they left the kitchen. David and Terry looked up guiltily and turned quiet. Haddie's chest tightened as she left them alone.

"Why?" Haddie asked jerking a thumb back toward the kitchen.

"You've got a lot on your plate, with David and

worrying about everyone, me included. Just a couple days. Then you can figure out what to do with him. If he gave up and turned himself in to the police, he'd have to tell them a lot more than you want them to know."

Haddie sighed. Liz was right. David consumed her and she couldn't help but worry about her friends. One less concern would help. She grabbed Liz in a hug. "Thank you. Best friend ever."

Liz picked a pair of sweats out of a drawer. "Besides, these are really short, even on me. I owe him for being such a turd most of the time."

CHAPTER 57

HADDIE LEFT Cooper with Liz and ran back into the storm with David and Terry. The air smelled fresh as the temperature dropped. Rain poured off the house in noisy waterfalls and drops drummed on the roof of the Highlander.

As she climbed into the driver's door, David went for the back seat behind her. *He hates me.* The sour smell inside wrenched her stomach. She turned on the heat to counter the chill and their damp clothes.

Closing the passenger door, Terry wiped back wet hair. "I'm not sure what to tell Livia."

Haddie started the car and almost replied without thinking. Usually they kept their activities from Livia, as she did from David. Terry had been gone longer this time than any other, and David sat in the seat behind her.

Terry looked over at her as she backed up without comment. He nodded, as if understanding. "I guess bring me to my car, over by the park."

"Are you going to be okay?" She expected the FBI to be watching both his apartment and Livia's. She imagined them picking up Terry as soon as he pulled into his parking lot.

"We'll see. I told you. Look for the blog. If I don't post tomorrow, then you'll know what happened."

Haddie pulled back her hair. *I just need a moment to rest and think.* She'd slept in the car in shifts, but felt like she hadn't in days. Making sure David was okay had been her only focus; now everything seemed to be falling apart. Terry would be going back into the real world and risking himself, and David planned the same.

The streets were quieter with the rain and the late hour. She would miss Eugene. *I'll miss David and my friends.* Haddie forced back tears.

"Will you go after Bruce?" Terry asked.

They pulled up to a red light and she sighed. "Dad will, so, yes." She planned on checking in with him in the morning, before he jumped into something rash. Kiana would not let him out of her sight.

"I'll keep tracking the packets. Assuming I'm not in some FBI lab."

He directed her to his car, parked in an empty lot. The rain had lessened. Terry unbuckled his seatbelt. "Alright, Buckaroo. Wish me luck."

"Be careful, Terry."

He chuckled as he opened the door. "You, too."

The storm dulled his words as he stepped out and glanced back at David, who hadn't made any move to switch to the front. Shrugging, Terry closed the passenger door and jogged for his car.

Haddie's jaw tightened. *I didn't ask for all this.* "I'm not a chauffeur. Get up front and talk with me."

The rain pattered on the roof, off tempo with the windshield wipers. Terry's car started and his lights lit more of the storm.

She gripped the steering wheel. "I feel bad that I had to keep all this from you, but look how you're reacting. Is it because I killed your kidnapper who was about to shoot me? Is it because I have powers I never asked for?"

He didn't answer immediately. The heat blew from the vents, and she flushed despite being soaked. She stared into the mirror, but he leaned away, toward his window.

"Yes." David opened his door.

Haddie sucked in a breath as he stepped out. Was he coming up front, or just leaving? *I don't want to lose him.* He might not be able to handle who she really was. In the beginning, she'd found it difficult to accept herself. Now, there were bigger things to worry about. She whipped her head around as he passed her window and walked around the front of the SUV.

David climbed in the front seat, closed the door, and wiped his face. "I don't know what to think. Can you blame me?" He focused on the glove box.

She needed to give him time. He'd just found out. "Do you think I'm a monster?"

He shook his head. "No, but I don't know what you are. Terry tried to explain some of what has been going on. That terrifies me even more."

She'd hoped that Terry might make David more comfortable with her situation. They'd been talking the entire time she helped Liz with Cooper.

David motioned out the window. "Can we go?"

Haddie wilted and backed up the Highlander. "So, where does that leave us?"

"I love you, Haddie."

Her heart leaped, but he didn't seem finished. There was more.

He swallowed. "I need to think about all this. I'm tired and sore. I need to rest. Can we talk tomorrow?"

She nodded. As she drove toward his apartment, she fought to see through the tears and rain. He'd been kidnapped and then he learned that Haddie was something – different. *I'm being selfish.* Bruce could still have people ready to harm David.

When they pulled into his parking lot, he reached for the door handle as if he would leave without a word. She twisted her hair and spoke. "Can you go somewhere for a while? Keep out of sight?"

He opened the door. "I won't hide." The rain had lessened, but water poured off the building in noisy waterfalls.

"I love you," Haddie said as he stepped out.

David nodded. "I love you." He closed the door.

Haddie leaned back and shut her eyes, her fist wedged against the back of her neck and her hair pulled so tight it prickled her skin. She took a sharp breath and jumped out of the car. David turned at the noise. Running through the rain she caught him under the overhang.

She grabbed him in a hug and held him. Her face would look like she'd been beaten, but she didn't care. Slowly, his hands came up and held her shoulders. Not an embrace, but he didn't push her away.

"I have to go away. Come with me," she pleaded.

He shook his head wordlessly.

"Can I call you tomorrow?" She didn't let go.

David nodded.

"It'll be a burner, something that can't be traced."

He still didn't respond and seemed to grow still.

I might lose him. "Don't hate me," she whispered.

CHAPTER 58

WELL AFTER MIDNIGHT, Haddie reached the cabin where Rock stayed with Meg and Sam. The rain had muddied the dirt road leading to it, but she didn't have trouble driving through the pine forest. Dad's white Transit was parked out front of a short wooden house with a wraparound porch. The lights were on, and the yellow glow beckoned Haddie.

As she climbed out, the scent of pine and fresh rain welcomed her, but the worst of the storm had either not made it this far east or abated. *Sam said they'd stay up.* Rock's silhouette appeared in the window, and she smiled.

Haddie had spent the ride worrying. What was David going to tell the police? Did it matter? What would Dad do about Bruce? What was she supposed to do? She had no answers, but as she walked toward the porch, Rock gave her hope that for the next few minutes at least, she might forget her worries.

He jumped away from the window and the door opened, letting a warm yellow beam into the cold wet night. Sam stood behind the screen wearing a long pink T-shirt with blue and white lettering, "Trans rights are human rights." She beamed at Haddie and pushed back Louis.

"Hey," said Haddie. She opened the screen door and grunted as Rock butted into her. "Hi, Boy. Sorry I've been gone."

He nuzzled against her leg, and Louis joined the fray while Sam gave her a hug. The house smelled like chili and home cooking. There was no fire in the fireplace, but the heat blew warm air through the vents.

Meg stood a few steps into the rustic living room wearing a yellow nightshirt. She had a broad smile. Sam's ferret, Milk, sat on her shoulder yawning.

"I'm glad you're okay," Sam said.

Rock wormed between them, and Haddie knelt to give him a hug. "I missed you. All of you."

As Sam closed the door to cut off the night chill, Meg moved in while Haddie wrestled with a squirming Rock. Grabbing her in an embrace, Meg whispered in Haddie's ear. "I knew you'd be okay. The angels are watching over you."

They had. Haddie's already puffy eyes teared and she held Meg tighter.

Sam walked to a doorway to the left and flicked on a light. "First, hot water for tea. I've got fresh clothes laid out for you on your bed, first door to the right down the hall. If Merlin is sleeping on your vent, Meg can move him to my room. Do you want me to heat up chili?"

Haddie laughed. "Yes. Thank you. I'm hungry."

Meg grabbed her hand and led her toward the back as Sam ran water in the kitchen.

Ten minutes later, Haddie was curled up on the deep couch with a crocheted blanket and Rock's chin on her thigh. She held a glass of tea that swirled hot and cold as it melted through the ice. The scent of chili filled the room. Jisoo's muted cry called from the kitchen. Milk's nails skittered about on wood floors as he played with Louis. Meg sat on the other end of the couch petting Rock.

For the first time in days, Haddie felt like she was home. She wouldn't be going back to her apartment or Eugene. Andrea wouldn't need a call. The FBI would have already checked there with the warrant for Haddie's arrest. Probably the same could be said for the university.

"When do you leave again?" Meg asked.

Haddie took in a shallow breath. What was her plan? "I don't know. Right now, I just want to enjoy being home."

Meg smiled and nodded slowly.

CHAPTER 59

THOMAS LEANED against the headboard of the hotel bed with Kiana nuzzled against him. Her painted cast stretched diagonally from under the blanket. The room had a wet, overused smell, but she had the scent of fresh flowers from her shampoo. The air conditioner clattered under the window, though the night had cooled off outside.

Biff had rented a room at the same hotel, and they'd all gotten back from the hospital an hour ago. Crow would be in bad shape for a while. *I'm going to have to call in some favors.* He couldn't approach Bruce in Texas without some help. From the sound of the man's bragged comments, something would be going on in New York shortly. It had the sense of something catastrophic, if Bruce meant it to begin the decline of civilization. A bomb or chemical warfare seemed the most likely.

Terry had agreed to getting his people to investigate New York for anything unusual. He'd made his usual jokes, but behind that façade, he'd taken the matter seriously.

"Are you going to be able to sleep?" Kiana turned her head up to look at him.

He had to keep her safe. "Yes." With the cast, she took risks trying to be part of the operations.

"I can hear those gears turning."

"Old age, everything squeaks." He put his phone on the nightstand. They should get some sleep. His concerns would wait until the morning.

"You're hardly old."

She commented with light-hearted intent, but it darkened his mood quickly. Couldn't he enjoy his time with her without thinking about the inevitable end?

"Old enough to need some sleep." Thomas slid down, adjusting Kiana, and put his arm around her. Enjoying the moment, he turned off the light.

CHAPTER 60

HADDIE PLAYED with her blackberry tart. Sweet and bitter, it fit her mood, but she couldn't eat. Scents of fresh coffee and baked pastry filled Roma's, and the evening crowd packed the tables. *I should be hungry.* Her stomach hung on the edge of queasiness. Her head felt light, and her chest tingled. "It'll be fine," she said to herself.

She wore a wig of long, brown hair that she let drop across her shoulders and light sunglasses to mask some of her face. Her face felt stiff from all the makeup.

The couple ahead of her sat engrossed on their phones. The two men sitting at the table beside her laughed and joked. Conversation blended from one table to the next. It would rise to a raucous level and then ebb down to general chatter. Many of the customers were students, and that hurt somehow. She hadn't been focused at school, but she resented that it had been taken from her.

Haddie took a deep breath, trying to subdue her nerves. David had insisted on the meeting this afternoon, after just one night's sleep. *Is this it?* Would he break up with her finally?

What future did they have anyway? She loved him. But her life would be dangerous until Bruce was gone. If they did survive that, she'd outlive David. He would grow old. She would leave him when it became apparent that she didn't age. *How can I do that?* How did Dad do that? He would leave Kiana.

She sucked in a sharp breath as David walked past the window. He wore a dark-green polo shirt and moved as if in a hurry. Her heart raced. *Don't be nervous.*

The front door chimed. The wall separating the front entrance and counter from the sitting area blocked her view, but she imagined his quick footsteps across the floor.

His face, tight along the jaw, softened as he found her in the room. His cheeks rose in a smile, causing the lines around his eyes to crease. Her heart fluttered. The last time she'd seen him, there had been no happiness left. David strode through the arch.

Once again, he carried a small white lily and placed it on the table. He nearly plucked her out of the chair for a hug.

"I'm sorry." He drew tightly against her and sighed in her ear. She could feel his heart pounding against her chest.

"I'm sorry," she whispered.

"No. I was . . . scared." His lips brushed against her neck as he spoke. "No more hiding who you are. I love you. You're just you, and I can accept it. I promise."

"I love you." She fought the tears.

His hands rose up her back and he loosened his almost desperate grip. He didn't pull away, just held her until she almost began sobbing. To have him accept her made all the difference in the world. Whatever she had to face, his support would give her strength.

David pulled back, and his fingers moved up gently to

her face. Tender, they pulled her lips to his and kissed them as if there was no one else in the room.

The world and her worries disappeared. They could have years before she would have to hide her inability to age. Dad had done it. She wanted every moment. *To wake up every day by his side.*

Haddie let out a small breath as he pulled back from their kiss.

He looked into her eyes. "Hungry?"

"Yes, if you're doing the cooking," she said.

ALSO BY KEVIN A DAVIS

If you haven't read the Origin story, *Shattered Blood,* then download a free ebook or purchase the paperback or audible on Amazon.

AngelSong Series

Penumbra - Book One

Red Tempest - Book Two

Coerced - Book Three

Demons' Lair - Book Four

Infrared - Book Five. (End of the AngelSong Series)

Website KevinArthurDavis.com

Facebook @KevinArthurDavis

KevinADavis on Twitter and Instagram.

Please join my mailing list if you'd like to be kept up to date on this series and the upcoming Khimmer Chronicles series.

ACKNOWLEDGMENTS

My wife April continues to support me in innumerable facets of my career. She's proofed my guest author blogs, reworded answers, and given me advice that I sometimes don't want to hear. I wouldn't have been able to get this far without her.

Robyn Huss, my editor, has the uncanny skill of taking my version of these stories and making them shine. On top of that she has to readdress my reluctant grasp on grammar; just when it seems like I've learned not to do something, it comes back in a new draft.

I will dearly miss David Farland; our loss still feels unreal. Please pick up one of his books and enjoy the magic he endowed upon the world. Writers, study his lessons at Apex Writers.

Jody Lynn Nye's workshop will always be my recommendation for any aspiring writers.

My writing groups from JordanCon (the infamous Fireside Group), DragonCon, and Apex are fundamental in making sure I keep on track.

Thank you.

CPSIA information can be obtained
at www.ICGtesting.com
Printed in the USA
BVHW072052160522
637101BV00021B/321

9 781737 391487